The Dogs of firing on t

Si Cwan clambered up model fighters and eased himself into the cockpit. "Kebron, this is going to be a tight fit for you," he warned.

"I'll take a deep breath," said Kebron, looking around for a fighter that was to his liking.

"Soleta, have you any experience with flying vessels of this sort?"

"No," she said cooly.

"Have you ever been in a solo firefight of any sort?"

"No."

That was not what Si Cwan was hoping to hear. They were going to be outnumbered as it was. His main hope was that the Dogs would tuck and run, as they tended to do simply to protect their numbers whenever a battle seemed more trouble than it was worth.

"Perhaps it would be better if you remained here, then."

"That would be the logical course of action," Soleta agreed. Whereupon she selected a fighter and vaulted into the cockpit. . . .

STAR TREK
NEW FRONTIER

7

THE QUIET PLACE

PETER DAVID

POCKET BOOKS

New York   London   Toronto   Sydney   Singapore

This book is a work of fiction. Names, characters, places and incidents are products of the author's imagination or are used fictitiously. Any resemblance to actual events or locales or persons, living or dead, is entirely coincidental.

An *Original* Publication of POCKET BOOKS

POCKET BOOKS, a division of Simon & Schuster Inc.
1230 Avenue of the Americas, New York, NY 10020

STAR TREK is a Registered Trademark of
® Paramount Pictures.

A VIACOM COMPANY

This book is published by Pocket Books, a division of
Simon & Schuster Inc., under exclusive license from
Paramount Pictures.

ISBN: 0-671-02079-X

First Pocket Books printing November 1999

10 9 8 7 6 5 4 3 2 1

POCKET and colophon are registered trademarks of
Simon & Schuster Inc.

Printed in the U.S.A.

SIX MONTHS
EARLIER . . .

"THE DREAMS CAME AGAIN, MOTHER."

Malia had been clearing the dinner dishes from the table in the simple, quite unadorned home she shared with her daughter. She stood over the sink about to dump the evening's dishes into it. Over by the table, her daughter, Riella, was slowly wiping the surface of the table with a cloth. She was doing so in a rather distracted fashion, and Malia knew better than to speak to her daughter when she was in that sort of mood. The girl had moods, Malia was quite aware of that. Oftentimes she appeared quite distracted, as if her mind were elsewhere, or even elsewhen. It gave Malia a bit of a hopeless feeling, frustrated that she was unable to help her daughter. She tried to tell herself that this too would pass. But she had the depressing sensation that, in fact, she was fooling herself.

3

It was the dreams that Malia feared more than any-thing. It had been a while since Riella had spoken of them. Malia had hoped that meant that they no longer haunted Riella. She knew, though, that it might just mean Riella had stopped telling her about the dreams because she knew how much they upset her mother. Naturally that just added to Malia's overall sense of helplessness. The notion that her daughter should be acting in a way that was intended to spare her mother grief . . . it was too much.

Then Malia chided herself silently. Here she was giv-ing herself all manner of mental angst over her feelings of inadequacy when the only one she should be con-cerned about was Riella. Riella, who had a delicate beauty to her, like a carefully crafted doll, so fragile that even a harsh word seemed capable of shattering her. Riella was just old enough that the last fleeting fragments of her childhood innocence were still cling-ing to her, while the features, movements, and figure of the woman that she had only recently become were fresh and pristine. She wore her young womanhood around herself like a cloak of spring newness.

Riella had finished cleaning the table and had not said anything further, apparently waiting for her mother to step in and fill the gap. She obliged her, prompting gently, "The dreams? Are you sure?"

"I think I know my own dreams, Mother." There was no impatience in her voice, nor anger. It was as if she were simply resigned to a state of being that was anath-ema to her but about which she was helpless to do any-thing.

"I did not mean to imply you didn't, my dear. It's just, that, well . . ."

Then her voice trailed off, for Malia had the distinct

impression that Riella wasn't listening to her. Instead, Riella was gliding across the room with that remarkably graceful step she had, so light and airless that it seemed as if she were floating rather than walking like a mere mortal. She stopped at the window, looking out to the far horizon. The sun on Montos set early this time of year, and although it was not quite down, the twin moons were already visible in the gradually darkening sky.

"I'm going out, Mother."

This pronouncement was quite surprising to Malia. "Out?"

"Yes. Out."

"Are you sure?"

This time Riella half turned to face her. Her thin lips were upturned in a small smile. "You keep asking me if I am sure of things, Mother. You don't seem to trust me overmuch tonight."

Malia's cheeks flushed against her very pale skin, and the antennae on her brow twitched ever so slightly, as they were wont to do whenever she became a bit agitated. "It's not a matter of trust, Riella. It is simply that, well . . . I trust you, but—"

"But it is the rest of Montos that you do not trust?" She shook her head. "Mother, that does not sound like a terribly appealing life you've created for me, now does it? Montos is supposed to be my home. How can I be afraid to walk the streets of my own home?"

"You should not be afraid. That's my job," Malia added ruefully. Then she grew serious.

"Mother . . . I almost never go out. I'm starting to feel trapped by these four walls, as if I'm a prisoner. Am I a prisoner, Mother?"

"No. Not at all; of course not. I would never stop you

from . . ." Her hands fluttered about aimlessly for a moment, and then she said simply, "No. But I just don't want you to become agitated."

"I'm willing to take that risk," said Riella. "It can't be worse than the dreams."

"I'll go with you, then."

"I'd rather be by myself."

"Riella, I—"

"I would rather . . . be . . . by myself," she said, and there was unexpected firmness in her voice. As disconcerting to her as the dreams were, clearly there was still a strength to her that she could draw upon as needed. Then, paying nominal deference to her mother, she added, "If that is acceptable to you, of course."

"Of course it is. However, you have to take your medication first."

"Mother," sighed Riella, "must I continue to take that tonic? I'm hardly a child."

Her mother wasn't listening, however, and Riella certainly knew better than to argue with her when she was like this. She got the bottled tonic from the cabinet and said, "I know you're not a child, but that's not the point. You've been taking my special body-building tonic every day since the day you were born, and I'm going to make sure you take it until the day you die . . . and for several weeks thereafter." She had poured a dosage of the liquid into a spoon and extended it to Riella. "Open and hold," she said firmly.

"Mother . . ."

"Open and hold. I have spoken." Although there was amusement in her voice, there was also the clear tone of someone who expected to see things done her way.

Riella, knowing that there was no point in going around about it, held her nose as she customarily did since the smell was so disagreeable to her. Her mother poured the contents down her throat, and she clamped her mouth tightly to make sure it stayed down. Once Riella had swallowed it, she looked at her mother as if to say, "Happy now?" In response to the unspoken inquiry, Malia made a sweeping gesture to the door, indicating that Riella could leave as she desired.

For a moment she wanted to walk to her daughter, who had been speaking to her as if addressing her from one of the far-off moons, so distant she seemed. Walk over to her, hold her tightly, tell her everything that she was feeling, explain how much she wanted to help her and how completely inadequate to the task she felt. But then the moment passed, and Riella turned and walked out the door, leaving Malia alone with her frustrations and the conviction that she was simply not up to the task of raising Riella and helping her cope with her dreams.

She hoped she wouldn't have to kill her.

Riella was aware of the gazes that followed her. Certainly her appearances in town were infrequent enough that her mere presence was enough to attract attention. Plus her visual appearance was distinctive enough, with the unusual duskiness of her skin differentiating her at a glance from the uniformly pale Montosians. Then there was the exoticness of the fact that she had no hair, instead she sported a pate that was smooth and gleaming as a water-caressed pebble. Indeed, it had drawn so many stares that she had taken to wearing a short brunette wig. She had picked it up just as she was leaving her mother's house . . .

Her mother's house.

She heard the wording in her head and couldn't help

but be struck by the distance of it. Her mother's house. Not home, and certainly not her home. Even though she lived there, even though her mother cared for her as best she could . . . still, there was something about it that made her feel separate and apart. She didn't live there; she dwelt there. She had no idea why she felt that way. There was nothing that her mother had ever done to make her feel the least bit off-put or unwanted. A kind and good woman, who worried about her perhaps even more than she needed and would probably rather plunge a knife into her own heart than risk doing any harm to her beloved daughter. Her mother worshiped her, she knew that.

And yet . . . there was . . . something . . . just something, niggling away at her.

She brushed the stray thought away. It was nothing. She was allowing the dreams to push her imagination to newer and greater fever pitches and fanciful flights, and they were beginning to affect how she viewed her own mother, her own home. What a sad state she was coming to. She felt very much the ingrate.

She heard her name being mentioned. People are prone to that; they can generally pick their names out of a buzz of crowd noise. When one is a celebrity, one learns to control one's reactions as one's whispered name spreads through a throng of people. It is, after all, impolitic for one's head to whip around in response. It undercuts the coolness that comes with celebrity. Riella was not tremendously experienced in the ways of the world, but she certainly had enough self-possession not to look around upon hearing her name being bandied about. Indeed, it would have served no purpose, for she knew without looking who was discussing her.

It was the boys. It was always the boys.

Sometimes she would glance out the window of her small house (Home! Home, damn it!) and she would see the boys walking past. They would point in the direction of her window, and whisper or laugh or whatever, and she would hear the words "scary" or "nervous" or "creepy" mixed in with her name being mentioned. Admittedly, the words "beautiful" or "exotic" floated into the mix as well, and that brought her some comfort. However, she desired to be known for something other than her looks or her reputation for being odd. Unfortunately, she couldn't quite make up her mind just what she wanted that notoriety to stem from.

She walked down the one main street that ran the length of her small community, and she caught their reflection in the display window of one store. They were following her. She sensed that they weren't stalking her; they were just provoked by curiosity and were trying to saunter along while looking as if they weren't paying the least bit of attention to her. She wanted to be flattered by it, or amused. Instead, she just felt nothing, as if they didn't matter to her.

She was beginning to wonder what in the world *did* matter to her.

She stopped and turned to face them. There were four of them, clustered together, and they had been in the midst of whispering to each other when they froze in their tracks upon being "seen." She knew the tallest of them; his name was Jeet. His face and body were a puzzle-style array of pieces that might, given time, arrange themselves into a semblance of handsomeness. As it was, he simply looked gawky. "May I help you with something, Jeet?"

Jeet looked uncomfortably at the others. "No," he said after a brief hesitation. "We were just . . . walking."

"You weren't walking after me, were you?"

This prompted an array of furiously shaking heads. Riella found it mildly amusing. "You're quite sure, now?" she further prompted, and the shaking was now replaced by rapid head bobbing.

She studied them a moment more. No one moved, as if they were in some sort of face-off or duel. Finally she said, "All right, then. Enjoy the evening."

"You too, Riella," said Jeet, and then the boys quickly beat a retreat.

She regretted that they did so. Truthfully, she wouldn't have minded if one of them, or even all of them, had stayed with her. But at the same time that she found herself desirous of company, she wanted solitude as well. She didn't pretend to understand it. She really wondered if it was possible for her to understand anything anymore.

The dreams flittered around her consciousness.

She continued to walk, and soon there was nothing along the road except Riella herself, the simple structures of the small town left far behind. The sun had set completely, but the moons provided enough reflected light to guide her . . .

. . . to where?

Ahead of her was a ridge of rocks, where mosslike vegetation was growing so thickly that it provided a spongy surface upon which one could sit quite comfortably. She came to this place every so often, just to get away, to sit and contemplate whatever was going on in her life (such as it was). She came there seeking answers, or absolution, or . . . something. Answers to questions that she couldn't frame, answers that she probably wouldn't understand even if they were presented to her.

"Why am I like this?" she asked no one in particular. "Why can't I rest? This doesn't happen to other people. Why is it happening to me?" The answers, unfortunately, were no more forthcoming at that point than they ever had been.

The moons rose higher in the air, and she lay back on the rocks. The smell of the moss was quite pleasant, making her nose tingle. She interlaced her fingers, rested her head on her hands, and stared up at the moons. She fancied that they were a pair of luminous eyes gazing down at her, set in a gigantic face that was as black as night, causing it to blend in and be indistinguishable from the sky.

What if she could talk to that face? If she could ask it any question, what would she ask? Probably *why*. Not any specific why. Just why. She would be satisfied with any answer she would get.

She felt her eyelids growing heavy, and she fought with all her might against it. She knew that it was absurd; she couldn't stay awake forever. Gods knew that she had tried. She had been awakened by the dreams in the middle of the previous night and hadn't fallen back to sleep since. Maybe she'd never have to sleep again. Wouldn't that be wonderful? Maybe a miracle had been visited upon her and she would never again have the dreams inflicted upon her. All she had to do was never indulge in slumber, ever again.

Even as that pleasant scenario occurred to her, her eyes closed almost of their own accord, and a haze of black filled her mind.

And the call came to her . . .

. . . and there were voices whispering to her, and crying to her, and shapeless forms moving about gracefully; at first they didn't seem to notice her. But then they

did, and they angled toward her and surrounded her, and they began to scream, louder and louder, and yet the louder they screamed, the quieter they were. How was it possible? How could one scream and make no noise whatsoever?

She threw her arms up defensively, trying to ward them off, and then they were upon her and through her, insinuating themselves into her and she tried to run, but there was nowhere for her to go. She cried out, shouting for help, and they slid effortlessly into her mouth, and they were everywhere, invading her, demeaning her . . .

And they called, Riella! Riella! Come to us, stay with us, help us, need us, love us as we love you, and there was laughter and sobbing, all tangling together. She had no idea what to do or where to go, and there was no escape, and they were calling her name again. . . .

And there was a man, a man with red skin, and he was stalking towards her with a grim and frightening visage, and she heard a name but couldn't quite make it out—Zorn, or something like that, and it was still frightening to her, and he was reaching towards her . . .

"Riella!"

From far in the distance, she heard her name once more, but it sounded different somehow. And she felt warmth as well . . . warmth, she realized, that was the sun on her face. She came to comprehend this when she awoke, blinking against the brightness of it and then shielding her face, squinting so hard that tears welled in the corners of her eyes. In her confusion and disorientation, she wondered how in the world the sun could have come out in the middle of the night. "Riella, where are you?" came the confused, almost desperate voice again, which she now recognized as her mother's.

It was at that point that Riella realized, belatedly, that there was no sinister condition or situation involving the sun's normal time of rising. The stupid thing was right where it was supposed to be—in the morning sky. She was the one who was out of place.

Through her slitted eyes, she spotted her mother just over a ridge, looking around with what was clearly growing concern. Riella tried to sit up. Her spine was sore and creaky from having reclined all night on the moss-covered rocks. Spongy as the surfaces might have been and as comfortable as her impromptu bed had initially appeared, spending an entire night reclining on them had resulted in one rather hellacious backache. She forced herself to a semi-upright position and called out to her mother. The morning air was sharp in her throat and lungs, and what emerged from her mouth was little more than a croak, but it was enough to catch her mother's attention.

"Riella!" Malia cried out and ran straight to her daughter, throwing her arms around her and hugging her so ferociously that Riella heard a crack in her spine. The noise alarmed her until she moved slightly and discovered that her back felt better. Her mother had inadvertently helped her out. "I was so worried!" Malia continued.

"There was nothing to worry about, Mother. I was just fine."

"You didn't come home! The entire night—"

"Yes. I know that. I fell asleep here."

"Why? Is something wrong with your bed at home? Or did someone hurt you? Drag you out here, or—"

"Mother . . ." Riella couldn't help but feel some degree of amusement at her mother's flustered attitude. In a way, it was rather charming. She put a finger to her mother's lips to still the torrent of words. "Mother . . . could we just, perhaps, go home? Please?"

"Yes, honey. Of course." She let out a sigh, put an arm around her daughter's shoulders, and as they began the slow walk back home, Malia asked, "The dreams? Did they . . ." There was no need to complete the sentence.

Riella considered the question a moment, and then, slowly, she shook her head. "No," she said.

"No?"

"No. I had no disturbing dreams at all. Slept rather peacefully as a matter of fact. It was . . . quite pleasant."

She wasn't practiced at lying to her mother, and she couldn't be sure if she had been particularly successful this time. But Malia simply nodded, patted her daughter on the shoulder, and together they set off for home.

NOW...

I.

MORGAN LEFLER TOOK ONE LOOK at her daughter and knew that something was wrong.

Robin had returned to the quarters they shared looking rather quiet. The fact that she was back at their quarters was not unusual; she had just gone off shift. It was the quiet part that caught Morgan's attention. Customarily, when Robin came off duty, she would tend to burble to her mother excitedly about everything that had gone on that day, whether big or small, important or not-so-important. So, the silence that marked Robin's return this particular evening was more than enough to snag Morgan's attention.

"What's wrong?" she asked, in the tone of voice that mothers had been using in interacting with their daughters for centuries without count.

17

To which Robin gave the customary response in such situations, "Nothing."

Morgan considered that rather useless reply for a moment and then decided to take another angle. At that time, Morgan was engaged in studying some recent research published on the subject of wormholes, so rather than press the issue overtly by turning away from her work, she continued to scan the information on the computer screen while chatting with Robin in a fairly offhand manner. "That's nice. So . . . how was your day?"

"It was fine."

"And your meeting with Si Cwan?"

That clearly surprised Robin. She looked up at her mother, her eyebrows knit together in confusion. "How did you know I had a meeting with Si Cwan today?"

"I didn't. It was just an educated guess. Whenever you work with him on something lately, you come back here just a little more thoughtful than usual. Tonight you seem extremely thoughtful, so I reasoned that you had an extremely important meeting."

"Oh, well . . . no. No, I mean, it wasn't all that important. Just planning a diplomatic mission, that's all."

"Really. Where to?"

"It doesn't matter," Robin said. She slapped her thighs briskly and rose to her feet, clearly ready to change the subject. "So . . . how was your day?"

"Well . . . since you asked, this article on worm—"

"Here's the thing," Robin said, crossing the room quickly and leaning on the edge of the desk. "Lately, Si Cwan seems to be keeping me at a distance."

"I see. At a distance you say."

"Yes, that's right."

"Lately."

"Yes."

"And what about not lately? That is to say, how has he been towards you in previous weeks. Or months."

"Oh, he's been polite. Respectful. Attentive to my opinions."

"And how has that changed? Recently, I mean."

"He . . ." Her voice trailed off as if she were losing steam. She frowned, apparently trying to consider a reply that sounded reasonable, and she couldn't quite come up with one. "Okay, maybe that hasn't changed."

"Then what are you complaining about? Oh. Of course," she said with a smile. "You're complaining because it hasn't changed. There's something going on between you and our esteemed Thallonian nobleman, isn't there? Or at least, you'd like there to be."

"The latter. Much more the latter," admitted Robin.

"Honesty with your mother. I'm impressed. There was a time not so long ago when such a thing would have been unthinkable."

"Oh, don't be silly, Mother."

"I'm not being silly. You have a tendency to draw inwards at crucial emotional times, Robin." She turned the computer screen completely away from her now and focused her full attention on her daughter. "You do a superb job putting forward the attitude and behavior of a very social animal, but you also have a real tendency to withdraw into your . . . your 'den,' as it were. Particularly when something that makes you uncomfortable is being presented to you."

"That's absurd, Mother. I don't withdraw anywhere. Excuse me."

"Where are you going?"

"To the bathroom."

"We're in the middle of a discussion, Robin."

"No, we're not. You're in the middle of treating me as if I'm a child, telling me that I run away and withdraw. Me, I'm just going to take a very quick shower and attend to other calls of nature."

"You're withdrawing."

"And you're ridiculous. I'll be out in ten minutes and we'll continue right where we left off, if you insist."

She went into the bathroom and emerged some time later, clad in off-duty attire. "There. How long did that take me? Ten minutes, like I said? Fifteen?"

"An hour and nineteen," said Morgan.

"No, it didn't. That's"—then she looked at the chronometer and saw that, sure enough, an hour and nineteen minutes had passed—"*absurd.*" The word rolled unconvincingly off her tongue.

"So let's see," Morgan said coolly, engrossed once more in her work and this time not even bothering to look in her daughter's direction. "Let's see if I've got this figured out. Si Cwan is about to embark on some diplomatic mission. The truth is, you'd like to accompany him. It doesn't matter to you overmuch if you're actually *needed* on the mission, but you want to go anyway. It's a desire not particularly spawned from any mission imperative, but instead because you'd really like to have the opportunity to spend some time with him away from the ship. You figure that, if he suggested you accompany him, it might be an indicator that he shares some of the still-nebulous feelings you have for him. But he doesn't suggest it, indicating to you that he sees you only in terms of your function as his shipboard liaison rather than as someone he'd actually like to spend time with. This leaves you lost in thought as you try to determine whether you're being unprofessional, or unreasonable, or just simply too much the coward to tell Cwan exactly how it is that you do feel; presuming you've worked out your own emotions on the matter sufficiently to be able to articulate them. There. Does that more-or-less summarize the situation as it now stands?"

Robin slowly nodded and then, as if catching herself, she quickly shook her head. "No, that's not it at all . . . that's . . . the truth is, I . . . you see . . ."

"Robin," and Morgan reached over and took her hand gently. "Robin, I bear some degree of responsibility over this. If I had been there for you when you were a teenager, and you were first dealing with these kinds of heartbreaks and difficulties, I could have guided you, helped you through. Instead, you seem a bit adrift."

"Oh, Mother," and Robin patted her shoulder. "It's not really your fault."

"I know. I just thought saying that would make you feel better."

Robin rolled her eyes. Then she fixed a gaze on her mother and said, "All right, but you're here now. What would you suggest I say or do?"

"That's obvious. You're not a teenager any more, Robin. You're a Starfleet officer, for God's sake. You should have enough confidence to say what's really on your mind. I mean, hell, if you make a mistake at Ops, you have to worry about ramifications for the whole ship, and you do that job perfectly well. Here the only consequences are personal, and certainly they're not life-threatening or even remotely catastrophic. Do the job and stop nattering about like a teenager with a crush on the boy across the schoolyard."

"You're right. By God, Mother, you're right." Robin squared her shoulder. "If I have feelings for Si Cwan, then I should tell him. I owe it to myself, and in a way I owe it to him."

"That's right."

"Because, damn . . . I'm a good catch."

"You certainly are," smiled Morgan.

"And he should have the right to know that someone as high quality as me is interested in him."

"Exactly the attitude to have."

"And I can do this without withdrawing. Wish me luck, Mother."

"Good luck, Robin."

Robin strode forward. Morgan watched her go, watched the door slide shut behind her. She hesitated a moment, as if reluctant to speak, and then sighed as she called, "Robin. You do realize that's the bathroom."

"I know. I'm just composing myself. I'll be ten minutes."

"Now, Robin."

"Mother, I assure you—"

"Now, Robin!"

The door slid open again and Robin emerged with a tread that could best be described as stomping. "You don't have to talk to me as if I were a child, Mother," she said stiffly.

'Well, then try not to act like one."

Robin blew air impatiently through her lips and then, with that same stompish tread, walked out of their quarters. Morgan just shook her head and went back to her reading.

With each stride that she took down the corridor, Robin felt confidence seeping into her. The truth was, she had no reason to doubt herself. She had proven herself as a competent and dedicated officer on the *Excal-*

ibur. She had served on away teams. She knew the ropes. Indeed, there wasn't a single good reason that she should not be part of the mission. The only type of reason was a bad one—Si Cwan had gotten to her.

When she'd first been assigned to be his liaison in his duties as the official "unofficial" ambassador of goodwill aboard the *Excalibur,* granted she'd found him intriguing. No reason she shouldn't, really. This was a Thallonian noble, after all. Scion and possible last survivor of a royal family, he tried to use goodwill and his considerable personal charisma to stitch together the tattered remains of Thallonian influence. The star-spanning Thallonian Empire, of which he had been a part, was gone. It was obvious after five minutes of conversation with him that he was more than aware of that. What made Si Cwan different from the others of his royal ilk is that he cared, truly cared, about the people who had been affected by the collapse of the Empire. He really, genuinely wanted to make things better, safer. He wanted to make certain that the assorted worlds that had once comprised the Empire, now left to their own devices, would not spiral downward into chaos and anarchy. He did not seem interested in leading so much as guiding.

Yes, first she had been intrigued by him. And then she was impressed by him. Then she admired him. Then she thought about him more often than not. And then . . . then . . .

"Then what?" she asked herself as she entered the turbolift and ordered it to bring her to deck 12, where Si Cwan's quarters were.

Si Cwan was not the type to be effusive in his sentiments. It seemed undignified somehow. Beneath him. Even though his titles and rank in the extinct Empire had no relevance in his status quo on the *Excalibur,* he still maintained a sort of regalness that demanded a reserved, restrained attitude. Consequently, Robin was unable to get any sort of read off him at all as to just how he might feel about her. That was quite frustrating because Robin had always prided herself on her ability to intuit what other people were thinking. Unfortunately, she was getting no such sense from Si Cwan at all. That didn't necessarily mean that he cared nothing for her, but it wasn't a strong indicator that he felt something.

The problem was that the more time she spent with Si Cwan, the more confident she should have become in her dealings with him. Instead, although she had maintained an outward air of poise, inwardly she was a conflicted mess. She was reasonably sure that her quandaries and internal discontent hadn't spilled over into her interaction with him; certainly no one else had commented to her that anything seemed remotely off. Still, there was that niggling, damnable uncertainty.

So, when she and Si Cwan had been discussing the impending diplomatic mission to the planet Montos, they had talked in cool, dispassionate terms about who would be the best people to accompany him. What she had wanted to say was that, as his liaison, it would be best if she attended with him. But she didn't trust her judgment. She wasn't sure how much of that sentiment was being generated by genuine belief that she was relevant to the mission or how much came just from her desire to spend an extended amount of time with him. Rather than err on the side of misjudgment prompted by inappropriate or irrelevant concerns, she had kept her silence and been willing to discuss just about anyone except herself.

That had been a foolish error, and one she would not repeat. Because, dammit, she *should* go along. That's all there was to it.

No. That's not all there was to it. Si Cwan deserved to know the reason—all the reasons—that she wanted to accompany him. There was simply no way for any sort of progress on their relationship (whatever that might be) to occur if he didn't know what was what. Matters might still be nebulous, in a state of flux, but she had to tell him just what the flux was going on.

She walked up to his quarters feeling newly emboldened and rang the chime. She heard a voice from within say, "Come," but she barely paid attention to it as her thoughts swirled within her head. Her fists clenched tightly from building tension, she strode in, her eyes closed tightly (as she occasionally did when she was faced with a situation that was emotionally stressful) and blurted out, "Look, I've been keeping this to myself for a while, and I'm not even sure I know what I'm feeling because it needs to get out there so we can talk about it and see what's what, but I have to tell you that I think I'm attracted to you and developing very strong feelings for you that extend beyond our duty-related relationship."

She opened her eyes.

Seated quite comfortably on Si Cwan's couch was Captain Mackenzie Calhoun. He was holding what appeared to be one of Si Cwan's Thallonian texts in his hands, and he was staring at Robin Lefler with a carefully neutral expression.

Then he sighed heavily.

"It's all right," he said. "I hear that all the time."

All the blood drained from Robin's face and poured down into her feet; consequently, she thought she was going to pass out, but she wasn't able to move as her boots were firmly anchored. "Captain, I . . . I . . ."

He raised an eyebrow and waited expectantly.

"Captain, I'm . . . I'm not attracted to you at all, sir."

"Oh." A small flicker of what appeared to be disappointment—or possibly amusement, although Robin wouldn't have been able to discern it at that moment—danced in his purple-hued eyes. "Well, I hear that all the time, too."

"That is to say . . . I'm not . . . I mean, I . . ." She cleared her throat, but didn't succeed overmuch for there was still a deep raspiness in there. "Is Si Cwan here?"

"No. He's not. As you know, we have a diplomatic mission on its way to Montos. Si Cwan felt that, since they were ready to go, there was no point in delaying the departure. So he, and Lieutenants Kebron and Soleta, departed an hour ago on the runabout, Marquand II. However he had some historical texts here in his quarters that he invited me to read. He simply asked if it wouldn't be too much trouble if I read them here, however. He didn't want them circulating around the ship; they're quite old and sacred and, well . . ." He shrugged. "We all have our quirks, I suppose."

She nodded, still feeling so mortified that she was having trouble composing anything resembling a coherent sentence, or even a coherent thought.

Calhoun paused and then said, maintaining that careful deadpan, "Would I be correct in assuming that the sentiments you were expressing were intended for him?"

"Captain, I . . ." She took a very deep breath. "I would be most appreciative if you could . . . maybe . . . well, forget everything I said. Or ever said. Or will say."

"That might be a bit of overkill, Ensign. But I understand your chagrin. I think you needn't worry."

"Thank you, Captain. And I . . . I didn't mean to insult you, sir. I wouldn't want you to think you aren't attractive because, you know, I'm sure that someone other than me would—"

"Robin . . ." He raised a hand as if to ward off the barrage of verbiage. "It might not be a bad idea if you stopped talking now."

She bobbed her head. "Yes, sir. Thank you, sir." She turned on her heel and bolted from Si Cwan's quarters . . . leaving Calhoun shaking his head and chuckling slightly to himself.

II.

XYON HAD NEVER ACTUALLY ATTENDED an execution before. Unsurprisingly, he didn't want to start now. The reason it was unsurprising was that it was his own execution in question.

For all of its space-going facilities, Barspens was still a relatively barbaric world when it came to its customs and amusements. Holovids, television, even printed matter had never really caught on as a means of entertainment. Public executions, on the other hand, were still a very popular pastime, a predilection that Xyon would have been more than happy to observe from a distance. Being the star player was definitely not what he had had in mind when he had accepted the commission that had led him to this damnable backwater planet.

For what seemed the umpteenth time, Xyon prowled

28

the entirety of his cell. The young man moved with a calm and easy stride that belied the stress of the situation he found himself in. His movements were smooth, like wind on glass, and even though he was taking his time (for indeed, what need was there to rush?) any observer would have been able to tell that there was speed and strength contained in his limber body. He was clothed in deep red and purple, and his long hair hung loosely in his face. Normally he tied it back, but he wasn't feeling particularly in the mood to care about such niceties. In contrast to the lightness of his hair, his eyebrows were quite dark, as were his eyes that roiled with the intensity of a raging sea. His thin lips were pursed in thought, and his slightly elongated jaw gave him the look of a bird of prey in flight. He had no weapons, for they had all been taken from him. He did, however, have a self-sustaining determination, a confidence that he would triumph over his enemies and whatever obstacles that happened to be thrown in his way. This usually managed to see him through whatever dire situations he was in.

That confidence had not wavered, despite his current predicament. Still, he would have felt just a touch better if, during the thirty-eighth inspection of his cell, he had managed to find some means of egress that had escaped his notice the previous thirty-seven times. Unfortunately, such was not forthcoming.

A brisk knock came from the door. He knew from experience that it was not only intended as a means of informing him that someone was there, but also as a warning to back away lest something rather unfortunate and painful occur. Informed by experience from previous encounters, he wisely backed away to the far side of the cell.

The door opened outward (the hinges positioned on the exterior of the door so that he couldn't get at them) and, as he expected, the shock prods were the first things to enter the cell. The three-foot-long prods were held firmly and wielded expertly by the guards in the corridor. Xyon heard a voice boom, "It is time, out-worlder. Time for your trial and execution."

"You're making a serious mistake, Foutz," Xyon said warningly.

"Not as serious as the mistake you made in coming here. Now you may walk of your own accord or you may be jolted into submission. It is entirely up to you."

"Oh, is it. Hmm. Let's consider it a moment. Excruciating pain that will leave me numb and unable to walk or lack of same. That's quite a choice you've left me."

Foutz was visible in the corridor just outside the door. He was of average height, although he did make the customary Barspens squishing noise when he moved slightly from side to side, as Barspens tended to do. That was to be expected when dealing with a race that glided across the ground on appendages that could best be described as tentacles. He carried himself quite well, though, with as much dignity as a perpetually squishing individual can have. His clear eyelids clacked over his eyes, which continued to glower at Xyon as he said, "If you desired an abundance of choices, then perhaps you should never have come to our world and attempted to rob us in the first place. Before you did that, you had a universe of options. Now you have precious few. Value the ones you do have."

"Very wise words, Foutz. I'll recall them fondly when I'm busy breaking your neck."

Foutz didn't smile, which was natural since he had more of a flap than a mouth. He gestured to the guards and they stepped back, allowing Xyon room to step out of the cell into the corridor. Xyon's body tensed a moment as he automatically scanned the situation and tried to determine whether the opportunity to make a break was presenting itself. Unfortunately, nothing seemed forthcoming. The guards were too cautious and too experienced, and they were quite determined not to rob the Barspens people of their afternoon of fun by doing something as careless as allowing the main participant to get away. So Xyon relaxed, conserving his strength in hopes that he might have a subsequent opportunity to use it.

It was quite early in the morning. *Why are these things always at the crack of dawn?* Xyon couldn't help but wonder. Being executed was bad enough. But having to lose one's life while still rubbing the sleep out of one's eyes was positively barbaric.

He blinked against the sunlight, and almost went deaf at the roar that went up when he stepped out into the day. Squinting from the glare, he saw people lined up on either side of the narrow street. There were the Barspens, packed in four-deep, waving flags and shouting imprecations and having a grand old time. There was, mercifully, a stiff breeze coming in from the north, blowing in Xyon's face and causing his hair to blow about in what he hoped was a vaguely heroic-looking manner. At least he knew he was the hero. All of these imbeciles were under the impression that he was the villain of the piece.

He waved at the people in a friendly fashion as if unaware that the blood they were all howling for was his. His hands were not bound; it was a measure of the confidence the Barspens had that he was not going to be able to escape. He seemed quite cool and composed.

One would have thought he was strolling to a pleasant outing on the beach instead of to his own rather grisly end.

One of the shock prods nudged him from the back. It was at the very lowest setting, not even enough to shock him really. Just a mild buzz to get his attention. They wanted him to start walking. Xyon obliged them and began to saunter down the street, deliberately adopting a spring-kneed gait that caused him to bounce along in a fashion that gave him a resemblance to a hand puppet. His arms swung back and forth in an almost jaunty manner, vaguely in sync with the odd up-and-down motion of his legs.

"Thief! Bastard! Despoiler! Wretch!" These and more, they shouted at him. He wished he could write it all down and examine it under more pleasant conditions. It's rare that one person manages to garner that much negative feedback. It could almost be considered something of an accomplishment.

It was a long walk, but naturally Xyon was in no hurry to complete it. He ignored the shaking of fists, the vituperation bordering on hysteria. He did not, however, ignore the good-sized rock that came winging his way. He spotted it just out of the corner of his right eye, aided and abetted by the fact that a light scan of the crowd had detected the assailant just before he let fly. What happened next was so fast that a number of people didn't even see it. While the rock was bare inches away from his head, Xyon snagged it and, without slowing or hesitating, flung the rock back towards its point of origin. It struck the thrower squarely in the forehead. He had been in the middle of bellowing some insult, but before he could complete it the missile that he had hurled had been returned to him courtesy of

Xyon's catapultlike right arm. The heckler in the crowd wavered in place for a moment, then his eyes rolled up into the top of his head and he keeled over.

Several more brave souls picked up rocks, preparing to throw them, and Xyon's head swiveled in their direction, fixing them with such a fearsome glare that they lowered their missiles and settled for contemptuous howls that couldn't be turned back against them. Xyon barely glanced at them from that point on.

They drew closer to the place where Xyon's combined trial and execution was to take place. He hated to admit it, but he found it a bit refreshing to be in a society that made so little pretense of offering up anything resembling a fair or impartial judgment procedure. He had heard that the Cardassians had similar lack of interest in fairness, but he had endeavored to steer clear of them in the past. He wondered bleakly if he'd have opportunities to steer clear of them in the future.

There was a large platform, and Foutz—who had gone on ahead—was just mounting and making an inspection of the various instruments of death that awaited him. Even from where he was, Xyon's sharp eyes could see an impressive array of sharp instruments. There were stains of assorted colors upon them, indicating that members of various races had met similar, nasty demises. Xyon was quite certain that he wasn't going to be going the way of the others; however, the manner in which he was going to avoid sharing the fate of those who had preceded him wasn't immediately presenting itself.

Nevertheless, he knew he wasn't going to die this day because this wasn't how it was supposed to happen.

There was a short ramp that led to the top of the platform. The roaring of the crowd was almost deafening, which was quite painful for Xyon's sensitive hearing. He gazed balefully at the chanting throng of Barspens around him and amused himself to a degree by imagining what it would be like to open fire on them with a single high-powered pulse rifle. Since none seemed to be forthcoming, he trudged up the ramp after the guards prodded him meaningfully once more. As he approached the top of the platform, there was a joyous roar as Xyon's torture and death became imminent.

As before, Foutz made no attempt to smile since such niceties were not within his abilities. Instead, he raised a hand and that gesture alone was enough to still the crowd. He waited until there was dead silence, and then he bellowed, "Outworlder! You stand accused of stealing from the people of Barspens! Of robbing us of sacred treasures! Of defiling our beliefs! For one of our race, the punishment would be banishment! For an outworlder, banishment would be only a return to the place from which you came, so the punishment can only be death! How do you plead?"

Xyon did not answer immediately. He stood straight and tall and proud and looked contemptuously toward the crowd as if it were he who held their lives in his hands, instead of the other way around.

"Well?" Foutz prompted.

"Why should I bother?" he asked. "You are a joke, Foutz. You and all your little friends here, gathered around in hopes of watching me scream and cry and beg for mercy, so that you can derive some sort of demented entertainment. Your sacred objects?" He raised his voice so that all could hear him. "Your sacred objects were pilfered by your own government!"

"Blasphemy," Foutz said promptly.

"If the truth is blasphemy, then yes, it's blasphemy," Xyon shot back. The guards with their prods were ringing him, and he had no hope of moving fast enough before they could stun him into immobility. But if he stood there, just stood there with his hands calmly folded in front of him, there was nothing they could or would do. So that was how he remained, his fingers delicately interlaced. "The truth is, people of Barspens, that your leaders love their little quests. Their crusades. So they go off to other worlds and take from those worlds the so-called artifacts that they then claim are sacred to Barspens." There were shouts of denial and angry catcalls, but Xyon spoke over them, drawing enough air into his lungs so that he was able to shout and make himself heard over the protests. "If you truly want to know why I'm here, ask the people of Ysonte. Yes, that's right, Ysonte, a small world that most of you have probably never even heard of. They do not have much. They have little advancement, not much in the way of weaponry. But they have elaborately carved gems and statues that were produced by Ysontian artisans over a period of centuries. Gems and statues that your leaders helped themselves to when they swarmed over Ysonte and snapped up whatever it was that caught their eye."

"Liar! Deceiver! Agent of the evil one!" All the predictable epithets were hurled at him, but he could also see looks of vague uncertainty on the faces of some of them. Not very many, just a few. But it was enough to give him even a scrap of hope that the situation was not completely hopeless.

"The Ysontians have done nothing to you!" Xyon continued. He took a step forward, but did so in a manner that was very much an imploring one and could not possibly be construed as an attack. Foutz, who was standing some feet away on the platform, was looking from Xyon to the crowd and back again with growing concern. "They have done nothing but commit the hideous sin of trying to live their lives in peace. But your leaders saw to it that that wasn't possible. They stole the most precious and valued artifacts of Ysonte. And it's not as if the Ysontians were using them to profiteer in some ways. No, my good people of Barspens, we are talking about simple works of art that brought joy and pride to the hearts of Ysontians everywhere."

"All of this is claim without foundation and irrelevant in any event," Foutz interjected.

But Xyon was having none of it. He whirled towards Foutz, and he must have done so in a manner that seemed a bit too aggressive for the guards. For the moment he turned, a shock rod touched the area just behind his-knee, and Xyon felt his left leg go out. He hit his knee on the platform with such force that it probably would have hurt like hell, except that his leg was numb from the shock. He did not, however, let out any yell of pain. He'd be damned if he gave the bastards the satisfaction of hearing it. Instead, he swallowed deeply and continued, as if his prone condition was simply a choice he'd made for the purpose of relaxing, "So your leaders brought them here and passed them off as long-lost artifacts, making themselves heroes in your eyes. They couldn't care less about the unhappiness and anger they left behind. But they didn't know that the Ysontians would hire me."

"Hire you!" Foutz said triumphantly as if he had just uncovered some deep secret. "You see, my friends! He was hired by some alien race to steal from us that which is rightfully ours! He would say anything—"

"No one buys my integrity," shot back Xyon. His leg

wavering, he nevertheless brought himself up to a standing position once more. He saw the guards out of the corner of his eye, watching him, waiting for any move that could remotely be considered threatening. He made sure not to budge an inch. "No one purchases my soul. I speak only the truth. It's an annoying habit of mine, as annoying a habit as pompous blowhards such as you, Foutz, have of distorting the truth to suit their fancy."

"You stole our precious artifacts from our very churches!"

"I took back, from the places you had them on display, that which you had stolen—"

"The Unblinking Eye of Mynos, the Jeweled Sceptre of Tybirus, all those and more, you ruthlessly—"

"Oh, stop it!" Xyon said in obvious annoyance, making no attempt to hide his impatience. "You stole those items because they looked vaguely like things you had described in your texts, and you attached names to them that they had no business bearing. You're glorified thieves and scoundrels, caught up in your own sanctimoniousness and self-righteousness. You—"

"Enough!" Foutz spread his arms wide and called out, "You have heard him admit his crime! What say you, my friends?"

"Death!" came the shout, and again, *"Death!"*

"Now there's a shock," Xyon muttered.

Rough hands seized him and dragged him forward. In the center of the platform were two large, sturdy columns, with heavy leather thongs that were attached to him. The guards bound Xyon's hands making it impossible for him to pull away. Xyon, however, did not appear particularly perturbed. He spoke in a low voice, "You're sealing your own fate, Foutz."

Foutz did not hear him at first, and leaned in more closely. "What?"

"I said you're sealing your own fate."

"Really." If Foutz had been capable of smiling, certainly that would have been the time for him to do so. "And how do you reckon that?"

"Because this is not how I am to die. Not at your hands. I have a destiny to fulfill, and anyone who gets in the way of that destiny tends to meet rather horrible ends."

"Is that a fact?"

"Yes. It is. And to be blunt, I think I'm being more than fair in letting you know about it. After all, I could just keep my peace and allow you to meet some hideous end all by yourself. Instead, I'm being generous enough to make you aware of the foolishness of your actions."

The leather thongs pulled tightly on his arms. His shoulders ached, and the sun was remarkably hot considering how early in the morning it was. Considering the circumstances he was facing at that particular moment, it was all that Xyon could do to keep his normal self-possessed manner about him. He was rolling in confidence still; but it was not the easiest thing for him to maintain.

Foutz leaned in closely to him. The Barspens' breath was not especially pleasant. "You," he said, "are going to die very painfully."

"Possibly. But not today."

"No. Today. And do you know what else?"

"I expect you'll tell me."

"There have been others who have been in a similar position as you."

"Yes, that much I was able to surmise," Xyon said,

glancing once more at the multicolored bloodstains that decorated the assorted cutting implements.

"In their cases, I have generously offered them a merciful death. Because I acceded to their pleadings and beggings and admissions of wrongdoing. That is simply the generous sort of individual I've always been."

"You're my new role model for compassion," Xyon told him.

As if Xyon hadn't spoken, Foutz continued, "You, however, are unrepentant. You do not care about the wrong you have done or the noble individuals whose honor you have besmirched. Therefore, no matter how much you beg or plead, I will do nothing to make your passing easier."

"What a startling coincidence. I was just about to say the same about you."

"The only hope you have—"

"I have hope?" Xyon raised a skeptical eyebrow. "Make up your mind."

"The only hope you have is if you tell us where the artifacts are now. You might actually survive to see another sunrise if you cooperate."

Previous inquiries to that effect had been fruitless, but now Xyon said, "As a matter of fact, I would be happy to tell you that."

Foutz made no effort to hide his surprise. He turned to the assembled throng that was still chanting cries of vengeance and bloodthirstiness, and called out, "The condemned wishes to try and make restitution by telling us where our holy artifacts are!" This announcement resulted in a rather tepid cheer. The crowd was sufficiently worked up that the last thing they wanted was any possibility of a reprieve. At that moment they were far more interested in blood than repentance. Foutz turned back to him and demanded, "Where are they?"

"They're off planet," Xyon informed him cheerfully. His nose itched at that moment and he would have given anything to be able to scratch it. "Ysontian agents have, by this point, recovered them from where I'd hidden them before I was stupid enough to fall into your hands. I utterly underestimated your abilities, I freely admit that. I suppose I get sloppy sometimes knowing that imbeciles such as you can't possibly put an end to me. My fault. It won't happen again."

"No," Foutz said drily. "I daresay it won't." Then he turned back to the crowd and shouted, "There is no repentance, my friends! Now there is only death and dismemberment!"

Over the rousing cheer that pronouncement elicited, Xyon inquired calmly, "In that order? Because if so, then the latter won't really be of much interest to me, will it."

Foutz turned to him and picked up one of the sharp instruments, a small curved blade. "I can't decide whether your tongue should be the first to go. The temptation is there since it means I won't have to listen to you anymore. On the other hand, it will interfere with your ability to scream during your execution. What do you think?"

"I don't believe you're really interested in what I think."

"Oh, but I am. I truly am."

"All right. I think you should let me go because it may be your very last chance."

"That," Foutz told him coolly, "will not happen."

"Told you you wouldn't be interested."

That appeared to be all Foutz needed to decide him. He gestured to the guards, and they pried open Xyon's mouth. This prompted the loudest cheer of all from the crowd as they anticipated the beginnings of the torment they had been so eagerly awaiting.

Xyon didn't struggle in their grasp. Once again, he wouldn't give them the satisfaction. There was a small brazier filled with coal nearby, waves of heat rolling from it. Foutz stuck the curved blade into the coal, calmly waiting for it to warm up to a sufficient temperature. The crowd began to chant Foutz's name. Apparently he was quite popular in these parts. He pulled the blade from the coals, and it throbbed with a deep red intensity. Foutz slowly started towards him, milking the drama for all it was worth. It was at that point that Xyon came to an unpleasant realization—he knew the circumstances of his eventual demise, but there was nothing in those circumstances that indicated whether he had a tongue or not. It was entirely possible there was a genuine threat being presented to him, and his considerable sangfroid was becoming increasingly difficult to maintain in the face of the heated blade coming closer and closer to his forced-open mouth.

Foutz saw the flicker of uncertainty in Xyon's eyes and seemed to derive pleasure from that. He brought the blazing knife up in front of his face, his steely eyes peering around the blade at Xyon. "Any last words?" he said.

"Yes, but I doubt you'd understand them."

Foutz brought the knife forward, and Xyon braced himself for the agony that he was about to feel.

III.

AND THAT WAS THE POINT when the explosions began.

The roaring of the crowd had been so loud at that point that, at first, they didn't hear the detonations of weaponry around them. But the next wave of explosions unquestionably seized their attention, particularly when nearby buildings suddenly erupted into flying debris.

Foutz's head snapped around and he began to stammer in confusion. People were pointing, shouting, running, and Xyon suddenly felt the pressure released on his jaw as the guards backed off and looked skyward.

A barrage of small vessels was descending from on high, and Xyon had never seen anything quite like them. They were wildly decorated with pictures of crouching, slavering beasts with wild eyes and bared fangs. Descending upon the helpless Barspens as they

42

were, the ships seemed like nothing so much as a pack of animals hurtling towards its intended victims.

The small ships flew with almost demented abandon, zigzagging and unleashing wave after wave of concentrated fire power. Xyon quickly realized that they were not firing directly into the crowd. Rather they seemed intent upon attacking as much property as possible without actually killing anyone. But Xyon had the instinctive feeling that the attackers didn't care one bit about preserving life. This naturally meant they had another goal in mind, but Xyon couldn't even begin to guess what it was. Nor was he interested in doing so; at that point, he had other considerations uppermost in his mind.

"Steady! Steady!" Foutz was shouting, but no one was paying attention to him, including the guards. The platform had not been struck yet, but it was an obvious target, and the guards clearly realized that. They hesitated a moment more and then, with a significant look at each other, they suddenly bolted, their tentacles carrying them away with remarkable speed. "Come back here! Cowards!" shouted Foutz.

Then more explosions rocked the area, and Foutz obviously came to the realization that remaining in the area wouldn't be a particularly bright idea. Descending to the ground wasn't going to be much better; the crowd was in total panic, trampling each other in their haste to try and get somewhere, anywhere that they would be safe from assault. Foutz began to make his tactical retreat . . .

. . . and came to the abrupt realization that it might have been wise to tie Xyon's feet as well as his hands. For Xyon, although his hands were still bound by the leather straps, was still quite mobile when he didn't have guards on either side of him. Just as Foutz started to pass him, Xyon gripped the leather straps and swung his legs up. They snared around Foutz's neck and upper shoulders, and Foutz staggered under the abrupt pressure around his throat.

Foutz tried to get a word out, but Xyon's legs had closed too solidly on his throat. He couldn't say anything. But he could hear, as Xyon brought his head close to Foutz's ear and whispered, "A universe of options. Remember? That's what you told me about. And remember how I said I'd remember those words fondly when I was breaking your neck?"

"Y-yes," Foutz managed to gasp out.

"Well, I lied. Not about the neck breaking part. About the fondly part."

Foutz's eyes widened, but before he could say or do anything else, Xyon twisted his hips around with a quick, sharp turn. The crack that came as a result was most satisfying. Furthermore, the jolt was so abrupt that the knife which Foutz had been holding flipped out of his hand. His right hand outstretched, Xyon managed to snag it just as it started to fall past him. He released his grip on Foutz, allowing the newly created corpse of his tormentor to slide to the floor. Manipulating the knife deftly, he sliced through the leather thong that bound his right wrist. The heated blade parted the leather with no problem, then Xyon cut through the strap on his left hand. Within a moment, he was free.

It was not a moment too soon, for one of the ships angled straight towards him and opened fire from its gunports. Xyon leaped clear of the platform just as it erupted into hurtling shards of wood. He hit the ground rolling and came up quickly, rubbing his wrists a moment and barely glancing over his shoulder at Foutz's body. Not a moment's grief or regret did he waste on the corpse of his fallen foe. Instead, his only priority was keeping his own head on his shoulders.

He saw a convenient pile of debris that had once been a building, and it seemed a reasonable place for him to hide. As explosions rocked the air around him, the smell of burning wafted toward him and Xyon charged across the open space and dove behind the debris for shelter. Then he clambered up behind the pile, peering over the top to keep an eye on what was happening with the invaders.

It was at that point he spotted what he could only assume to be the flagship.

It was larger than the others, painted even more fiercely if that were possible. The smaller ships deferred to it, banking away as it touched down in an area that had previously been crowded with both people and buildings but now contained only some assorted rubble, the people having run off.

Upon seeing the respect and deference with which the other vessels treated what was obviously the ship containing the leader, Xyon came to the conclusion that he was dealing with idiots. Well-armed idiots, to be sure, but idiots nonetheless. How else to explain such stupid behavior? The last thing any reasonable individuals should want to do is point up for the benefit of an observer who their leader is. It made him or her a spectacular target. If Xyon had been armed with anything remotely formidable, he would have known which ship to take down and conceivably put a major dent in the offensive of these individuals, whoever they were.

Then again, Xyon certainly had little enough reason to harbor any sort of grudge. As vicious and unprovoked as the attack might have been, it was also spectacularly well timed. If not for these new arrivals, Xyon's tongue might be flopping around on the floor of that platform, and who knew what other essential pieces of him might have joined it by that point.

The flagship, with a firing of reverse thrusters, had settled into a tidy landing. From his safe observation point, Xyon was able to hear gears shifting as an exit port cycled open. There was a burst of haze, which indicated that the atmosphere or temperature inside the ship was different (probably cooler) than the surface of Barspens. The other, smaller ships were settled as well, and they were likewise opening up.

When the creature shambled from the flagship and looked around, Xyon had to blink his eyes several times to make sure that he had not lost his mind, that he was seeing what he was seeing properly. Xyon's first assumption was that some sort of pet had emerged from the ship and would shortly be followed by the true leader of the group. Then the creature angled its snout around, sniffed the air, its nostrils flaring slightly, and its lips drew back in a contemptuous sneer. "All right!" he called in a gravelly voice that sounded like two sides of a fault line scraping together. "Come out, you sons of *tharns*."

At first Xyon thought the creature was addressing whoever might be left after the initial wave of assault. But then others similar to him started to emerge from his ship and the other ships as well, and Xyon realized the thing—no, *he*—had been speaking to his own troops.

The leader was definitely the largest of them. He wore gray, lightweight armor that left bare his arms and legs, presumably to allow greater maneuverability. Those arms and legs were thickly muscled and covered with coarse brown fur. His hands and feet were flat and broad, with thick pads on the palms and (Xyon presumed) the soles of his feet. His toes and fingers ended in formidable-looking claws, and when he took a few steps forward while still sniffing the air, his toenails clacked on the rocks beneath his feet. His head was set close to his broad shoulders. His ears were perked up, his snout long and vicious looking with visible fangs curling out from beneath his dark lips.

Worst were his eyes. They were solid black, it appeared, and pitiless. Dead. They seemed dead to Xyon. And Xyon had a feeling that if those eyes spotted him, he might very likely be dead as well.

Then he came to a fairly hideous realization. The sniffing nose of the creature was pointed in his direction. It was possible that it (he, dammit!) was zeroing in on him. Xyon didn't move, didn't so much as breathe. Even though he was slightly visible if someone was looking right at him, he didn't want to take the chance of moving because that alone might be enough to attract attention directly to him.

He saw the ears of the creature twitching. It wasn't just sniffing, it was listening as well. Xyon was certain by that point that his heart was pounding so loudly that the annoying organ's beating could be detected. Even the blinking of his eyes sounded thunderous to him. The only thing he had going for him at that point was that there was so much rubble floating through the air, and the scent of weapons' discharge, that it might obscure whatever scent Xyon might give off that could be detectable.

Waiting. Still waiting. The creature hadn't moved.

Then, finally and amazingly it looked away from him. "This way," it said roughly, and they moved off.

Even so, Xyon still didn't let out a sigh until they were safely out of range.

Not all of the creatures looked like their presumed leader. They were of the same general type and caste, but varied in height, fur coloration, and other aspects. Granted, Xyon still owed them a debt of timing. However, he felt under no compulsion to repay it in any way. He had the distinct feeling that if he came forward and tried to thank them, they'd just as soon rip him apart as look at him. Besides, they clearly had something on their mind, and far be it from him to interfere with their plans.

But . . . even so . . .

Even so . . .

The thought of not interfering was immediately bothersome to him. Who knew what they intended to do? Who they intended to hurt? Who knew?

Well, they did, certainly. They knew exactly what they intended to do. Which meant that Xyon was going to have to know, too.

The young man made no effort to spare himself an internal scolding. Damn it all, when was he going to learn to keep to his own business. Why did he go out of his way to get involved in the difficulties of others? There had to be more to it than his overdeveloped sense of confidence, stemming from his secure belief that his death would not be immediately forthcoming. He was beginning to wonder if it was overwhelming ego or perhaps just sheer stupidity. The creatures were heading north. Xyon's own ship was south. There was every reason in the world to head as far away from the creatures as possible and not a single good one to follow them.

Xyon turned towards the south, took three steps,

froze, and then with an angry sigh, spun and headed north.

Krul liked watching Rier work.

Rier in addition to being the leader and the best fighter of the Dogs of War was also the best tracker. It had taken him no time at all, using his own abilities as well as information garnered from terrified citizens, to learn what he had wanted to learn.

There had been some resistance, credit the Barspens with that at least. Once the Dogs of War had come to ground, individuals had managed to pull together local militia to muster a repulsing attack. They had been spectacularly unsuccessful, of course. The Dogs were too well prepared, too vicious, too thorough in their ability to rend and tear and destroy with brutal efficiency. They had left a string of bloodied and shredded bodies behind them as they had hunted down Sumavar with the sort of speed and efficiency that marked all of their operations. They had known the general area that Sumavar was hiding out in; tracking him down to his specific location had not taken much time at all.

Krul had heard much about Sumavar before they had landed. Once upon a time, he had been one of the premiere warriors of the Thallonian Empire. Now, though, he was older—albeit no wiser. He was past his prime. Yet he had been given a responsibility and had taken it quite seriously. But the Dogs of War took their responsibilities seriously as well; at that point they considered it their bound duty to track down Sumavar and extract from him the information they desired.

Tracking him down had been easy enough. Not all of the Barspens questioned knew who Sumavar was or where he resided, but enough did. He was, after all, an outworlder, and the Barspens certainly knew enough about *those* types. Indeed, the fact that the Barspens were so renowned for their dislike of those other than themselves had been the key to Sumavar's being able to remain hidden for so long. Who would think to look for someone on a world of renowned xenophobes? Apparently, however, Sumavar had managed to grease the right palms or do the right favors for the right individuals to garner himself some sort of special dispensation. They had left him alone, he had kept to himself, and it was a perfectly reasonable arrangement all around.

The arrangement, however, had come to a halt naturally because the Dogs of War had tracked him down.

Give Sumavar credit: He had put up a fight. Apparently, he had heard the explosions and, anticipating a battle, had assembled a battery of weapons with which he had intended to defend his home. He had been quite successful too, at least for a brief time. The Dogs had suffered some light casualties during the initial assault, and Rier was not particularly happy about it. Indeed, his instinct had been to tear Sumavar limb from limb for daring to fight back against the Dogs of War. But several of the Dogs, including Krul, had managed to remind Rier of just how counterproductive such an activity would be, considering that they needed Sumavar alive in order to obtain the information they wanted.

So instead, once they had managed to beat past Sumavar's defenses, smashing into his house from all directions and overwhelming him through sheer ferocity and force of numbers, Rier had simply settled for breaking Sumavar's arms. Both of them, one after the other, snap snap, and he hadn't even asked a single question yet. The stunned Thallonian warrior had sunk into a corner, gasping and choking back tears and looking really rather unimpressive. If this was what a typical Thallonian was like when faced with pressure, thought Krul, no wonder the fools had lost their empire.

"Does that hurt?" Rier had asked.

Sumavar, his red face already turning a lighter shade of pink, nevertheless looked defiantly up at Rier and then spit at him. Rier, without hesitation, slammed down with his right foot and broke the large bone in Sumavar's left thigh. This elicited a howl of agony from Sumavar's throat, and in a fit of uniform mockery, the Dogs raised their voices in imitative baying. Sumavar would have reached over automatically to cradle his injured leg, but since his arms were not exactly functioning at that moment, naturally his abilities on that score were somewhat limited.

"Try that again," Rier said challengingly. "I dare you."

Sumavar did not take the dare.

"Very wise," said Rier. He glanced at his followers, who nodded approvingly, and Rier loped forward and hunkered down near Sumavar. "You can guess what we want."

"I have no idea." Considering the pain he must have been under, Krul couldn't help but think that Sumavar was keeping his voice remarkably steady.

"Hmm." Rier scratched the underside of his muzzle. "We could, of course, go back and forth and we could torture you some more until you admit that you know what we're here for. But then you'd just be telling us what we already know and would likely be so close to death that you wouldn't last for the second part of the questioning. So, I think we'll just jump forward, if you don't mind. The one you call Riella. She eludes us.

You, we have reason to believe, know of her whereabouts. Tell us where she is and we will let you live."

"I don't know where she is. I never heard of her."

"Don't be a fool." Rier sounded almost sympathetic to Sumavar's plight. "Bones knit. You can heal from this. You can still recover. You do not have to die. You have my word."

"The word of a Dog of War?" Sumavar laughed in pained contempt.

"Yes. The word of a Dog of War. Such pacts are immutable. Even such as we have an understanding of honor. Tell us what we wish to know, and we will leave you alive with no further harm come to you."

For a long, silent moment, Sumavar stared levelly at Rier. Then he said calmly, from a very far away place, "I don't know anyone named Riella."

At which point the torture began in earnest.

There was much screaming, screams that carried a great distance, and no one, but no one, came to help. Krul found it amusing. They must have heard. They must have. There was no way they could not. But they realized that it was only one person being tortured, and thank the gods it wasn't them, so they hid in what was left of their ruined hovels and the great, blustering, supposedly barbaric race called the Barspens kept their distance while the Dogs of War molested unmolested.

Rier was very judicious in what he did, although naturally he could have killed Sumavar any time. But there is no craft to execution. The trick was keeping him alive long enough to tell them what they needed to know. Rier had no need of any torture instruments. Between his claws and his teeth, he had more than enough to accomplish what he needed to do. The torture session went on for a good hour before Sumavar finally told them what they wanted to know, and after he did so, Rier continued torturing him to make sure that none of the answers changed. They didn't.

Finally Sumavar lay there, barely recognizable as a bloodied and pulped mess, his breath rattling in his chest. Rier shook his head sadly and simply muttered, "What a waste. Do you have any idea how foolish this was?"

And then, to the surprise of all the Dogs, including Krul, Sumavar actually smiled. "You . . . are the fools."

This comment actually drew the bizarre half-smiles that were all that the Dogs of War were generally able to manage. They glanced at others as if trying to determine whether any of them knew what he was talking about. "Are we?" Rier finally asked. "And why would that be, dead man?"

"You seek . . . the Quiet Place."

None of them had mentioned it. The words themselves had an almost electric effect on the Dogs of War, and Rier drew closer to Sumavar. "Yes. We do."

"You will die . . . envying me. You will envy me . . . because I am already dead. And your suffering . . . has yet to begin . . ."

And then he laughed. He laughed deep in his throat, and the noise was clearly annoying to Rier, because his head and neck lanced forward like a snake and his teeth clamped onto Sumavar's throat. With one quick pull he ended Sumavar's life. He carefully wiped away the blood on the edges of his muzzle, and then he turned to the others. "Tell the rest of the Dogs that they can have their fun for another few minutes, and then it's time to leave."

"Rier," Krul said slowly. "What he said . . . about the Quiet Place . . . do you think it was true? Do you—?"

Rier looked at Krul with open annoyance. "Of course not. What do you expect him to say, Krul? 'Hurry to the Quiet Place because riches untold and the secret of immortality await you there.' Of course he's going to try and warn us off. He doesn't want us to go there. I'm surprised you'd even have to ask."

"I'm sorry, Rier. It's just . . ."

Rier's paw moved so quickly that Krul didn't even have time to react. He struck Krul on the side of the head, sending the Dog to one knee. The others who were standing around guffawed in appreciation of seeing someone other than themselves being slammed around.

"Don't waste my time again, Krul," Rier warned him.

Krul bobbed his head in acknowledgment. Deep within him, anger stirred, but he shrewdly suppressed it. The last thing he needed to do was toy with the idea, even for a moment, of going up against Rier. There was no question that he would lose. Rier was half again as tall as Krul, far faster and smarter and ferocious than Krul could ever hope to be. If Rier thought, even for a moment, that Krul was considering challenging his authority, he would break the smaller Dog in half without a second thought.

So Krul, wisely slunk away, as the rest of the Dogs spread out to do as much damage as possible before they, and their brethren, took their leave.

Krul didn't even glance behind him as he moved away from the place that had served as the home for the now-deceased Thallonian warrior. Instead his mind was in a turmoil, considering the possibility that maybe, just maybe, Sumavar had not been simply trying to scare them off. What if he knew something they didn't?

What if there was some sort of danger in the Quiet Place that had not been considered?

As he pondered these and other options, his nostrils suddenly flared. He smelled blood, and not far away. There was prey waiting for him, and if it were bleeding, it wouldn't be in much of a condition to fight him. That was the kind of prey that Krul most preferred. Truth to tell, Krul wasn't much of a warrior. He held his own, and when prey ran screaming from him, he was able to run it down capably enough. But when he was going up against someone or something that was capable of putting up a fight, he was more than happy to leave the chore of taking it down to one of the other, more aggressive Dogs.

But a wounded victim? That was most definitely within Krul's abilities to handle.

A burned out building, a target of the initial strafing of the Dog's attack run, appeared to be the source of the scent. Moving quickly on all fours, Krul made his way through the rubble, inhaling deeply, closing his eyes and letting faculties other than his sight guide him. He licked his dark-colored lips in anticipation, and every muscle in his body was tense with eagerness. He tread carefully, though, for the rubble was sliding about beneath his paws and it made traction a bit difficult for him.

He moved over a crest of one of the piles of rubble, the smell of the blood so overwhelming that he felt as if he were going to leap right out of his pelt. The source was just beyond the rise, and he padded over to it, body tensed and ready to lunge.

There was nothing there.

No. He was wrong. There was blood, all right. Blood on a red shirt that had been left lying flat on a small pile of rubble. Krul had been downwind of it, so the smell of the blood had wafted right to him. But there seemed to be no purpose to it. Why in the world would anyone leave a blood-stained shirt there for no purpose? Obviously, the answer had to be that there was a reason. The only reason that came to Krul's mind, though, was . . . *a decoy*.

And barely had his mind processed the information when his assailant leaped onto him from behind.

Krul cursed his own stupidity. He should have realized that if the shirt was upwind from him, then whoever might be coming around upon him would likely be downwind. Even as the thought occurred to him, he'd been flattened. Driven to the ground by an assailant of unexpected speed and strength. Nevertheless, it was going to take more than a simple sneak attack to get the best of one of the Dogs of War. He tried to bring his jaws around to snap at whoever was on his back.

He had a brief glimpse of his attacker. He was barechested, of course, with thick hair that hung wildly around his shoulders. There was a thin ribbon of blood across his chest. It seemed eminently likely that he had gashed himself in order to bloody the shirt and draw Krul's attention, taking care to stay downwind of the Dog so that he himself wouldn't be detected. Krul's grudging admiration for the pink-skinned, humanoid creature upon him rose exponentially. That didn't stop Krul from being utterly determined to haul the humanoid off him and tear him to pieces.

Unfortunately the humanoid wasn't giving him a chance. Krul tried to dig his teeth into his attacker, to get a limb within range, but the humanoid was too quick. Before Krul even knew it, the man had his arms down, under and through Krul's arms, and his fingers were interlaced and clamped onto the back of Krul's neck. Try as he might, Krul couldn't dislodge him. He flipped over onto his back, tried slamming the man into debris, but still he failed to make any headway in removing him. "Get off me!" he howled, as if that would make any difference. At the very least, he hoped that the sounds of struggle might attract other Dogs to his aid.

But the humanoid had been too careful. He had succeeded in luring Krul off on his own, and he wasn't about to give up his advantage. Krul felt his neck beginning to creak under the pressure.

The human brought his mouth close to Krul's ear, and he whispered, "I want to know what you know."

"I'll tell you nothing!" snarled Krul.

"I wouldn't bet on that," said the humanoid, and he readjusted his grip. He released Krul's left arm and his fingertips brushed against Krul's forehead. It was a sloppy maneuver on the part of Krul's attacker, and he intended to take full advantage of it. He started to yank free—and then his mind went blank.

He had no idea what was happening. All he knew was that he felt somewhat disoriented. It seemed to pass almost in no time at all, except the next thing he knew, his wrists were being tied behind his back. He looked around in total befuddlement. It was as if time had jumped. One moment he was in the midst of a battle; the next moment, it was over and he was the clear loser. "What did you do?!" he started to yowl, but his demands were quickly truncated when a strip of leather was lashed around his mouth.

"Stop it," said his attacker.

Krul tried to speak, tried to protest, but he couldn't open his jaws at all. He had been tied up too thoroughly; he couldn't make a single move. His mind was still awhirl; bare minutes ago he had been the predator, and now he was the prey. It made no sense to him.

He was flat on his stomach. He tried to sit up, but then a boot pushed on the back of his neck, shoving him back down again. "There is a cost," his assailant said, "to killing. Every time you kill someone, a little piece of you dies along with your victim. I very much believe that. Which is not to say that I'm averse to killing, but the victim has to be worth it. You are most definitely not."

"I'll kill you!"

"Possibly. But not today," said the humanoid, with the tone of one who had said that phrase a number of times before.

"You'll learn nothing from me, if that's your plan!"

"You mean I'll learn nothing about Riella? Or the fact that she's hiding out on a world called Montos? Or that she holds the secret to the Quiet Place? Is that the nothing you're referring to?"

Krul froze. It was impossible for him to hide the terror on his face. "I . . . told you . . . nothing! . . ."

"True. But your leader—Rier was his name, I believe—isn't going to know that. As a matter of fact, if you make any endeavor to follow me or hunt me down before I get off this rock, then trust me, I'll be sure to get word to Rier that you told me everything I needed to know without the slightest hesitation. I think I can readily imagine what your leader will do to you in that circumstance."

"He'll . . . kill me!" Krul choked, hating his own weakness, but having no choice. "Please, don't tell—"

"Then stay here like a nice Dog of War. Feign unconsciousness if you wish when they find you. Better for them to think that you were simply knocked cold. Your stock won't go up, but you won't be considered a traitor—just inept, which you are."

"Who are you!"

"Just someone passing through. Pay me no mind, I'll be gone before you know it."

Krul was about to issue a protest, and then a rock (gripped firmly in the humanoid's fist) slammed down into the side of his skull. Krul's head sagged and, with a barely audible sigh, he gave up consciousness. Just before blackness enveloped, he thought he heard a faint chuckling sound, and he swore to himself that he would never forget it. That sooner or later, he would face his assailant again, and the next time around, it would be Krul who had the last laugh.

Telepathy had never been Xyon's strong suit. Most of his psionic powers were low level and instinctual. But when he had encountered the creature that called itself Krul, what he found was a remarkably simplistic creature with not much depth and tremendous reliance on instinct. As a result, Xyon was able to divine more information from Krul than he would have been able to glean from a more sophisticated, resistant mind. Unfortunately, what he had managed to extract didn't make a tremendous amount of sense to him.

He lay the rock down next to Krul's insensate form and tried to collect his own scattered thoughts. Who was this Riella? What was this Quiet Place? He'd never heard of it.

Montos, however, he had heard of. A backwater world, nothing particularly remarkable about it. Not heavily populated, and the residents there were largely an inoffensive lot. But the people living there (one of them in particular) had suddenly become targets, although they didn't know it yet.

The things that Xyon had heard about the Dogs of War were beginning to come back to him. They'd been the results of some sort of genetic experiments, that much he remembered. And the group name, Dogs of War, had been given them by some United Federation of Planets reporter, apparently culled from an earth poem or something. The name had stuck, as press-designated names often did. Apparently, even the Dogs themselves had taken to fancying the name, because they were now calling themselves by a term that translated as Dogs of War, although in their language it meant more like "unstoppable rampaging mindless beasts." The "mindless" part Xyon somewhat agreed with; "unstoppable" was clearly an exaggeration.

In the distance, he heard snarling and rending and tearing, and he knew that the Dogs were stampeding throughout the area. They would continue to do so until they ran out of prey or got bored, at which point they would then head to Montos and go after this Riella person, a "she," judging by the information he'd garnered from Krul. Xyon couldn't help but feel sorry for her.

And then he moaned softly to himself because he knew himself all too well. He knew what that feeling entailed. He was going to have to do something about it. Knowing that the unknown Riella was going to be subject to the vomitus attentions of the Dogs of War was all the impetus Xyon needed to throw himself into yet another determined quest.

"Gods, I'm an idiot," he muttered, but unfortunately he didn't find himself in much of a position to do anything about it.

He checked Krul over and found no weapons on him. That was unfortunate; Xyon could have used some. It was understandable, though; the Dogs were practically living weapons. When they were up in their ships they didn't hesitate to unleash whatever firepower they had, but once on the ground, they obviously preferred close-up rending and tearing with their claws. Charming creatures.

Xyon began to make his way past the newly created rubble and the burning buildings. He stuck close to the perimeter and managed to avoid the centers of activity where the Dogs were going about their business. As adept at remaining inconspicuous as Xyon was by nature, in this case it wasn't particularly difficult at all. The Dogs were making so much noise that a blind elephant could have avoided detection simply by listening for where they were and going where they weren't.

Within minutes Xyon had managed to work his way back to the place where the flagship had landed. He had made only one brief stop: At the platform where he had, only a short time earlier, been faced with a rather nasty prospective end. There he had grabbed several of the more easily transportable cutting implements and shoved them into his belt and the tops of his boots. He wouldn't have minded having a phaser, disruptor, or blaster at his side, but he was obviously going to have to make do.

The main entrance to the ship had been left wide open. This screamed *trap* to Xyon, for it would have been the work of but a moment to cycle the door shut behind them. So, the obvious conclusion was that they were trying to draw potential victims into the ship for the equally obvious reasons.

Xyon was trying to determine a way in when it presented itself to him in a most unexpected fashion—specifically, when a low growling and the sound of claws on rocks alerted him at the last possible second. If he had turned to see the Dog of War leaping at him, that would have been enough to finish him. But he knew what was coming, and instead Xyon dropped to the ground, allowing the Dog's lunging charge to carry the creature clear over his head. The Dog was larger than Krul had been, more heavily muscled, and obviously more confident. That confidence, however, turned out to be its undoing. It hit the ground and started to scramble around in order to face Xyon once more, but it was too slow. Xyon leaped atop the Dog's back and wasted no time at all. He gripped the creature's head on either side with fingers that were like steel cords, and he twisted as hard and as quickly as he could. The Dog's neck snapped with only slightly less resistance than Foutz's had. Xyon rolled off as the Dog's carcass slumped to the ground.

The way in now presented itself. It wasn't going to be pleasant, but it would at least get him close enough.

He removed the armor from the Dog's body and set to work.

Nothing got past Vacu.

It's not that Vacu was particularly bright. In point of fact, he wasn't. He was, however, easily the most massive of all the Dogs of War. He was a head-and-a-half taller than Rier and routinely had to bend over whenever passing through any portal. If he had had brains or intestinal fortitude to match his build, he would have been the most devastating Dog of all. None would have been able to stand against him.

His lack of fundamental intelligence, however, was a

major drawback. Instead, he was more than happy to be treated well and follow orders. That was something he excelled at. And in this instance, the order from Rier had been quite simple: Stay out of sight just inside the entrance port. And if anyone who is not one of us enters, kill him. There was no way that Vacu could possibly get confused over that.

So, he had remained hidden, at least as well as someone of his bulk could manage. And he had waited to see who, if anyone, entered.

It had been fairly quiet, and Vacu was impatiently shifting from one foot to the other since he really didn't have anything else to do. And that was when he heard a noise at the door and braced himself in anticipation of possibly getting to kill someone. His nostrils flared as he tried to detect the scent, and what he picked up was tremendously confusing to him. It smelled somewhat like Shukko, but the scent was different somehow.

"Shukko?" Vacu said softly and peered out from his hiding place. Then he gaped at what he saw, his black eyes going as wide as they possibly could.

It was Shukko, all right, but he looked terrible. His fur was stiff and matted with blood. His paws were up and covering his face as he staggered. He wasn't saying anything. Considering the amount of blood on him, it was possible that someone had cut his throat.

"Shukko!" Vacu cried out, louder this time, and he emerged from his hiding place, crossing quickly to his pack mate.

He drew within two feet and the smell was even more wrong. There was death . . . death was clinging to Shukko, but it didn't seem possible because Shukko was standing right there. Clearly he wasn't dead, but he didn't seem quite alive. It was too much for Vacu to figure out.

He did not, however, have time to figure it out, because Shukko drew an arm back and hit Vacu as hard as he could in the side of the head. Vacu staggered slightly and looked at Shukko with crossed eyes. "What's the matter with you, Shukko?" he demanded.

Shukko hit him again and Vacu still didn't come close to toppling over. He did, however, start to realize just what was wrong, and he grabbed at Shukko's head and yanked as hard as he could. The fur-covered head tore off and Vacu found himself staring at a bloodied and distinctly non-Dog face that peered up from beneath an armor plate. It took him that long to realize that Shukko was, in fact, dead, and suddenly the creature with the non-Dog face yanked a piece of pipe free from the wall and swung it as hard as he could. He struck Vacu with full force in the skull and Vacu went down, his ears ringing. "Stop it!" Vacu managed to get out thickly, feeling more annoyed than anything else, and then several repeated blows to the head were enough to knock Vacu cold.

Xyon quickly stripped off the rest of his makeshift costume and tried not to let it get to him—although he desperately needed a bath. He couldn't believe how many attempts it had taken him to down the behemoth he had encountered, and he couldn't shake the feeling that somehow he had gotten off lucky.

Fortunately, the ship was lightly manned. Most of the Dogs were out and about, enjoying themselves and having just a grand old time spreading carnage and destruction wherever they went. That left Xyon with enough leeway to do what needed to be done.

He made his way quickly through the ship, trying to steer clear of any random members of the skeleton crew left behind. Considering he was covered with the blood of one of their associates, the odds were that they would be able to smell him with no trouble if they came anywhere within range of him.

His plan was simple: Find the engine room and disable the engines so that the main ship would be stuck on the planet, giving him the lead time he'd need to get to Montos before they did. He was reasonably sure that he could make his way to the engines, wherever they were, in fairly short order.

He took one turn, then another, ducked through some sort of circuitry tunnel, emerged on the other side, and stepped through a door . . .

. . . and found himself on the bridge of the ship.

It was fairly small, really, constructed for maximum efficiency and use of space.

There were two Dogs there, apparently running systems checks or in other ways performing routine maintenance. They turned and looked at Xyon with open-jawed astonishment.

"Hello," said Xyon, and suddenly he had a knife in each hand. Before his presence had fully registered on the Dogs, he had left fly with the twin blades. They sped through the air and landed squarely in the chests of the two Dogs. The creatures didn't even have time for a howl of protest as they pitched forward. Xyon gave them no further thought as he shoved them out of the way so that he could inspect the weapons and guidance arrays. There was a viewing port set into the front section of the bridge, giving him a clear sight line to the surrounding area.

He studied the consoles before him and quickly came to some interesting conclusions. He tapped what appeared to be a pivot control and discovered that he was absolutely right. The entire bridge section swivelled a full 360 degrees. Apparently they were positioned squarely on top of the vessel and the full-turn capacity was how they managed to view everything around them.

Nestled all around the flagship, like so many contented little guards, were the smaller ships.

Xyon discovered the weapons array and he grinned in a most satisfied fashion. "You creatures like carnage?" he murmured. "Here's some carnage for you."

Rier's first hint that something was wrong was when he heard a series of explosions coming from the general area where the vessels had landed. Other members of his pack who were with him likewise reacted with surprise, looking in confusion at each other as if automatically assuming that the other would have some sort of explanation. "Come on!" shouted Rier, and they left behind their amusements as they bolted in the direction of the ships to see what was causing this rather unexpected assortment of detonations.

When they drew within sight of the landing area, they froze, unable to believe it. The upper section of the flagship was turning, opening fire on all the ships around it. It was ripping into the ships with no particular accuracy; instead it was just shooting and shooting in all directions as it continued to turn relentlessly. However, since the vessels around it were not moving, it had no problem blowing the lot of them to kingdom come. The Dogs let out a collective howl of fury as, one by one, the ships erupted in flame. Shrapnel and assorted bits and pieces of the ships spiralled through the air, crashing into rocks and debris like so many flaming meteorites.

"Who's doing this!" barked Rier, but no answer was forthcoming. The other Dogs ducked back, but Rier refused to be intimidated by his own ship. He charged forward, darting between the random blasts, making his way deftly towards his flagship. With every yard he covered, he bristled more, became more furious as he contemplated the way he was going to avenge himself on whomever it was who had the nerve to interfere with the Dogs of War.

Then Rier skidded to a halt. He saw the gunports angling down and around towards the flagship itself. "No!" he shouted, but even as he cried out in protest he was backing up as fast as he could.

The weapons lashed into the flagship, cutting a swath through the unshielded hull. Rier saw where the track of the blasts was taking it, but there was nothing he could do as the guns blasted into the engine room. Immediately the engines exploded, flame belching heavenward in a blazing column that made all the fur on Rier's hide stand on end. From behind him there was distressed yipping from the other Dogs, but they—like he—were completely helpless. Fire erupted in concentric circles, enveloping the remains of the smaller ships. It seemed an eternity, but in reality it was only seconds as the entirety of the Dogs' landing force was reduced to scorched or melting metal.

The other Dogs, numbering two dozen, gathered around Rier, staring in astonishment at a landing fleet gone completely awry. No one said anything. No one could think of anything *to* say.

"Atik," Rier said after a time. "Fista. Omon." In response to their names, three of the Dogs—Rier's prime lieutenants—appeared at his side. Atik had the blackest fur of any of them, so dark that one could stare at the shadows for a time and never see him. He was also the only one of the Dogs who carried a weapon, having fallen in love with a set of two, razor-edged swords captured during one foray. He had started wearing them on his back, referring to them as his "long claws." Fista, litter brother to Krul, had a lean and hungry look about him, and his fur was a mottled gray. Omon moved with assurance and swagger. His gestures and mannerisms were always big and full of confidence, his dusky red fur slicked back and meticulously maintained. "Spread out," continued Rier. "Scour the area."

"Whoever was responsible, Rier, is surely dead," Atik said in his customary just-above-a-whisper tone.

"Not if he set it for automatic sequencing, he's not," Rier replied. "He could have rigged it and gotten out before the first shot was fired. Unless, of course, you have something better to do, Atik. Considering, however, that we're stuck here until the rest of the pack realizes we're overdue and sends rescue ships, I don't see any problem with you spending some of your precious time in trying to determine who did this to us. And if—"

Then they blinked in surprise as, from the rubble, there was a stirring. Immediately the Dogs tensed, having absolutely no idea what to expect.

From the smoke, from the debris, rose a huge form. It was Vacu. He looked extremely puzzled and stared blankly at his pack brothers. His fur was completely blackened, and he coughed up a huge lungful of smoke. He staggered towards Rier and the others, who remained motionless as he drew nearer and nearer. Finally he stopped several feet away from them, stared at them as if not truly believing that they were there, and

then said, "Ouch." At which point he fell forward
again.

"Perfect," muttered Rier.

Xyon reached his ship without any further incident.
That was something of a relief; considering everything
that had gone on since he'd set foot on the damned
planet, it was nice to have at least one thing go smoothly for him.

"Hello, Xyon," his ship greeted him when he stepped
into the cockpit. He referred to it as a cockpit because it
was really too small to be reasonably called a bridge,
being large enough only to accommodate two or three
people at most.

"Hello, Lyla," he replied. "Fire up the main thrusters
and let's get out of here."

"Is someone trying to kill you?" inquired the ship.
Naturally, it was capable of multitasking, so even as the
ship conversed with Xyon, it brought the engines on
line and heated up the main thrusters. The ship itself
was not remarkably large or even particularly pretty to
look at, being somewhat irregularly shaped since Xyon
had a consistent habit of building on to it here and there
whenever he had the resources or the luck to find something he could adapt. But the ship was fast and maneuverable, with a stolen cloaking device and enough
weaponry to see him through most fights. At least,
most fights that enabled him to hit and run.

"Of course someone's trying to kill me. It wouldn't
be a normal day, would it." He ran a quick systems
check.

"Your respiration rate is three percent above the
norm. Bio scans reveal three contusions, and eighteen
burn marks."

"Well, running one step ahead of a fireball the size of a small moon will do that to you. Come on, Lyla, get us out of—"

There was a thump at the front view port and Xyon's head snapped around. A dog was there, outside, with fur as black as night and a sword that looked like it meant business. It should have posed no threat at all, but the dog swung the blade around and struck the view port. To Xyon's astonishment, a narrow crack ribboned across the port.

The Dog stared straight into Xyon's face, as if committing every centimeter of its structure to memory. Xyon felt a chill go down his spine even as he called out, *"Lyla! Leaving now would be a truly excellent idea!"*

The sword was drawn back to strike again, and then with a roar of its thrusters, the ship lifted off. The black-furred dog seemed to hesitate a moment, as if trying to decide whether to try and continue hacking its way in. At the last moment, the Dog threw itself clear. It was not a panicked move, though, that much Xyon could tell. Instead, the creature had simply calculated whether there was time to accomplish its task, discovered that there wasn't, and exited its position. But Xyon had the uncomfortable feeling that the meeting was only a preliminary one. Even as the ship, *Lyla* by name (he had named it after the on-board consciousness that powered it), broke free of the planet's gravity, Xyon did not believe that he had managed to achieve safety, but simply had obtained a momentary stay of execution.

IV.

SHE HAD COME TO THINK of him as the Red Man. At first he had showed up only every few dreams, but lately he was always there, omnipresent. He watched her as if she were some sort of microbe, and his form was frequently different. Sometimes he was normal sized, no bigger than an average man; other times he was gargantuan, his face taking up the entire sky and leering down at her. At times like that, she felt the most powerless. She wanted to fight back, but she had absolutely no idea how to go about it. She endeavored to reach into inner resources, to pull up bravery and determination and everything else that a young girl could possibly require under such circumstances. But she kept coming up empty. All she could do was turn and run, even in her dreams. Her pumping legs would carry her over the vast wasteland, and as before, the voices *would come to her, whispering things, asking her to join them, to stay with them, to become one with them. And as always they were so quiet, so quiet. All except the Red Man, the master manipulator, overseeing all and laughing, confident, in his power.*

"Go away, go away," she would call to him, and still he ignored her. And on one occasion, one particularly horrible occasion, his gigantic face had filled the sky and his hand had reached down for her. Reached down and seemed ready to scoop her up, possibly to throw her, possibly to crush her . . . she couldn't even begin to guess. All she knew was that she couldn't get away, and she raised her arms in front of her face to ward him off even as she sobbed and cried and begged for mercy that would not be forthcoming . . .

And then she woke up.

Her instinct was to cry out, to shriek her mother's name, but thanks to long months of training, she stifled the impulse. She had had a good deal of practice in keeping her mouth shut, for she had not wanted to continue to alarm her mother. Consequently, she had foregone the habit of sleeping somewhere outside so that her mother wouldn't be concerned as to her whereabouts. She certainly didn't need mother wandering all over the planet trying to find where her wayward daughter had slumped into slumber on yet another evening.

On the other hand, she didn't want to rouse her mother from sound sleep by waking up screaming. So she had developed a most disconcerting compromise, training herself to stifle her instinctive response so as not to disturb anyone. It took a supreme effort of will. As disconcerted, as disoriented as she was in her dreams, she had to reorient herself that much more quickly. It was the only way she could prevent herself from crying out.

She managed it this night, although just barely. Her mouth was open to scream for help, but at the last split instant, she remembered. Her desperate reaction was instantaneous: She sank her teeth into her lower lip so hard that blood trickled down, and she felt as if her entire lower jaw was going to go numb from pain. But she was at least successful, containing the urge to cry out and suppressing it.

Her room was dark, and she sat up in bed, reaching up with one sleeve to wipe the trickling blood from her chin. She wished that she could have felt some degree of triumph, or even vague pleasure, in her success, but all she felt was dread. For someday her control would be insufficient, and then would return the cries in the night, and her mother would learn with sinking heart that the dreams had not ceased. That, in fact, they had become more persistant, more clear than ever before, even though that clarity was still confusing in most aspects. She had wanted to spare her mother needless anguish, instead she had lied to her and hidden the truth. Even though she'd done it for her mother's own good, she still felt guilty over it.

She heard footsteps just outside her door, and for one panicked moment she thought that perhaps she had had less control than she thought. That perhaps she had indeed cried out in her sleep and, as a result, summoned her mother inadvertently. She flopped back onto the bed, trying to appear as relaxed as possible, ignoring the sweat that filled the sheets and matted down the back of her nightclothes so that she felt a chill cutting through her. Just before the door opened, she realized she was holding her breath from nervousness, so she did the best she could to feign steady and relaxed breathing.

The light from the corridor just outside played across her face and, even with her eyes closed, she could sense her mother peering in at her. The tableau remained frozen that way for ages, then the door slowly closed. As forced as her "normal" breathing had been, Riella now let out a long, unsteady sigh, her heart fluttering within her chest.

Then she heard something else, something that confused her greatly. Her mother was talking to someone, but she had not known that her mother was expecting any guests. This was a particularly singular state of affairs because Riella couldn't remember the last time that anyone had come to the house. Guests were not only a rarity, they were nonexistent. This was naturally more than enough to provoke Riella's curiosity, but she didn't want to do anything to draw attention to herself.

Cautiously, ever so cautiously, Riella swung her legs down and off the bed. With exaggerated care, she stepped onto the floor, pausing to see if there was any creaking of the floorboards beneath her feet. There was nothing. She strained her ears and heard muttering from the other room. Her mother's voice, definitely, and one other. She thought—although she couldn't be sure—that it was a male voice. That was even more unusual. She had spotted her mother chatting, from rare time to time, with other women in the town, but never a man.

She smiled to herself. Could it be that her mother had a secret life herself that she was trying to keep from Riella. That there was a man involved, and her mother thought Riella would be upset over a possible romance? How charming . . . even quaint. As if Riella would begrudge her anything in the world, considering how wonderful a mother she had been to her.

She crept ever so slowly to the door and opened it as narrowly as she could. The voices were definitely coming from the sitting room, which was connected via a small corridor. Riella suspected that, if she was very careful, she could sidle into the hallway and peer around it without being spotted herself, particularly if she did so on her hands and knees. She had to fight the urge to giggle; she felt like a little girl, a child, sneaking around the way she was.

She got down on her hands and knees and slowly made her way across the floor. At one point her knee caught on the trailing end of her nightdress and she almost fell flat on her face. This miscue was, in and of itself, nearly enough to send her into fits of giggles, but she managed to contain herself. She pulled the offending cloth out from under her knee and kept going.

She settled upon an angle of observation that did not permit her to see everything, but she was able to spy on their legs. They were sitting opposite each other, and she could make out their calves, shoes, and an occasional hand gesture. The man was wearing black gloves, which she thought was a bit curious, particularly considering how temperate the weather was.

Then her blood froze as she heard the topic of discussion.

"I'm telling you, I think the dreams have stopped. She tells me everything. If she were still having the dreams, I'd be the one to hear about it."

The man replied softly, ever so softly, with what seemed to Riella to be great control. She had to strain to hear him. "That," he seemed to say, "would be most unfortunate."

"Why unfortunate? Maybe she's not the one . . ."

"No. She is the one," said the man. Riella could see his gloved fist clenching. "I know it. I simply refuse to believe we've wasted all this time on her. Once the dreams start, they don't stop. Not in all the history of our people."

"But maybe this time . . ."

"No. Far more likely that she has simply fooled you."

"Why would she be trying to fool me?" demanded her mother. There was clear irritation in her voice. "What would be the point?"

"Perhaps she doesn't trust you. Perhaps she has figured it out . . ."

"No. She hasn't." Her mother was speaking with a tone she had never heard before. In all her life, she had never heard her mother talk with anything other than love, affection, and concern. Now she sounded angry, impatient. Even a bit cynical. "She has not figured it out. She trusts me implicitly."

"If she did, then she would tell you about the dreams."

"That's a circular argument, Zoran."

The name struck Riella with such force that it was almost like a physical blow. She recoiled from it, and it was all she could do not to let out a gasp of shock. That name, *Zoran*—that was the name. The name from the dreams. She was sure of it. She had had a vague sense of it in her nighttime imaginings, but now that she heard it articulated, she was positive that was it. But what could it mean? Who was he? And why in the world was he having any sort of dealings with her mother?

"Do you have any explanation, then?" Zoran was asking her.

"Maybe . . ." Her mother steepled her fingers, apparently giving the matter some thought. "Maybe she simply doesn't want to worry me. That could be it, you know. Sometimes the best explanations are the easiest."

"You may be right. Then again, you may be wrong. We cannot afford to take the chance. I want you to start talking to her about them again."

"She'll be suspicious."

"You cannot have it both ways, Malia. Either she trusts you implicitly, in which event she will not attribute your inquiries to anything other than a mother's concern. Or else she already suspects you, in which case no damage will be done because she is aware that all is not as it seems."

Riella felt as if her world was spinning around her. All of *what* wasn't as it seemed? It didn't make any sense to her. Perhaps . . .

Perhaps she was still dreaming. Yes. Yes, that made as much sense as anything. Maybe more. The entire scene had an almost dreamlike quality about it.

"Matters may be coming to a head, in any event. We may not have much time," Zoran was saying.

"Why not?" Malia sounded worried. "What's happened?"

"The Dogs of War have been sniffing around. They captured one of my people while the fool was 'enjoying' himself at some backwater tavern. It's possible that he managed to withstand their questioning—likely, in fact—but it's also possible that he didn't. If that's the case, then sooner or later the trail is going to lead the Dogs of War here, straight to your so-called daughter."

So-called? Yes . . . yes, it had to be a dream.

"Am I going to have to . . . ?"

The question trailed off. Riella was befuddled,

having no idea what the rest of the query could possibly be.

"Kill her?" Zoran grunted. "That would be unfortunate. But if the Quiet Place represents the source of power that legends say it does, she cannot be allowed to fall into the wrong hands."

Riella clapped a hand over her mouth to contain the shriek that was building in her. This was beyond a dream. This was a nightmare.

Then she heard a creak of a cushion and the one called Zoran leaned forward. She had the briefest glimpse of his face.

It was red. The red face from her dreams. The face that had hung in the air and laughed and sneered at her, and seemed to be in control of her life.

She skittered backwards, crablike, and banged into the wall with her shoulder.

Instantly the atmosphere seemed to change in the adjacent room. "What was that?" she heard Zoran demand.

"What was what? I didn't hear anything."

"I thought I did. Some sort of thud."

"Possibly some animals outside, rooting around in the garbage. They do that sometimes."

Riella wasn't waiting to hear the rest of the conversation. She virtually flew across the floor, making no sound, and she slithered back into her room, not even daring to breathe. She clambered into her bed, readjusted her sheets and then performed one of the greatest accomplishments of her young life: She managed to feign something approaching normal breathing while her true desire was to scream and keep screaming until someone showed up to awaken her from the living nightmare in which she was trapped.

There was a sound at her door and it took all her will not to jump at the sound. She remained instead absolutely immobile. She didn't know if her mother (mother?) or Zoran or both were peering in at her. What she did know was that she dare not give the slightest indication that she had overheard anything.

"She sweats a good deal," she heard Zoran whisper.

"Perhaps she's in the midst of a dream right now."

"Perhaps. Question her in the morning. Learn what you can. I will remain in the vicinity. Report to me what she tells you, and we will determine her future from that point."

"All right, Zoran."

"And Malia . . ."

"Yes?"

There was a significant pause, and then he said, "Do not make a muddle of this. Two corpses are as easy to arrange as one, and on a nowhere world like this, I assure you there will be very few inquiries. Do we understand each other?"

"Threats are not necessary, Zoran."

"No. Not necessary. Just one of the perks. Good evening to you, Malia."

Riella listened to the departing sound of his footsteps, heard the front door close, listened as the sound of his feet receded into the night. During that time, her "mother" didn't move from the spot. Then she heard Malia slowly approach her, and it was all she could do not to scream as the woman's fingers brushed against her check and delicately rearranged a few strands of hair, as lovingly and solicitously as any mother might. Then her mother walked out of the room, leaving Riella with her mind awhirl.

She had no intention of sleeping that night. In point

of fact, her intention was to bolt from the house at the earliest opportunity, to get as far away as possible. But the night held its own terrors now as she envisioned Zoran waiting somewhere for her. Perhaps he was watching the house specifically to see if she'd run away. Or maybe, somehow, he would just know, and come after her in the dark, and . . .

"Riella. Come on . . . wake up, sleepyhead."

Riella blinked against the light pouring in through her window. Her night clothes were so soaked through that they made a peeling noise as she sat up. She looked around and there was her mother, as cheerful and pleasant as ever. She riffled Riella's hair and said, "I can't remember the last time you slept this late. I couldn't bring myself to wake you earlier, because you were sleeping so soundly. You must be feeling very relaxed."

"Very," Riella said gamely. In the harsh honesty of daylight, she was beginning to wonder whether the entire unreal experience from the previous night had been just that, unreal. It was possible that she had imagined the entire thing. It certainly made more sense than thinking that somehow her mother was in a bizarre conspiracy with a red-skinned man who had haunted her dreams.

"Well, I made you a nice lunch; you slept straight through breakfast. Why don't you get yourself washed up and come into the kitchen."

"All right, mother." Already the shreds of the night's recollections were falling away, the fantasy replaced by the reality. Obviously her dreams were becoming more and more sinister, presenting themselves convincingly as realistic scenarios rather than surreal exploits through an illusionary planet's surface. Everything was, in fact, unchanged. She could see that now. She had cooked up the conversations of the previous night from her fevered imaginings, but none of it was based in reality.

Her mother was heading for the door of the room, but she stopped in the door frame, turned and said, "If you're sleeping that soundly, then those dreams you were having must have really gone away." Then she paused and added, "Have they?"

Riella's breath caught in her throat and once again she was faced with the temptation to scream. "Yes," she said hollowly.

"Because if they hadn't gone away . . . you would tell me, wouldn't you?"

"Of course I would, Mother. Why wouldn't I?"

"No reason," her mother said gamely. "No reason at all. Is there?"

"No. None."

"Well," Malia rubbed her hands together. "We can speak more of that later. Because, you know, I worry so much."

"I'm sure you do, Mother," said Riella, as visions of the previous night flashed through her mind. "Believe me . . . I'll bet it's not half as much as I worry."

V.

SI CWAN HAD NOT BEEN exactly sure of what to expect when informed that he would be meeting with the ruling council of Montos City, for Montos was very much off the beaten path for the Thallonian Empire, and he had never actually had the opportunity to go there. Montos had kept very much to itself, and since it was not a particularly advanced world (beyond minimal capability for space travel and the like) and not especially inclined to challenge Thallonian rule, Si Cwan's people had not given it overmuch attention.

But these were different times. The worlds of Thallonian space were on their own, and even the smallest planets had new priority. Particularly when threats appeared on the horizon that had not been there before.

So Si Cwan had mounted this diplomatic visit to Montos at a time when things were still relatively peaceful, but they could heat up more quickly than any-one on Montos might anticipate. Accompanying him were Zak Kebron, the massively built Brikar who was chief of security, and Lieutenant Soleta, the Vulcan sci-ence officer of the *Excalibur* who was the only one be-sides Si Cwan to have any sort of extensive experience with Thallonian space. Even Soleta had not been to Montos. Naturally, that meant that the planet presented some scientific curiosity to her. During the voyage to Montos, Si Cwan had wondered whether or not it might have been a good idea to have brought Robin Lefler with him as well. Ultimately, though, it probably hadn't been necessary. Besides, he reasoned, she spent an in-ordinate amount of time attending to his needs and re-quests, and she doubtlessly enjoyed the break from having to deal with him.

Upon arriving on Montos, they were escorted to the council chamber. They had been greeted respectfully by their escort, who even seemed just a bit intimidated by the sight and presence of Si Cwan and quite daunted by the glowering and formidable presence of Kebron. Once they had arrived at the council chamber, however, they had been left to stand there—with no chairs or even the slightest amenities—to face a raised podium surrounded by half a dozen chairs, three on each side. No one seemed to be showing up to sit in any of the chairs, however, or even to give them a few moments of their time. At least half an hour had passed since they had first set foot upon Montos, and Kebron, for one, was beginning to lose any semblance of patience.

Normally Kebron was one of the more temperate of individuals. He could afford to be. Anyone who bore a marked resemblance to a walking land mass could af-ford to view the world with a certain degree of equanimity. But Zak Kebron also did not suffer fools gladly, nor did he particularly enjoy having his time wasted.

"We should leave," he said finally.

"Don't be absurd, Kebron," Si Cwan told him. "We've not come all this way simply to turn around and leave again."

"True. But if we have to, we will."

"They will be along directly."

"We do not know that," Kebron said reasonably. "We may be targets."

Soleta, who had been occupying herself by running analyses of the atmosphere with her tricorder, glanced over at Kebron with an eyebrow cocked. "Targets?" She seemed neither worried nor dismissive of the notion. "Why do you say that?"

"We are in one place. There is no one else around. One avoids being a target by moving."

"You're being paranoid, Kebron," Si Cwan told him.

Kebron, who had no neck to speak of, swiveled his entire torso to face Si Cwan. "Yes. Your point being—?"

"That there's no point in being paranoid all the time."

"Who told you to say that?"

Si Cwan rolled his eyes. "I'm sure someone will be along—"

"I am not. Your problem, Cwan—one of many—is that your imperious attitude precludes your being able to accept that someone might be setting you up. You do not believe you could be outmaneuvered or manipulated in that way."

"And do you know what your problem is, Kebron?"

"Yes. My problem is you."

Before Si Cwan could respond, there was the sound

of the chamber door scraping open. Si Cwan couldn't help but notice that Kebron subtly—at least, as subtly as he was capable of doing anything—interposed his bulk between Si Cwan and the door. For some reason, this amused Si Cwan greatly. For all the antipathy that Kebron had developed towards him, nevertheless his sense of duty compelled him to protect Si Cwan from any potential attack. He was further amused to see that Soleta instinctively drifted behind Kebron as well. It made sense; Kebron's first line of defense was, naturally, his considerable bulk coupled with his fairly impervious hide. Most assaults had little chance of getting through.

The individual who came through the door, however, didn't seem to present all that much of a threat. He was pale skinned, as Montosians usually were, and his antennae were slightly droopy. He was clearly rather elderly, with graying whiskers sticking out at odd angles from his pointed chin, and when he walked it was with an odd bit of a bow-legged shuffle.

He carried a triangular stone in one hand. The triangular shape had obviously not been its natural state; it had been carefully honed and polished into that condition. What was most odd about him was that he appeared to be talking to himself. He waved the stone around, muttering in a soft, rapid-fire voice, as if he were holding an animated chat with people that only he himself could see. Clearly he represented no threat, but it was difficult to determine just what it was he did represent. Si Cwan and the others looked at each other with openly quizzical gazes, for none of them knew just quite what to make of the newcomer.

He sauntered across the room to the chair that was on the raised platform, eased himself into it, and continued to talk to himself for a few more moments. Then he looked over at Si Cwan, his attention finally focusing on the ambassador and his associates.

"Meeting come to order!" he called out authoritatively as if addressing a considerable assemblage, and he rapped the flat bottom of the triangle on his desk. "This meeting of the ruling council of Montos is now called to order." He squinted at Si Cwan. "And you are?"

Si Cwan was never one to allow himself to be thrown by anything. He drew himself up quickly and said with his customary self-possession, "Lord Si Cwan, late of the royal house of Thallon. And these are Lieutenants Soleta and Zak Kebron of the starship *Excalibur,* representing the interests of the UFP. Do I have the honor of addressing one of the members of the ruling council?"

"No."

The brisk negative response confused the hell out of Si Cwan. "Did you say no?"

The old man looked around, apparently under the impression that perhaps someone else had spoken and he simply hadn't spotted him. When he satisfied himself that no one else had spoken on Cwan's behalf, he nodded and said, "Yes. Yes, I believe so."

"Then, sir, who are you?"

"I am Fr'Col." He said it with a faint air of surprise, as if he couldn't imagine why in the world Si Cwan would even need to ask. Wasn't it, after all, self-evident.

"And you are not a member of the ruling council?"

"No. I am the entirety of the ruling council."

"Can we go home now?" Kebron said under his breath. The question was addressed to Soleta, who had sharp enough ears to hear the muttered sentiment. Naturally she maintained her reserve and didn't even acknowledge the comment.

"May I ask where the rest of the council is?"

"Yes," the person who had introduced himself as Fr'Col said. And then he sat there and twirled his triangular stone around as if it were the most incredibly fascinating thing he'd ever seen.

Si Cwan felt himself losing his patience. It was an impulse that he fought against. It had taken him many months of concentration and self-discipline to tone down the imperious attitude that many, including most frequently Kebron, had told him he possessed. Although Cwan still felt as if they had overstated the matter, nevertheless he had endeavored to act a bit less like displaced royalty, simply out of interest in helping life go more smoothly. It was one thing to be imperious when you were in an environment where people scuttled about at your slightest whim and lived for the opportunity to perform one, just one, task on your behalf. You did not encounter that sort of attitude on a starship, however, where even after all this time, Si Cwan still couldn't help but feel that there were many aboard the *Excalibur* who regarded him simply as a guest. Certainly there was precious little kowtowing aboard the starship, and the crew's attitude didn't seem likely to adjust itself in the near future. Since there was only one of him and a thousand or so of them, it seemed to make sense that he should be the one to try and make some changes in expectations. It had not been easy. And he had certainly not been particularly humble. He still deported himself with an air of someone who was accustomed to being obeyed. This was a problem since no one on the ship was really particularly obliged to obey him. But he had worked to adjust and, to some degree, so had others aboard the ship (except, naturally, for Ke-bron, who seemed perfectly sanguine about the notion of just taking Si Cwan and stuffing him down a photon torpedo shaft at the earliest opportunity).

The bottom line was that Cwan tried to be a bit more tolerant of lesser mortals, of which there was a staggering overabundance. And so, with that forced patience that came as naturally to him as light came to a black hole, Si Cwan said, "All right. Where . . . is the rest . . . of the council?"

"Not here."

"Not here. I see. Would it be possible to bring them here?"

Fr'Col considered that a moment. "Yesss," he said slowly, nodding and scratching his chin with the triangle. "Yes, it would. But you wouldn't want to do that."

"I wouldn't."

"No."

"Why wouldn't I?"

"Well!" Fr'Col said as if the notion was appalling to him. He seemed incredulous that Si Cwan would even have suggested such an idea. "They'd stink the place up something terrible."

Si Cwan felt as if he was losing his mind, but it was Soleta who spoke up and said, "They are dead, are they not."

"Of course," Fr'Col replied.

"The rest of the ruling council are dead." Si Cwan said it slowly as if he needed to explain it to himself. Fr'Col's head bobbed in confirmation. He placed the triangular stone on the small desk next to him, then picked it up again for no discernable reason. "May I ask how that happened?"

"Yes."

There was another pause, and Si Cwan had to fight the impulse to step forward and rip out Fr'Col's throat with his teeth. "How did it happen?"

"They got old. I object!" he suddenly switched tone and slammed the triangular stone on the desk.

"You?—" He looked at his companions. Kebron's face was inscrutable as always, and it wasn't as if the Vulcan Soleta had a remarkably expressive mien either. He looked back at Fr'Col. "You object . . . to what?"

"Things," Fr'Col said ominously.

Dead silence then.

Si Cwan felt his patience slipping away, and with visible effort he forced himself to maintain his equanimity.

"May I ask what . . . things?"

"Yes."

More dead silence.

"I'm going to kill him," rumbled Kebron, not making an effort anymore to keep his voice down. Fr'Col, however, did not seem to notice.

Si Cwan, however, did. And like tissue paper in water, his forbearance suddenly dissolved. He suddenly seemed to grow about a foot in height, and the air in the chamber appeared to darken with his anger. "Listen to me carefully, old man. Perhaps you didn't hear me before. In case you have forgotten during this interminable conversation, I am Lord Si Cwan, once a Thallonian noble, and there was a time that I wouldn't give this pissant world of yours a second thought, or even a first thought. But times have changed. The worlds of Thallonian space, out of a sense of mutual protection, can and must draw together. That means every world, even small worlds such as yours. There are formidable forces out there who would just as soon step on you as look at you. The Redeemers, for instance. Those religious zealots are presently spreading their reign of fanatacism in the M'Gewn star sector, and the starship *Excalibur* is embroiled in a conflict with them there. But we had been asked by the ruling council of this world—we had thought—to come here. Did you or didn't you?"

Fr'Col scratched his chin thoughtfully. With a moment of apparent lucidity, he said, "I seem to recall something about that. Gothil did that, I believe. Before he passed away last week, that is."

"Wonderful. Well, the fact is that you are here, now. If you are all that is left of the ruling council, and you need assistance, then spearhead a movement among your people to elect new members. If you are fit to lead yourself, then do so. Either way, make a decision and let us proceed together to follow the lead of the United Federation of Planets and create an alliance and unity among the worlds of what was formerly Thallonian space. The might of the Thallonians no longer exists to protect small worlds such as yourself, and now is the time to forge new alliances that will see you through to the next century and beyond. Do you understand what I am saying, Fr'Col?"

"Of course, I understand; you don't have to shout."

Si Cwan was about to tell him that he hadn't been shouting, and then he realized that, in fact, he had been. His voice had become progressively louder as his frustration level had risen. He cleared his throat loudly and then said, "My pardon, Fr'Col."

"I don't want your pardon," Fr'Col said with surprising fire. "I'm not even entirely sure I want you. We don't have all that much need for alliances or guidance here on Montos, Ambassador. We've had some dealings with other races. We've done some trade here and there, although we've never really come out with much in the bargain. We've traded valuable minerals and gotten useless junk in return. Objects that former members of the council thought was going to be of use, but never really served much purpose here. Historically, we've kept more or less to ourselves and been left alone."

"Because of Thallonian influence."

"So you say. But you could stand on the highest mountain in these parts every morning and wave your arms, and the sun would come up. You could then turn around and claim that Thallonian influence caused the sun to rise, but the claim doesn't make it so. You see what I'm saying?"

It was all Si Cwan could do to suppress a smile of amusement. Apparently, the old man did have some spirit to him after all. "Yes. I do." Then his demeanor grew serious. "But claims shouldn't automatically be dismissed out of hand. Danger doesn't have a habit of dispensing copious warnings; it simply presents itself, and if you are not prepared for it, it can go rather badly for you."

Fr'Col appeared to consider that, stroking his wispy beard once more. Then, abruptly, he slammed the stone down like a gavel. "It shall be considered!" he announced. "I shall need to consult with my people, however."

"Of course. Perhaps we can have the opportunity to address the—"

But Fr'Col wasn't listening to him. Instead he had slid off his chair and proceeded to amble to the door. Moments later he had left the room.

"That went well," Si Cwan said after a time.

"In what reality did that go well?" Kebron demanded.

"You have no experience with small worlds such as this, Kebron," Si Cwan informed him haughtily. "We are dealing with basic physics here. Objects at rest tend to stay at rest—"

"Unless acted upon by an outside force," Soleta finished promptly.

"Precisely. On a world such as this, the tendency is to keep doing things the way they were done yesterday, and the day before, and so on. Complacency sets in, as does resistance to change. Occasionally it takes a while just to get the attention of those in power. But once you have, then—"

The doors swung inward, and Fr'Col entered. He muttered to himself as he walked to his chair, eased himself into it, then rapped authoritatively with the triangular stone as he called out, "Meeting come to order! This meeting of the ruling council of Montos is now called to order." Then he lay the stone down, interlaced his fingers and stared at Si Cwan. Cwan waited for his pronouncement or decision.

Fr'Col stared at Si Cwan, his entire face a dark scowl, and then he said, "And . . . you are?"

"I'm going to go wait in the ship," said Zak Kebron.

VI.

THE HOUSE LOOKED UNASSUMING, which naturally prompted Xyon to assume the worst. It stood on the edge of a dirt road with walls made of some sort of bricklike material.

The hairs on the back of his neck rose. That alone would have been more than enough to alert him, for he generally tended to trust his hunches. But standing around outside with concerns and raised hairs wasn't going to accomplish a damned thing. He considered the possibility of sneaking around the back, climbing up through a window, rooting about. All of those were possibilities. On the other hand, he wasn't sure just how necessary any of that would be. It would have been one thing if he were trying to infiltrate a fort or some sort of outpost, but this was simply a house, a house where there was definitely someone in residence, for he had caught fleeting glimpses of her through the windows. It was an older woman, a pale-skinned sample of the type on this world. She definitely had something on her mind. Xyon could discern that even from the furtive glances he'd caught of her, particularly because she kept glancing toward the second story of the house. On the second story, there was a room with shuttered windows. There was only one room like that, and Xyon had the feeling that whatever was causing the older woman concern, it was in that room.

In all likelihood, it was the mysterious Riella.

Montos was not a particularly populous world: There were a couple of outlying tribes that were somewhat nomadic in nature, and the rest of the small populace resided within the proximity of the central city. It had taken Xyon no time at all to check out the more remote areas before determining that Riella wasn't to be found there; instead he turned his attention to the more populated regions.

During his search, he had been guided naturally by what people he questioned told him, but also by his gut instinct. He had a knack for detecting duplicity, and lying to him was generally something of a waste of time. Nevertheless, despite his natural gifts, he had anticipated it being an extremely arduous, time-consuming, and even boring process. He could not have been more wrong; it didn't take long at all. Apparently, the girl had something of a reputation, both in her manner and in her preference for seclusion. Of course, Xyon was no fool. He knew the male mentality well enough to know that all manner of attitudes could be ascribed to a young woman who, quite simply, didn't provide the local males with the kind of entertainment they'd prefer. The fault might very well lie with them rather than her.

In any event, the young men to whom he spoke had no trouble at all steering Xyon to the woman he sought. They had initially regarded him with some suspicion, for he was clearly of alien origin and Montos was not accustomed to having many visitors. Xyon had managed to allay their concerns somewhat adroitly, however, by the simple expedient of giving them their first taste of Romulan ale (several bottles of which he kept securely tucked away on his ship). He hadn't wanted the boys talking about his presence to the wrong people until he had time to accomplish what he needed to. That wasn't going to be a problem, considering that they were sitting around in a large circle, sporting rather goofy grins and giggling incessantly at one another under the impression that they were actually having a conversation. By the time they sobered up, with any luck, Xyon would be long gone.

With Riella? Xyon still wasn't sure. To a certain degree, he was improvising. His disgustingly annoying streak of sentimentalism was prompting him to take a hand in the matter, but he wasn't entirely certain as to how strong a hand he should take.

There were two things that were certain, however. The first was that nothing was going to be accomplished by skulking around outside the house. And the second was that the passage of time was only going to bring the Dogs of War closer, not place them farther away.

Opting to go for the direct approach, Xyon walked up to the front door and knocked on it with authority. He figured he had nothing to lose. If the woman inside (the mother, he suspected) proved intransigent, he could always gain entry to the structure via other means.

There was a stirring from within, and Xyon thought he detected two sets of footsteps. Then the door creaked open and a woman's face appeared. It was the same woman he had spied through the windows earlier. Her face was careworn, and when she looked at Xyon her eyes went wide in surprise. Very likely she was no more accustomed to seeing offworlders than anyone else on this backwater planet was.

"What do you want?" she demanded. Straight, to the point, suspicious. He could appreciate that attitude. It was probably the same way that he'd react.

"My name is Xyon," he said. "I admit, you don't know me and have no reason to trust me. But I'm here to tell you that you and Riella are in danger."

"How do you know Riella?" she said.

That, of course, was precisely the reply he'd been hoping for. He'd figured that if he'd asked whether Riella resided there, he might be met with obfuscation. By presenting it as a given, he'd gotten her to admit that Riella was there.

"It's enough that I know," he told her. "May I come in and—"

She cast a glance over her shoulder. Someone was standing there, probably Riella. "I would rather you didn't." And she started to close the door in his face.

Xyon put a firm hand against the door and stopped it from shutting. "I don't think you quite understand me, Madam. I said there is danger coming. I trust that word is not unclear to you."

Her voice cold, she said, "You are a stranger, sir. I do not know you, and yet you come here and spout about danger, talking about my daughter. The only danger that has presented itself in recent days is you. Good day to you." She pushed again, this time obviously applying all her strength.

Xyon, however, didn't budge. His arm was strong and

straight and didn't bend in the slightest, despite the effort she was putting into closing the door. Her inability to move him at all registered as clear surprise on her face. Nor did his voice, calm and assured, display any indication of strain. "You are quite right. I am a stranger. I could have left you and your daughter to your fate and not had it impede my life in any way. I chose not to do so, however. Now you can show some appreciation for that and help me to help you save your life. Or you can fight me, wasting time and further jeopardizing yourself. Let me come in and we can work out—"

The door was suddenly yanked open and Xyon took a step back in surprise, for the person he was staring at was most definitely not a young female named Riella.

He was tall and powerfully built, and he had fiery red skin. Xyon instantly recognized him as a Thallonian.

"You have been told to leave," said the Thallonian. "I suggest you do so."

"Who are you?"

"Someone who is welcome here. That makes one of us. Now be on your way."

"You don't care about danger either?"

"I assure you, child, there is nothing you know that I do not." The Thallonian dripped scorn. "Now be off with you."

"Perhaps you might want to let me speak to Riella about that," Xyon said. "After all, she is the one who is in danger, red man. Not you. Why don't I—"

Xyon had never seen anyone move quite as quickly as the Thallonian. Before he knew what was happening, he was on the ground, a pain in his chest from where the Thallonian had punched him. He was gasping, but he was determined not to rub his chest where the pain was. He didn't want to give the Thallonian the satisfaction.

The Thallonian, for his part, had barely seemed to move. Clearly he was a warrior of some sort. Xyon chided himself mentally; he had been horrifically over-confident. If the Thallonian had had a blade concealed in his hand, Xyon would be dead instead of just sitting in a rather undignified position with a sore rump.

Obviously, the Thallonian knew that as well, for he said, "You were lucky just now, boy. Do not push your luck. Understood?" Without waiting for a reply, he pushed the door closed and this time Xyon made no effort to stop it.

"Idiots," he muttered. Then he rose, dusted himself off, and studied the house carefully to see what would be the best means of sneaking in.

That was when his sharp ears heard something hit the ground from behind the house. Immediately he knew from the way in which it landed that it was heavy enough to be a body. Indeed, it probably was a body. Could it actually be that the Thallonian and the woman had tossed Riella's body out the back window? Were they vaguely under the impression that no one would notice? How stupid could they possibly be?

Then he heard a low moan. Perhaps the body was not dead after all, but instead only on the brink of death. That would reduce the Thallonian and "mother" to the rank of "attempted killers" rather than murderers. Cold comfort, that.

Then came a grunt, and he could tell from that grunt—along with the sounds of dirt and random pebbles being scattered—that the body was most definitely not only alive, but kicking. It was getting to its feet and obviously was intending to go somewhere.

It was then that Xyon ventured in the direction of the back of the house. He moved with the utmost caution, although he was understandably curious about what it was that he was going to find. He already had a sneaking suspicion, however. And once he got within range, he saw that his suspicion was correct.

He saw, dangling from the back window of the house, a short piece of a makeshift rope, cobbled together from what appeared to be knotted bedclothes. It hung halfway down the back of the house, with the remaining distance to the ground covered by the simple act of allowing herself to fall. It had not been a graceful drop because he could tell from both what he had heard and the evidence of toe-displaced dirt that she had landed quite clumsily. Dirt and debris were scattered everywhere, and he could even see a bit of the imprint from where she had landed and come down hard on her rump.

He caught the briefest glimpse of her as she ran from the house. She was limping slightly, and he hoped that she hadn't injured herself too badly. The abodes in that area were set relatively close together, so she quickly disappeared down an alley between two other homes, but it was going to take far more than that for her to shake him. With that confidence in mind, he set off after her and hoped that the confidence wasn't misplaced.

Never before had Riella run so fast.

She had walked so many times around the relatively small area that had circumscribed her life. She knew the paths, knew every bush. There was the large boulder a short distance from her house that she had clambered upon when she was a little girl. There was that remarkable moss-covered area where she had lain and stared up at the moons and tried to get some sort of sense of what the future held for her.

Now she viewed all those places as if she were seeing them through other eyes. Even the most mundane and familiar elements of her life were alien and frightening to her. It was a natural extension of her present state of mind, for the place that she had called home all this time had been transformed into a strange and unknowable place.

Her mother had spent the morning grilling her about the dreams, first gently and then with greater and greater belligerence. Every so often Malia would seem to realize that her aggressiveness in the matter was odd and drawing attention to things that she would rather not have attention drawn to. In those instances, she would rein herself in, although it was always temporary. Clearly she was running scared, and Riella knew exactly who she was scared of.

The source of the fear arrived a short time later. Riella had been hiding up in her room when he arrived. Her mother didn't know she was hiding, of course. Riella had simply pleaded fatigue and gone up to take a nap. Having done so, she then crouched down by her door and listened carefully. Even so, straining her ears, she had only picked up bits and pieces of the conversation. But what she was hearing, she didn't like. To be in a situation where one's mother is in league with a spectre who haunts one's darkest dreams.

Well, naturally, the impulse is to extract oneself from such a situation as quickly as possible. She caught the eyes of a few scattered citizens as she ran, but no one said anything or tried to stop her. They seemed, at most, mildly curious as to what had propelled her in this manner, but other than that they didn't give her plight overmuch consideration. Every so often she would glance over her shoulder, wondering whether or not she was being followed. She felt haunted, hunted. She felt as if, at this point, there was no escape in any aspect of her life. In her sleep, her dreams came after her, and in her waking existence, her mother had been transformed from a beloved parent into an ally of those who would harm her.

How could her mother do that? How was it possible?

Maybe she's not your mother. The words came unbidden to her mind, but once there, would not leave. Was it possible? Why not? At this point, anything was possible. But all the memories she had, of her mother being there from her earliest days: bouncing her on her knee, wiping away the blood from a cut, loving her, caring about her, and being there for her every day of her life. All of those contradicted the new notion that this woman was, in fact, her worst enemy, a betrayer, a . . .

She couldn't think about it anymore. She just had to keep moving, keep running.

Which was precisely what Riella did.

The problem was, she had no idea where she was heading or what she was going to do. She had no real friends on Montos. Her entire world was her home and the woman with whom she shared it. With those cut off to her, she felt completely adrift. Still, one does not necessarily have to know where one is running to in order to run away from something else.

And so Riella had bolted, as quickly as her legs would take her.

It did not take her long to leave Montos City behind. The land beyond the city was not particularly inviting. There had not been a good deal of rainfall recently, and the ground was hard and cracked. There were, however, some areas with small mountains and (so she had heard) caves. Supposedly there was some danger and local children had been warned to stay away from the area lest mishaps befall them. Indeed, there were stories (folktales, she hoped) of children who had gone exploring in the caves and come to unhappy ends, their spirits still wailing away in eternal undead misery. That, however, did not bother Riella in the slightest. Her waking life was nightmarish enough. The prospect of facing other peoples' nightmares didn't deter her at all.

Food, however, was a concern. She had not been able to go down to the kitchen to obtain anything to take with her. She had no food, no water. Her prospects of survival were not plentiful. But she wasn't thinking about any of that. She was running purely on instinct. Unfortunately, her instincts weren't particularly sound. When concerns over practical matters, such as food and water warred for attention in her mind, she automatically pushed them away as a sort of self-defense mechanism.

At one point the toe of her shoe caught in one of the cracks in the ground, and she fell hard, scraping her right knee. She scrambled to her feet, blood trickling down the front of her right leg. She started to wipe it away, but then just took a deep breath and kept going.

The sun had reached its zenith, and she felt as if the heat was like fist blows beating her down. She pushed her way through it, determined not to let anything slow her. But her determination quickly crumbled, and she started to sob. She had never been more angry with herself than she was at that moment. She felt so weak, so useless, so utterly helpless. She was faced with a difficult situation, and she wasn't rising to it. She was letting herself be overwhelmed by it.

She saw some mountainous area ahead of her, separated from her by perhaps half a mile. She licked her lips and found that there was no moisture on her tongue to improve their chapped condition. They were becoming as hard and cracked as the rest of her face. The elegant antennae on her forehead were sagging under the unrelenting heat. Her mother had always tried to protect her from the effects of the sun, being extremely concerned and cautious about sunstroke or burning. She said there was a tendency in her family towards such mishaps. Riella no longer knew what to believe.

Her antennae were feeling tight, as if they were shriveling up on her. They were giving her more and more discomfort. Her whole body felt too tight on her. She was having trouble breathing, even thinking.

Then she heard something behind her. Something with sharp nails. She heard it scrabbling along, and it sounded like a wild animal. She was afraid to turn around, as if—whatever it was—it wouldn't be real if she didn't look at it. It wouldn't present any sort of threat if she just didn't acknowledge its existence by seeing it.

She heard it drawing closer, closer, and she realized that her plan wasn't exactly fraught with merit. Taking a deep breath, she turned around to face whatever it was. No furtive glances here; let whatever was coming after her take her head on.

It was two creatures. If they were just wild animals, intent on tearing her apart—somehow, she was ready for that. With her despairing view of her life as it presently stood and her chances that were monumentally slim, part of her really didn't care what happened to her from now on.

But they were not simply animals. There were two of them, humanoid in shape, and they were barreling towards her, their maws slightly opened, their tongues hanging out as if they were panting from the strain. No . . . no strain, she realized. They didn't seem the least bit tired. Instead, they were almost excited by it, as if they were in some sort of hunt mode.

And they were wearing clothes. That was the thing that sent Riella over the edge, that set her legs into motion; with a stifled shriek, she pivoted and started to run. She heard what sounded like a delirious chortle of amusement from one of them, or maybe both.

Then one of them spoke. A clothed animal that spoke. And she spotted, on its back, what appeared to be twin-bladed weapons crisscrossing. She felt as if her mind were slipping away. "Riella?" it said.

She couldn't move, couldn't even speak. She managed a stunned nod.

The creatures exchanged what appeared to be looks of surprised pleasure. "We smelled your blood!" it called to her. "We couldn't pass up the scent . . . and look who it led us to! How delightful!"

She glanced down at her legs, flashing beneath her, the streak of dried blood on her leg where she had cut it. She cursed the blood, cursed the gods that had put her into this hideous predicament, and reflexively she started to cry out for her mother to save her, remembering only at the last moment that that blessed woman provided no haven for her.

That was when she hit it.

She had no idea what it was she hit. It was just suddenly there, and she couldn't see it, but she ran full tilt into it and whatever it was, it didn't budge so much as a centimeter. In this case of the irresistible force meeting the immovable object, the force didn't stand a chance. Riella staggered back, reality swimming around her, her arms outstretched to either side, and they pinwheeled slightly before she fell back and hit the ground. Then blackness enveloped her.

But she did not slide completely into unconsciousness. She was vaguely, distantly aware of her surroundings. She felt as if she were in a gray area, hovering between the whispers of her frightening dreams and the equally intimidating reality of the world around her. And in that half-place, she heard chortling . . . and then words . . . and then anger, and the sounds of a fight of some sort . . .

And then an explosion . . . a series of explosions in the distance.

Suddenly, she was lifted. It would have been truly disorienting were she not already so light-headed, and she tried to open her eyes, but caught only a glimpse of longish hair that might have belonged to one of the creatures or might have been someone or something else . . .

Then she released her hold on consciousness and slipped away into merciful oblivion.

Atik wasn't entirely certain what had just happened. One moment the girl was running as fast as she could; he and Fista were bearing down on her, enjoying the thrill of the chase in a way that they didn't have all that many opportunities to do.

Abruptly she had stopped dead in her tracks. For a moment, Atik thought that she was changing her mind and was actually going to try and fight them. That, of course, would provide some momentary and very minor amusement before they ultimately, naturally, knocked her cold and dragged her off with them as Rier had told them to. But then Atik realized that, in fact, she had struck something. That seemed impossible; there was nothing there. But strike it she had, for she was staggering backwards as if having sustained some incredible impact due to her forward motion. Atik and Fista exchanged looks of confusion, as if each hoped that the other might have an explanation for what had just happened.

"Some sort of trick on her part?" Fista asked.

It seemed a possibility, and Atik tensed, allowing for their prey to abruptly turn, produce a weapon, and make a serious fight of it. But that didn't happen. Instead she fell backwards, hit the ground hard, and just lay there, spread-eagled, staring blankly up at the sky, her eyes apparently unable to decide whether to remain open or not.

"There's something there," Atik said.

"Out here? We're in the middle of nowhere! What could be here?"

Fista was more than happy to allow Atik to take the lead. The warrior dog advanced cautiously, affording Riella a cautious look as he stepped around her and moved towards where her flight had come to such an abrupt termination. He reached out with one paw gingerly, trying to brace himself for the possibility of some sort of unseen force field that would conceivably affect him as adversely as it had the girl.

And there, in midair, he felt some sort of smooth surface. Despite the heat from the sun, the metallic substance was remarkably cool to the touch. He slid his hand along it and felt it curve downward.

"What is it?" asked Fista, approaching cautiously. He tended to do everything cautiously.

"It's a ship. It has to be. It must have some sort of cloaking device." Atik began to walk the length of it, tracing it. His nostrils flared. "Waaaait a minute. The contours are familiar. It's hard to pick up any scent off it, but I would wager anything it's the same damnable vessel that was on Barspens! Yes, that's—"

That was when the discharge of a disruptor smashed across the open plains with deafening power. Atik jumped three feet in the air, and even as he did so, his swords (his "long claws") were in his hands. He whirled, not knowing what he was going to see and yet being completely unsurprised when he saw it.

It was the creature from back on Barspens. The one who had destroyed Rier's flagship, the one who had barely eluded capture. The one whose face Atik had so totally committed to memory.

He was standing there with a disruptor cradled in his arms and a look of quiet confidence on his face. Fista was frozen, unmoving, his body stiff and alert. The blast had clearly been a warning shot. The insensate body of the girl was lying about equidistant between them.

Reflexively, Atik judged the distance between them. But the muzzle of the disruptor angled not-so-subtly in his direction. "I wouldn't," the creature said coolly, "if I were you."

"Who are you?" Atik snarled, although he did freeze in place.

"My name is unimportant," he said.

"If so, then why do you hesitate to say it."

"It's unimportant to me. Apparently, it's important to you; why, then, should I give you anything of importance."

Atik's expression grew more fierce, and a growl grew deep in his throat. He waited to see if his obvious fierceness had some sort of impact on the long-haired humanoid. It didn't. The disruptor in his hand didn't waver, and his expression remained quite calm. Fista, for his part, was starting to move.

"I don't want to shoot you," the newcomer said. "But I will if I have reason to."

Atik and Fista exchanged glances smugly. Clearly they had the upper hand, for the newcomer was obviously hesitant to use his weaponry. And if that was the case, then they could use the hesitation to their advantage.

Suddenly there was an explosion of sound and energy from the disruptor, and before Atik could move, Fista went down, a charred hole in his armor, barely breathing. Confusion and surprise were his last expression, frozen on his face.

"On the other hand," continued the creature, "I can also kill if the mood strikes me. Or if I get the impression that you think I'm so weak that you can take me down with no problem. A preemptive strike, if you will, to head off potential unpleasantness for both of us."

If the creature's intention was to realign Atik's opinion of him, he succeeded. Atik actually took several steps back, making certain to keep his long fangs immobile. He toyed with the idea of trying to throw one of the vicious blades in hopes of doing serious damage to this interloper. But he judged the speed and determination with which the creature had moved, and he came to the conclusion that such an attempt would be folly.

The creature was looking at him carefully, and finally said, "I remember you. You were the one hanging on my ship back on Barspens."

Atik nodded slowly. He still stayed where he was. But challengingly, he said, "You appear to me to be a man who likes a challenge."

"Do I?"

"Your standing there, holding a disruptor on me from a safe distance, where is the challenge in that? You should have the nerve to face me one on one, with matched weapons. I would be more than happy to provide you that opportunity, if you wish."

"That's most considerate of you."

With the slightest and most unthreatening flick of his wrist, Atik tossed one of the blades to the ground. It landed with a clatter atop the other. The creature stared at it with a distant curiosity.

"Pick it up," Atik urged him. "Put down your weapon, pick up the sword and let us face each other as equals."

"Why in the world would I want to do that?"

"Because you know you want to."

"I see." The creature scratched his chin thoughtfully. "And because I want to should be sufficient reason. Caring about the girl's safety, trying to get her away, not taking chances with her life, these are all secondary to what I want to do."

"Of course." To Atik it could not have been more clear.

The creature leveled his disruptor at him and said calmly, "What I want to do is kill you. Shoot you down, right here and now. Send your soul screaming after that of your friend. Since that is what I want to do, why . . . I suppose I should give in to that, shouldn't I. Well? Shouldn't I?"

Atik's lips curled in a sneer. "You're afraid. That's all. You're simply afraid I'll kill you."

"You might," the creature said reasonably. "And then the girl will be left to your mercy, and that I cannot tolerate. If the only thing at stake is my life, I attach small enough importance to that that I'd have no problem risking it in a fight with you. I have some small experience with a blade and few enough opportunities to indulge. But one has to know the appropriate times. It's what separates us from the lower order of beasts, such as yourself." He flashed a smile and then said, "Step away from the girl."

Atik didn't move.

The creature squeezed the trigger and a chunk of ground to Atik's immediate right disappeared.

Atik moved. He stepped back as the creature advanced and lifted the girl in his arms. Every muscle in Atik's body was quivering with restrained anger.

Suddenly an explosion roared from the city, a gigantic plume of flame leaping toward the sky. Atik knew precisely what it was. It was the opening salvo of the Dogs of War attacking Montos City. In truth, it was at this point an unnecessary strike because the girl had been found. The ironic fact was that Atik and Fista hadn't actually been assigned to track the girl. The presumption had been that she was still in the city. They had simply been charged with scouting the perimeter. But in exploring the terrain, they had stumbled upon something that seemed to give them a minor hunting diversion. So they had seized upon the opportunity and, to their utter astonishment, had been led to the target of the entire Dog attack.

Although, truth be told, this did not entirely surprise Atik. He had always considered himself as a Dog of destiny, meant for great things, upon whom God (Dog, spelled backwards) had a tendency to smile from time to time. Because of this innate feeling of being intended for some great destiny, Atik tended to be on the lookout for any opportunity to seize a moment and make it uniquely his.

As a consequence, when the explosion went off, Atik was watching for the slightest reaction from the creature, and he got what he was looking for. The creature glanced off in the direction of the explosion, momentarily startled, but that moment was all Atik was looking for. He came right at the creature, full strength, full speed. He didn't bother with a roar designed to paralyze his intended victim with fear; he had the gut feeling that such a tactic wouldn't work but instead would simply serve as a warning.

The creature spun, his attention snapping back to Atik, but he was a hair too slow and Atik plowed into him. The two of them went down, and Atik heard the gun go flying from the creature's hand and clatter away. The girl thudded to the ground, and Atik knew, absolutely knew, that he had the creature cold. Tangled up as they were, with the creature helpless beneath his furious attack, the preordained end was only instants away.

And then Atik was airborne. He didn't quite know how it had happened. He only knew that one moment the creature's arms and legs were positioned beneath him, and then there was an abrupt thrust and Atik was flying through the air. Some sort of strange throw, something that Atik had not been remotely expecting.

He landed quickly and cleanly, though, and he was wielding one of his two long fangs, the other lying on the ground some distance away where Atik had tossed it as a defiant challenge to the creature. The creature, for his part, was simply standing there, his arms calmly at his sides, watching Atik with what appeared to be a confident smile.

They stood opposite each other, Atik waiting for the creature to make a move, either towards the fallen disruptor or the sword, each of which was about equidistant from him. But each was also just out of his reach, and Atik knew that, no matter which way the creature went, he would be able to get ahead of him and dispatch him quickly and cleanly.

The creature didn't budge.

A handful of seconds crawled by with the speed of an eternity, but Atik decided that the creature was simply paralyzed with fear, despite his outward appearance of calm. Figuring that nothing was to be gained by prolonging the agony, Atik came at him, whipping his long fang around with the intention of gutting the creature. Indeed, he had it all figured out in his mind. He would go for the belly first, allowing the creature's intestines to spill out all over the ground. The creature would see this, but naturally still be alive, and would react in a rather comical fashion. Either it would try to shove its organs back into place (always a chuckle to watch) or else it would try to run and slip and fall on its own vital juices. At which point the butchery could begin in earnest. The long fang was particularly useful for such endeavors, being far more elegant than the straightforward rending and tearing that the use of his claws entailed.

Atik thrust forward with the long fang—and just like that, the creature wasn't there.

Atik stumbled, momentarily thrown off balance, something having banged against his arm while he was lunging. For an instant, Atik thought that the creature had matter-transported out, or perhaps had turned invisible or used some other similar stunt. But then, from the corner of his eye, he saw the creature turning around to face him, and Atik moved to bring up his long fang once more . . . and discovered, to his shock, that his paw was empty.

A confused, gutteral noise came from his throat, and—ludicrously—he turned his paw over for an instant and looked at the back as if somehow the sword might have hidden itself there. Then he felt a gentle but distinct pricking sensation at his throat. He looked down. The sword point was touching up against it. He looked up and saw that the creature was holding it. He did not look the slightest bit strained or out of breath. As incredible, as impossible as it seemed, the creature had simply snatched the long fang right out of Atik's grip.

"Looking for this?" the creature asked.

Atik said nothing. He barely even breathed. The point pushed more meaningfully against the base of his throat.

"I hear," continued the creature, "that there's nothing more dangerous than a wounded animal."

Suddenly the sword flashed twice, across Atik's chest, in a crisscross pattern, the two diagonal lines intersecting. Blood welled up, staining his fur dark as Atik fell, clutching at himself. For a moment he expected that he was to meet the fate that he had been planning for the creature; then he realized that the cuts had not gone deep enough. They were still incredibly painful, however, and Atik felt the world swimming in front of him as the blood flow thickened, covering his chest. He went down to his knees, cursing himself for his weakness, certain that the next thing he felt would be the long fang flashing through the back of his neck on its way to beheading him. This wasn't right at all. This wasn't the destiny that he had been certain would be his.

But there was no cut, no impact. Instead he was startled by the sound of metal as the long fang clattered to the ground in front of him. He managed, through his pain, to turn his head and spy the creature standing a short distance away. He was holding the disruptor in his hand once more and had the girl slung over his shoulder.

"Well? Is it true?" he asked. "About wounded animals being dangerous, I mean."

Atik said nothing, merely glared.

"If it is . . . so much the better," the creature said with annoying cheerfulness. "The fact is, I love a challenge, and danger is intriguing. So, I leave you to lick your wounds. Do give your masters my warmest regards."

The only amount of satisfaction that Atik was able to take at that particular moment was that the creature didn't turn his back on him. Instead he backed up, keeping his disruptor leveled, even though Atik was clearly injured and not in much shape to be any sort of threat whatsoever.

Behind him, the oddly shaped ship that Atik had seen before rippled into view, the side hatch opening up so that the creature was able to step into it without taking a backward glance. He nodded slightly to Atik, as if giving him a tongue-in-cheek salute, and then the door irised shut.

Atik staggered to his feet, growling in impotent fury, as the ship lifted off. Moments later, as another explosion seized the town, and then a third, the ship with the target of the Dogs of War hurtled away into the sky.

VII.

THE REPORTS WERE COMING in from everywhere. Fr'Col didn't know where to look or who to listen to first. His people were crowding into his office, pointing and shouting and crying out. They were covered with ash, or bleeding from vicious cuts and bruises, and all through the air was the unmistakable stench of panic. Everyone was shouting at the same time, each clamoring for his attention or demanding to know what he was going to do about the present situation. He couldn't make himself heard; he couldn't even think.

"QUIET!"

The voice bellowed so loudly above everyone else that it immediately seized their attention. It was a heartstopper of a voice, a sound like an avalanche rolling straight through the room; indeed, two Montosians fainted dead away in shock from it. All eyes turned towards the source of the voice (the heads following immediately thereafter), which turned out to be the walking landmass from the Federation who had come in the company of the Thallonian, Si Cwan, and the Vulcan, Soleta. He glanced about for a moment, his fearsome gaze freezing any possible reply in the throats of those who were going to be presumptuous enough to try and make one.

"That's better," he rumbled, in a tone more closely approximating his normal one. With the momentary cessation of babbling, however, the explosions in the distance could now be heard. It seemed to Fr'Col that they were getting closer. "Now . . . what is happening?"

Naturally the cacophony recommenced, but this time it took only a look from Kebron to silence them, and Fr'Col took the momentary silence as opportunity to speak up. "Some sort of creatures, from what I've managed to gather," he said. It was not easy for him to focus; his mind tended to wander. He knew that was an ongoing problem; until now, it had never been a major handicap for him, for nothing of overwhelming importance, no major emergency, had ever presented itself to him. Those sorts of things simply didn't happen on Montos, an intrinsically polite society that considered such bellicose matters to be . . . rude, somehow. "Heavily furred," he continued, "piloting lethal ships, firing at random places in the city. No pattern. No . . . no nothing. Some of their ships have landed, and they're running about, attacking, grabbing whatever they want—"

"The Dogs," Kebron said immediately. "The Dogs of War."

Si Cwan looked at Kebron in surprise, impressed that the Brikar had come up with the only reasonable answer so quickly. "Yes. I think you're right."

Soleta looked at him in confusion. "The who?"

"Genetic breeding experiment that went awry. They spent time in the outer rim of Federation space for a while, then relocated their operations into the border area of Thallonian space," Si Cwan told her. "They were far enough out that they didn't present an immediate problem. We would have attended to them eventually, but we had more pressing matters than dealing with a group of barbaric space pirates. Unfortunately, the Empire collapsed before we were able to get around to it."

"Are they vicious?"

"Ferocious, Lieutenant," said Kebron, the formal-sounding use of her rank indicating the gravity with which he was treating the situation. "They made the mistake of attacking a Brikar colony some years back. We repulsed them . . . don't say it," he added as an obvious afterthought to Si Cwan.

"Wouldn't have occured to me to say it, considering this is not an appropriate time for sardonic banter. Don't you agree?" asked Si Cwan. Kebron nodded, which for him meant that the entirety of his torso bobbed slightly as if he were bowing.

Fr'Col took a deep gulp in his throat, fingering the triangular stone that he used for a gavel. "Can you help us?" he asked. It was not an easy thing for him to inquire. The people of Montos were rather dedicated to keeping to themselves and disdaining outside help. Asking for the aid now of these Federation people was very, very difficult.

The Thallonian seemed to realize, even appreciate that. His face darkened. "We would if we could. If our starship were here, we could likely dispose of them without too much difficulty. The Dogs tend to tuck tail and run when the odds even seem to move against them. But we have limited resources."

"If we had even some fighter ships, one-man vessels," Kebron mused out loud.

And Fr'Col thumped his stone vigorously on the podium. "We do!" This caused another round of mutual talking until Kebron once again shouted them down.

"How did you get such ships?" asked Si Cwan.

"I told you. We traded valuable minerals and got useless junk in return. That was the junk."

"Fighter ships were junk?" Clearly Kebron couldn't believe it, even though his face wasn't designed to display a multitude of expressions.

"They were until now. We never had any use for them."

"Are they near?"

"Take them to warehouse B!" called out Fr'Col.

Immediately this straightforward command was taken up as a war chant, and cries of "Take them to warehouse B! Warehouse B!" echoed throughout the room. Si Cwan, Soleta, even Kebron (although to a lesser extent) were caught up in a wave of excitement and bodies as they were ushered out of the room towards the storage facility where the only hope for Montos sat gathering dust.

Fr'Col suddenly slammed his stone triangle down on his podium. "I object!" he shouted, and then realized he'd forgotten why he'd objected. Fortunately, no one was in the room to hear him.

Si Cwan was less than enthused.

The fighter ships, such as they were, were not what he would have remotely termed "state of the art," although at least they weren't broken down in any respect. There were half a dozen of them, covered with thick dust.

The crowd of Montosians who had been huddling in Fr'Col's office were now grouped together in a quivering collection of trembling bodies. There were more explosions outside, and each time they would jump slightly and huddle even more closely together.

"They're getting nearer," Kebron said, listening to the explosions. He didn't sound particularly perturbed about it. If it were a purely natural thunder-and-lightning storm closing in on them, he wouldn't have sounded any more put out.

Si Cwan took one more glance at the ships. "I know these vessels. They're of Boragi design, aren't they." He looked around and saw that Fr'Col had entered the warehouse just in time to hear the tail end of his question. Fr'Col nodded in affirmation.

Cwan was more than familiar with the residents of Boragi III. They were a race that specialized in staying neutral under all conditions and circumstances. However, they had a remarkable knack for stirring up trouble among other races, and then coming in to pick up the pieces when the dust of the conflict had settled. It was obvious to Cwan that the Boragi had been hoping the Montosians might put their new-found toys to some sort of warlike use, preferably among themselves, leaving the Boragi free to engage in more trade and dealings with whichever side of the battle wound up surviving. They had reckoned, however, without the Montosians resolutely placid attitude. No such battle had been forthcoming, and there was no telling how long the ships had been sitting there unattended.

There was no way to find out except to check it for himself. Si Cwan clambered up the side of one of the fighters and eased himself into the cockpit. "Kebron, this is going to be a tight fit for you," he warned.

"I'll take a deep breath," said Kebron, looking around for a fighter that was to his liking.

"Soleta, have you any experience with flying vessels of this sort?"

"No," she said coolly.

"Have you ever been in a solo firefight of any sort?"

"No."

That was not what Si Cwan was hoping to hear. They were going in outnumbered as it was. His main hope was that the Dogs would tuck and run, as they tended to do simply to protect their numbers whenever a battle seemed more trouble than it was worth. "Perhaps it would be better if you remained here, then."

"That would be the logical course of action," Soleta agreed. Whereupon she selected a fighter and vaulted into the cockpit. It was all Si Cwan could do to suppress a smile. She was quite something else, Soleta was.

Then he turned his attention back to the weapons and control array. Time was not their friend, and the sooner they got out there, the better their admittedly slim chances would become. But that consideration had to be balanced against the preparations needed to fly the ship into battle without getting himself killed just from inexperience. There were two elements, and only two, on their side. The first was that the Boragi, as irritating and conniving as they could be, were quite skilled in the art of ship design and tended to produce solid—if not particularly inspired—weaponry. And the second was that they had tried to make it as simple as possible to operate so that the Montosians would be more tempted to use it.

He studied the weapons quickly, trying not to be distracted by the approaching series of explosions. They seemed to be fewer in number; obviously, as the bombing raid softened up the populace, more and more of the Dogs were descending to ground and taking on the people hand-to-hand. That sort of battle was generally more to their liking.

He heard a grunt and saw Kebron shoving himself into the cockpit of another vessel nearby. To say it was a tight fit was to understate the matter. But Kebron did not have a lot of choice. Several Montosians had climbed onto the vessel with him and were helping to push him down into place. "Thank you," he rumbled. He didn't bother to belt himself in; his own width was easily going to be able to keep him secure. Si Cwan had the feeling that the only way they were going to get Kebron out of the vehicle was to disassemble it.

"Fr'Col," Si Cwan said sternly, "I want you to understand something, and I want your oath in front of all these people: That when we return from this, after having saved your lives, you and your people will willingly join in the new alliance that we are endeavoring to form. That you will have seen the advantages of an agreement of mutual protection, for from that will grow mutual strength. Your oath, sir."

Fr'Col nodded. "Anything you say. I have no objections."

"Good." He looked over at Soleta, who was studying the controls in front of her with quiet, resolute determination. "Lieutenant, are you sure about this?" he called. "Are you certain you can handle it?"

"No," she said with her customary bluntness. "But I am a fast learner."

"Good. All right . . . lower the cowling," he said. The

weapons array was a somewhat quaint series of switch-
es rather than the touch-sensitive panels he was accustomed to, but he was certain he could adapt. He flipped
the switch that he surmised would bring the cowling
down and seal off the cockpit.

His vessel shuddered ever so slightly, and before he
knew it, blaster fire discharged from the front of the
ship and smashed into the far wall of the warehouse.
Montosians went running as debris rained down, dust
and smoke rising from the impact. When it cleared,
there was a large hole in the wall.

"You might want to consider the blue switch to the
left of that one," Kebron suggested without a trace of
irony.

"I believe I have a solid grasp of the learning procedure, Ambassador," Soleta said, constrastingly making
no effort whatsoever to keep irony out of her voice. "I
shall watch what you do, and then do the opposite."

Si Cwan let the remark pass without comment as he
flipped the suggested switch and the cowling settled in
around him. He had not even bothered to ask if any of
the Montosians there were going to join them in their
battle to save their own damned planet—considering
that there were ships to spare. The odds were that they
would be far more of a hindrance than a help anyway.

He found the controls that he hoped would actually
cause the ship's engines to come on line, and result in
the vessel lifting off. He breathed a silent prayer, partly
hoping that he wouldn't further embarrass himself—
and partly hoping that he didn't inadvertently incinerate
everyone else in the warehouse. He activated them and,
to his relief, the engines came on line. The thrusters
snapped to life and the ship hovered several feet off the
ground. He looked right and left and saw that Kebron's

and Soleta's ships were following suit. He couldn't help but notice that Soleta did not look the slightest bit out of her element. If he hadn't known that she'd never operated such a vessel before, he would have thought she had been flying for years.

Fr'Col had scuttled over to one end of the warehouse and flipped open a panel on the wall and hit a switch. There was a grinding of gears and one end of the warehouse slid open, providing them a means of exiting. There were shouts of "Good luck!" and similar best wishes, and the three vessels blasted towards the exit and out.

The moment they were out of the warehouse, Si Cwan opened up the vessel's engines to see what the ship was capable of doing. He had only seconds to fully master the ship's specs, he knew, before he was going to find himself in a combat situation. He rocked the ship back and forth slightly, getting a feel for how fast and maneuverable it was.

"Kebron to Cwan," Kebron's voice came over the combadge that Si Cwan wore. His sporting of one had been a matter of some small debate, considering that he was not a member of Starfleet, and so it wasn't exactly in keeping with regs for him to wear one. But Captain Calhoun had insisted, stating, "I want to know where my people are at any given time, and I'll be damned if I let regulations stand in the way of common sense." That had been that, and Cwan was rather glad at this particular point that Calhoun had been so insistent.

"Cwan here. Go ahead."

"Are you all right? I saw your ship moving in an erratic pattern."

"Just getting a feel for her."

The ground hurtled past beneath them. Their ships skimmed the tops of the buildings as they flew towards the area of the Dogs' attack. It was not difficult to spot; several miles to the east, smoke was rising from half a dozen areas and buildings that were in a state of ruin.

Then there was a sudden, warning beep from the console. He immediately checked the systems to make sure that there wasn't something wrong with the functioning of the ship itself. Instead, his perimeter alarms were informing him of something that, seconds later, Kebron did as well.

"Incoming," was all Kebron said.

It was all he had to say. Dog fighters were approaching from the other direction, and Zak Kebron, Soleta, and Si Cwan had been noticed.

There were six of them, coming in fast. Si Cwan wasn't thrilled; he was operating an unfamiliar vessel, backed up by two individuals, one of whom had never flown before, and they were outnumbered two to one. It wasn't the sort of odds he would have preferred.

"They're going to split. Three and three formation," Kebron's voice came over the combadge. And sure enough, he was absolutely right. The approaching Dog ships moved off left and right, coming in fast and endeavoring to outflank their attackers.

"I'll take the three on the right. You and Soleta, the three on the left," said Cwan.

"I can handle the three on the left. You and Soleta deal with the three on the right."

"I can take them. Soleta, stick with Kebron."

The Dog fighters were almost within firing range.

"That will not be necessary," Kebron said firmly. "Soleta, perhaps you should hang back as our—"

Soleta's voice crackled over the comm links. "Mr. Ambassador. Lieutenant. The two of you are beginning to annoy me."

Si Cwan gasped as Soleta's ship suddenly slammed forward, outstripping the both of them. Her blasters roared to life, firing at the approaching ships and missing them clean.

Instead, the blasts ricocheted off one of the partly demolished structures, spun off in trajectories that paralleled each other, caromed off two more piles of debris, crisscrossed one another and took out attacking vessels on either side. The two ships spiraled to the ground, chewing up huge troughs of dirt and debris as they skidded and then went up in huge balls of flame.

Si Cwan blinked in surprise, not quite certain that he had just seen what he thought he'd seen. Just like that, two of the six attacking ships had been taken out.

Quickly adjusting to the situation, however, the remaining four angled around and came in from all directions. Within seconds there was so much blaster fire around him that Si Cwan was having trouble seeing. Switching entirely to instruments, he maneuvered the ship as deftly as he could, dodging between the blasts. His ship shuddered under the impact as one or two of them glanced off him, but there were no direct hits. He was just in the process of congratulating himself when he heard Kebron's alarmed voice call, "Cwan! Pull up, *now!*"

He did as he was told without hesitation, and a Dog ship passed directly under him. The upper portion of the Dog ship literally scraped against the bottom of Cwan's; he could hear the ear-splitting sound of metal on metal. Then his ship peeled away and angled back around.

His proximity alarms were shrieking at him. He'd been targeted. There was a ship right behind him, possibly the same one that he'd just managed to avoid. It would have required formidable piloting skills for the Dog to have made that quick a recovery, but anything was possible. He looked to see if there were any weapons that fired to cover his rear, and saw that there were none. That was something of a design flaw, which he would have loved to take up with the Boragi should he actually survive this insane adventure.

He gunned the ship forward, angled off sharply, and then saw another Dog ship on the tail of one of the other fighters. He banked right, left, barely avoiding the explosions around him, and then to his horror he saw the rear of the other fighter go up in a burst of flame. "Kebron! Soleta!" He shouted both names, because he wasn't sure who it was whose ship had been mortally wounded.

No response came back to either name; suddenly he saw the injured ship, miraculously, pull out of its death dive. But there was no hope for it, just none. Two more of the Dog ships were coming at it from the rear, moving in for the kill.

Unexpectedly the aft thrusters of the Boragi flared to life, but only the aft thrusters, causing the ship to whip around sideways. It was no longer flying in any proper pattern but for an instant was simply hanging there in the air, a huge roadblock.

The Dog ships weren't able to correct course fast enough to allow for the demented maneuver, and as a consequence smashed into the crippled fighter. All three of them erupted in a blinding ball of fire and light, the explosion so powerful that Si Cwan's ship was carried by the force of the shock wave, skewing almost entirely out of his control. He slammed forward against the weapons console, slamming his chest so hard that he felt as if he'd nearly broken a rib.

As he fought off the waves of pain from the impact, he caught sight of one of the two remaining Dog ships, and opened fire. He struck the Dog ship broadside, sending it spiraling. He fired again, striking it clean with full force, and the ship blew apart. He then looked around for the sixth Dog ship.

Fortunately, or unfortunately, depending on how one looked at it, the Dog ship seemed disinclined to get involved. It reversed course and tore at full speed across the war-torn city. In the distance, Si Cwan saw other Dog ships, a handful of them, reconnoitering with the fleeing one. They were out of firing range, but he was still able to track them on long-distance scanners. He braced himself, waiting to see if the battle was going to continue. Just to add potential impetus, he flipped on a ship-to-ship communications beam, a broader channel than the narrow cast that filtered through the combadges he and the others wore. "All ships," he said, "we have the Dogs targeted in the eastern sector of Montos City. Converge on this point, with full weapon array on line."

He had no idea whether they were eavesdropping or not, no clue as to whether they actually heard him. For whatever reason—whether they'd had enough, or were running true to form and simply ducking out when a fight became too lopsided, or even too fair, or perhaps they had accomplished what they'd wanted to accomplish (whatever that was)— the Dog ships, as a single pack, moved off.

All except one.

There was one ship, a bit larger than the rest. Not necessarily a fighter, but more of a transport. It was on the ground, and Si Cwan flew towards it at full speed. If he was going to have the opportunity to dispose of one more of their ships, even if it was on the ground instead of in a more sporting combat mode, he was going to seize the chance.

It was situated near the shattered remains of one of the houses, a bit set apart from the others. As Si Cwan closed in, he saw several of the Dogs charge out of the house . . .

. . . and they were dragging someone.

He was astounded by what he saw, for even from that distance, he could make out that it was a Thallonian. The skin color was unmistakable.

Had the Dogs been by themselves, he would simply have opened fire. But as it was, he had to be more judicious. Targeting the area, he placed carefully selected shots, bracketing the fleeing Dogs without striking them directly. But still he came too close as the ground around them exploded from the impact of the blasts. He saw the Thallonian hurled in one direction, back towards the house, the Dogs in the other. Seeing the rapidly approaching ship, the Dogs lost no time in scrambling into their own vessel, apparently deciding that the Thallonian they'd been dragging with them was simply not worth the effort. Moments later the Dog ship was airborne and, like the others, hurtling away from the scene of their crimes.

"Si Cwan to Soleta. Si Cwan to Kebron. Are you there? Is either of you there?" he called over his combadge. But no response came from either. Were they both dead? Was that it? Had this misbegotten rescue mission gone that awry? All this just to try and gain some sort of alliance with this idiotic little world?

He tried to put his own scrambled thoughts in order. As cold and unfeeling as it might sound, even to Si Cwan himself, he simply couldn't dwell on the fate of the others right now. There was a fellow Thallonian down there, one who might very well need him. There was a clear area nearby where he could land his ship. This he did as soon as his long-range sensors assured him that the Dog fighters were indeed gone rather than simply staging a false retreat to try and lure him in.

When he opened the cowling of his cockpit, the first thing to hit him was the stench of burning. The entire area around him was charred, with ruined buildings and smoking corpses, blackened and scorched by the Dog weapons. From the distance he could hear the moans, the cries of "help me" from people he couldn't even see. Then he spotted one poor bastard, his legs gone, pulling himself forward pathetically hand over hand, leaving a twisted trail of blood behind him. He managed to crane his neck around and look at Si Cwan. Cwan wasn't sure the dying Montosian was actually seeing him, though, particularly because there was only a large socket where his right eye had been. He gurgled something low in his throat, then his head flopped down and he stopped moving.

Si Cwan had seen worse in his life. Much worse. Particularly when he was quite young and his father had felt it would be instructive to apprentice the young prince to the royal torturer for a time. Si Cwan had watched as the torturer had plied his trade and had taken very careful mental notes, for he found that working on intellectualizing what he was seeing was, indeed, the only way that he could actually deal with it. The last thing he wanted to admit to his father was that watching such activities was repulsive to him. His father would not have approved of such a soft attitude.

Although Si Cwan had seen worse . . . he could not recall when he had seen anything more pathetic.

He turned away, and hauled himself out of the fighter. He dropped to the ground a short distance below and made his way toward the Thallonian. The Thallonian was, happily, conscious, and Si Cwan (amusingly) felt a bit of pride about that. It took a great deal to put a Thallonian down for the count, that much was sure.

"Are you all right? Did they hurt you?" he called to the Thallonian.

The Thallonian was just standing up fully . . . then his head whipped around in response to Si Cwan's voice.

Si Cwan felt his next inquiry as to the general health and welfare of the newly rescued Thallonian dying in his throat as a familiar face gaped back at him.

Once . . .

Once upon a time . . .

Once upon a time, Si Cwan had had a young friend. An ally, who was by his side in all things and was utterly devoted to him. But the young ally had slowly come to believe that Si Cwan was weak and sympathetic . . . too sympathetic to the lesser beings who infested not only the lower strata of Thallonian society, but the Thallonian Empire as a whole. They had had a number of spirited debates about it as the young friend had tried to realign the noble Si Cwan's thinking. But the debates had become over the years more edged, and then angry. Si Cwan had never understood his friend's change in attitude. Perhaps it was because Si Cwan had, at his core, such an annoying streak of compassion, he was unable to comprehend how someone else could be so lacking in the same element. But that was definitely the case, and he had watched helplessly as his friendship with his erstwhile ally had fallen completely apart. There is no deadlier enemy than someone who was once loved.

The last time he had seen that individual, he'd been a target of an elaborate death trap that Si Cwan had escaped only by the slimmest and most fortunate of margins. He had wondered, in the time since that incident, when they would encounter each other once again. Curiously, he had never wondered *if* such a meeting would occur. It was as if they were destined to be at each other's throats, to meet repeatedly until only one of them was left alive. No, "when" had been the only thing open to speculation. In his imaginings, he had always figured that it would be in some great, dramatic context, possibly with the fate of entire worlds hinging on the outcome of the meeting. Somehow it had never occured to him that it would happen on some not-especially-important planet with nothing major at stake.

"Zoran," he whispered. He wasn't expecting to whisper. It just somehow came out that way. "Zoran Si Verdin."

Zoran wasn't saying anything, apparently even more stunned than Si Cwan that they were suddenly finding themselves face to face.

In the silence of the moment, a soft click was all the more commanding of their attention.

They turned as one and looked in the direction of the noise. There was a small globe lying on the ground barely ten feet away from them. It had a small pair of snarling jaws painted on it, jaws that were the symbol of the Dogs of War. A present left behind in a hurried departure that might not have been so panicked as it appeared.

Si Cwan knew it instantly for what it was. The only question was how much time he had before the thing went off. And considering that he surmised the click noise was the timing device having counted down to its triggering point, he could only surmise that the answer was: in no time at all . . .

. . . no time to consider Zoran. Without hesitation, he leaped towards a pile of debris that he could only hope was going to serve as some sort of shelter. The vault carried him to just within reach of the debris, then the bomb went off. The concussive waves carried him over the shelter, sent him tumbling, and he felt as if he were being carried high, high into the sky. The sun shone down upon him, and for a delirious second he thought he was going to be sent spiraling straight into its super-heated heart, there to incinerate instantly.

Then he crashed. He hit the ground with such force that it shook every bone in his body, and he lay there, unable to move, unable even to breathe—that was when he lost consciousness. The last thing he thought before passing out was that he hoped—whatever happened to him, had happened to Zoran first.

"Cwan. Si Cwan."

There was something large shaking his shoulder. He had no idea what it was, for his thoughts and attention were so scrambled. He felt wetness down the side of his face and wondered if he'd been crying. Then he realized that it was partly dried blood from a huge gash. He realized this by touching it, which was a serious mistake as it caused a bolt of pain to race through his entire head. But the pain, in turn, was something of a help to him since it brought him to full wakefulness that much faster, even though it left him with a headache lethal enough to split neutronium.

Through his bleary eyes, he found that he was looking at Zak Kebron. It would have been nice to say that Kebron looked concerned, but truthfully he looked about as blasé about the present circumstance as he did about most things. "Cwan. Are you all right?"

"I did not know . . . you cared." Each word was an effort, although a progressively easier effort with each one.

"I don't," Kebron replied. "But your quarters are nicer than mine. If you die, the captain promised them to me."

"Oh."

Then the presence of Kebron indicated something to Si Cwan. Slowly he sat up, and he felt a distant sense of loss. "If you're here . . . then . . . then that means Soleta . . ."

"Is over there." Kebron pointed and a stunned Si Cwan turned his head and saw Soleta a short distance away, picking through the rubble carefully as if searching for something.

Si Cwan looked from her back to Kebron. "I . . . I saw a fighter crash."

"Yes," Kebron said, "that was mine."

As Si Cwan slowly pieced together his fragmented concentration, he saw that Kebron's uniform was indeed quite a bit shredded. In fact, there were even a few chips in the supertough hide of the Brikar security chief.

"You survived it, then."

"No, Cwan. I died. But Starfleet ordered me back to work."

If Si Cwan had thought for a moment that he was hallucinating, the acerbic reply from Kebron put that notion to rest. "I saw your ship go up in flames, though."

"It takes a bit more to dispose of me than that."

But he was hurt. Si Cwan could tell. His speech was

slower. Although he was endeavoring to maintain his standard, wry tone, nevertheless the effort it took him to do so was quite apparent. Furthermore, the toll the impact had taken on his body was becoming more apparent. The longer Si Cwan looked at him, the more cracks in his thick epidermis became apparent to him. And from those more obvious wounds that Cwan had first noticed, a thick black liquid that he could only assume was blood was oozing from them.

Kebron saw where Cwan was looking. "Don't worry about that."

"What do you mean, don't worry. You're bleeding."

"No. I'm not."

"But—"

"I'm not."

"Kebron," Si Cwan said in mild exasperation, "you don't have to put on the stoic act with me anymore. You're hurt."

"No. You're ignorant. Now get up."

Si Cwan did so slowly, making sure that the world stopped whirling around him sufficiently so that he wouldn't topple over, and making a mental note to himself not to bother ever again to express any concern about Kebron's well-being. "Zoran," he said with sudden urgency. "Zoran . . ."

"What about him?" Kebron was naturally quite aware of who and what Zoran was, since he had been with Si Cwan when Zoran had laid the ambush that almost killed the both of them.

"Zoran is here . . . was here . . . is here . . ." His head snapped around so quickly in an endeavor to spot his nemesis that he almost toppled over once more. One of Kebron's large hands halted his fall. "There was an explosion . . . a bomb. The half-standing wall I got behind took the brunt of the impact." He looked to where the wall had been but saw there was nothing left.

"A moment of silence," Kebron said solemnly, "for the rubble that lay down its life for you."

"Damn you, Kebron!" Si Cwan shouted as he turned on him. "You know who Zoran is, what he's done. Lay aside your incessant sarcasm, for once!"

Kebron was silent for a long moment and Si Cwan had no idea what was going through the Brikar's head. Then, very quietly, he said, "Perhaps the bomb killed him."

"No," Cwan said forcefully. "If I survived, he survived. We have to—"

"Over here!" It was Soleta's voice. It was contrary to her long training, of course, to show any sign of emotion, but Si Cwan could hear the clear urgency in her tone. "There's a survivor here!"

Immediately Cwan and Kebron were running toward her. The entire way, Cwan was hoping, praying, that it was Zoran. Perhaps he was dying. That notion brought mixed emotions to Si Cwan, for the passing of Zoran— particularly if Cwan was standing there to witness it— would be a glorious thing. But if it came to that, Zoran might very well die without telling Si Cwan that which he, Cwan, most desperately wanted to know. Zoran was more than capable of doing that, of carrying much needed information to his grave, just to spite Si Cwan. The thought of Cwan begging, imploring Zoran for information, trying to appeal to his nonexistent good side or to the friendship they once had . . . that was not something that Cwan was looking forward to.

Truly, it was a screwed-up universe when one didn't know if one wanted an enemy to live or die, and might not be able to take true pleasure in either.

As they drew closer to Soleta, however, Si Cwan quickly saw that the question was moot. For it was not, as he had hoped, Zoran lying there amidst the rubble. Instead it was a woman, one of the Montosians. She was staring fixedly upwards, and Si Cwan knew immediately that she was not going to live much longer. Her eyes were already beginning to mist over. He wasn't even sure if she could see Soleta looking down at her.

"Who did this to you?" Soleta was asking her. Si Cwan didn't understand the question at first. Obviously, the explosions and devastation caused by the Dogs of War were responsible for leaving this woman half-buried under rubble. But then he understood as soon as he got a bit closer.

The woman wasn't simply suffering from having rubble fall on her, although certainly that would have been enough for anyone. There were bruises, cuts all over her in a systematic pattern. The antennae on her forehead, characteristic of Montosians, had been severed, and there was dried blood from the incision all over her face. This woman hadn't just been injured. She had been systematically tortured.

"Who," Soleta repeated slowly, "did this to you?"

"Dogs . . ." the woman managed to say. Blood was trickling from the edges of her mouth even as she said it.

"Obviously, they wanted some sort of information from her," Kebron said.

Si Cwan nodded in agreement. "Apparently, this little attack wasn't as random as it originally seemed. But . . . why her?"

Kebron shrugged or at least tried to. He wasn't really built for shrugging.

"Why? Why did they do this to you?" Soleta asked her. "What did they want to know?"

"Riella . . ."

The name meant nothing to Si Cwan, and he could see that it likewise rang no bells with the others. Furthermore, he could tell that they were running out of time. The woman was obviously fading fast. "Perhaps you can mind-meld with her," he suggested. "You can—"

"No," Soleta said quickly and firmly.

"Soleta," Kebron said, "as much as I dislike agreeing with Cwan, it might be more efficient to—"

"I said no." And it was evident from her tone that no further discussion was going to take place on the topic. She turned instead back to the woman and said, "Who is Riella? Why did the Dogs do this to you? Please . . ."

"Save . . . Riella . . ."

"We will," Si Cwan told her confidently, although naturally he had no idea whom he had just pledged to save. Then, hazarding a guess, he asked, "Is she your daughter?"

She didn't respond immediately, and when she did, her voice quavered as if she were exhaling some great secret. And when she did speak, Si Cwan couldn't quite make out what she had said. "Inkso?" he asked, puzzled. "What is . . . Inkso?"

"She said, 'Think so,' " Soleta told him, but she didn't appear to understand the words any more than Si Cwan did.

Then there was a gurgling deep in the woman's throat. Liquids began to ooze from her mouth, her nose. Her eyes had completely blanked over; she was no longer looking upwards, but instead into herself. And she said something so softly that Si Cwan missed it entirely. Then there was a rattle from her that he knew all too well . . . the last noise that a creature makes, which is surprisingly similar for a variety of races. She didn't move, her head did not slump over at all. But even so, it was clear that she was gone.

Si Cwan sat back on his haunches, shaking his head over the utter waste of life. He glanced over at Kebron and then did a double take. The blood from some of Kebron's wounds had crusted over and Kebron was calmly removing the scabs. Si Cwan couldn't quite believe it. Under the departed scabs, the wounds were healed.

"I told you it wasn't blood," Kebron said calmly when he noticed Si Cwan staring at him. "It's a special secretion that Brikar can generate that heals wounds."

"I've never seen you do that before."

"It is not . . . without effort. I felt it . . . necessary."

"Were the wounds that severe?"

"Yes," was all Kebron said, and Si Cwan could tell from the look of him that that was all he was going to say on the subject.

Then Si Cwan felt slightly dizzy again. Frustrated at what he saw as annoying weakness, he nevertheless knew that continuing to stand was going to be problematic. So, trying to make the action appear as leisurely as possible, he settled himself back down to the ground, draping his arms over his knees and shaking his head in a discouraged manner. "What an exercise in futility. Soleta . . . did you see anyone else around? A Thallonian, perhaps?"

She shook her head. "No. Just this woman. I suspect that the Dogs came here first, captured the woman and tortured her while attacking the rest of the city . . . to amuse themselves, if nothing else."

"But why? Why this woman? The things she said . . . 'Riella,' 'Think so . . .' None of it makes sense." He sighed, and then asked, "Did you manage to make out the last thing she said?"

"I believe so. But it did not make much sense."

"Well, what was it?"

"I believe she said, 'Quiet place.' "

The moment the words were out of her mouth, all the fatigue, all the frustration, all the muscle aches, everything that Si Cwan had been feeling up until that moment, vanished. He was on his feet and he gripped Soleta's shoulders with such ferocity that she actually winced. "Are you sure? Are you sure that's what she said? 'Quiet place?' "

"Reasonably, yes. What—?"

He released his hold on her shoulders and stepped back, obvious concern in his eyes. Soleta and Kebron were looking at each other in confusion, and then back to Si Cwan. "Cwan . . . what is it?" demanded Kebron. "Do you know this . . . 'Quiet place?' "

Si Cwan looked at his allies levelly and said, "No. Never heard of it." And with that, he turned on his heel and walked quickly away.

"Interesting," Kebron said thoughtfully. "Who would have guessed that Si Cwan was that bad a liar?"

VIII.

Xyon had absolutely no idea what to make of her, particularly when she woke up screaming.

The pale-skinned girl sat up abruptly in the bed that Xyon normally occupied. Her eyes were wide open, but when he went to her and passed his hands in front of her eyes, she wasn't focusing on him. "Calm down!" he shouted, but she didn't seem the least bit inclined to do so. Instead, she just shouted and howled and struggled about. She did this so violently that the shoulders of her dress slid down. Xyon found that to be momentarily distracting, which in turn proved to be something of a mistake. While his attention was diverted, one of her arms whipped around and smacked him upside of the head. He fell back, his ears ringing, and he shook his head and tried to reorder his momentarily scrambled senses.

In the meantime, the girl was practically tearing at her own face. He couldn't blame her entirely; he knew she had been through a lot and was frightened and disoriented. On the other hand, being whacked around on his own ship was not his idea of a good time.

Lyla's voice filtered through the speakers that were omnipresent in the ship. "Are you having difficulty, Xyon?" she asked solicitously.

By that point, Xyon had managed to pin her wrists and immobilize her. She was still thrashing about, however. "What gave you that idea?" he grunted.

There was a momentary pause, and then Lyla said, "That was sarcasm, was it not? I'm still learning my way around that one."

Xyon rolled his eyes; at that moment the girl started to sit up violently once more. She pulled one hand free, surprising Xyon with her display of remarkable strength, and then she clawed at his face. She managed to come into contact, raising a nasty welt on his cheek. By that point, Xyon had more than had enough. He hauled back and smacked her across the face, not out of desire to hurt or abuse her, but rather in the way that one customarily deals with a person who has totally lost control and fallen into a fit of hysterics: By hoping that the shock and suddenness of the slap would bring that person back to his or her senses.

This slap, however, had a far more profound and surprising impact than Xyon could possibly have anticipated. When he slapped her across the face . . . her antennae fell off.

He had not known exactly what to expect when he'd struck her, but certainly knocking a piece of her anatomy off had not been it. But that was exactly what had happened. The thing had just snapped off and clattered to the floor. Xyon stared at it stupidly for a moment. The girl, meantime, was still spasming in the bed, although the fits seemed to be subsiding somewhat. Xyon grabbed up the antennae and, in a move born of a combination of both alarm and chagrin rather than any reasonably thought-out course of action, he pushed the antennae against her forehead as if hoping that somehow the thing would adhere once more. This, naturally, did not work overmuch. He pressed firmly, released, and then watched the antennae fall off once more. Truly, he felt embarrassed over the incident. It was not as if he had tried, with some hostility, to remove the small forked things as some sort of retribution or act of sadism. It had just separated. Nor were Xyon's efforts going very far to accomplish anything.

She was lying there and now the panic seemed to have subsided. Slowly, she sat up and her attention focused for the first time on Xyon. "Who . . ." She blinked once more. "Who are you?"

"I'm Xyon. I . . ." He shrugged. "I rescued you."

"Oh." She didn't seem to know quite what to say in response to that.

"Are you all right?"

"Oh . . . perfect." She eyed him suspiciously. "Am I a prisoner here?"

"What? Uhm, no. No, not at all."

"Then I can leave."

"Nnnnno. No, you can't leave." He shrugged. "Sorry."

With mounting annoyance, she said, "If I'm not a prisoner, then I should be able to leave. One follows the other."

"Well, then I guess one shouldn't necessarily have expectations," Xyon told her, making no effort to hide his annoyance with her attitude. "For example, I saved your life from the Dogs of War, at no small personal risk. Under ordinary circumstances, one would think that such an action would rate, at the very least, a thank you. One follows the other. But I suppose that would be expecting too much, wouldn't it."

She opened her mouth to reply, then closed it again. Her face softened slightly and she said quietly, "Thank you."

"You're welcome."

"I'm sorry. I shouldn't be rude. I've been through more than you can imagine, and my head hurts so mu—"

She put her hand to her head to rub it . . . and felt the vacancy. Her eyes widened in shock. "My . . . my antennae! Where are . . . what . . . what happened to—"

A bit chagrined, he held them up. "I think you're looking for these."

Immediately the more conciliatory tone in her voice vanished, to be replaced by alarm and hostility. "What did you do? What did you do?!?"

"Nothing! I didn't do anything! They just kind of . . . fell off."

"Kind of fell off! Body parts don't just fall off!" She snatched them from his grasp and looked at them with growing horror. "You removed them! Why would you do such a twisted thing!"

"But I didn't! I didn't do any such thing!"

"Yes, you did!"

"No, I—" He put up his hands as if directing traffic. "Look . . . it really doesn't matter whether you believe me or not. I know what I did and didn't do. Your opinion isn't really relevant. All I can tell you is that I didn't, and I wouldn't hurt you, and to be blunt, you'd better pray that I'm being honest with you. Because if I did want to hurt you, there isn't a thing you could do about it." He sighed deeply and reached out a hand to her. "Listen," he began.

But she scuttled back on the bed, pressing herself against the wall, trying to get as far from him as she could, her gaze never wavering or leaving him for so much as an instant. This was sorely trying Xyon's patience. He understood that she was confused and scared, and that all of this must be tremendously disorienting for her. By the same token, he found himself seized by a desire to just slap her . . . this time not as part of an endeavor to snap her out of a fit of hysteria, but rather because she was, frankly, getting on his nerves.

"I want to get out of here," she said tersely.

"All right. Fine. Have it your way. The door's right over there." He pointed at it while making no effort to impede her path.

She looked at the door suspiciously as if she was anticipating a trick. But he could not have appeared more benign, sitting as unmoving as a stone statue. Within moments she was on her feet and then she was through the door.

Xyon still didn't move. He stayed right where he was, listening to the sound of her feet as she ran down the ship's single corridor which led to the fore section. Then she stopped running, which he had expected. After all, it wasn't as if she could go much farther than she had. The ship wasn't that big. Long moments passed; when no sound was forthcoming, he walked out of the bedroom with leisurely gait and headed for the front of the ship.

The girl was standing there, staring out the front

viewport. Her mouth was hanging open, and she was so stunned that he was able to close her mouth by pushing up on her chin, and she didn't even seem to notice that he had done so. Her gaze was fixed on the stars all around them.

"You see the problem with leaving," he said.

She nodded. Then she leaned forward, as if that gesture would bring her even closer to them. "They . . . they don't twinkle."

"Of course not. Twinkling is caused by distortion of light through your planet's atmosphere. Once you're out in space, they shine steady, like beacons."

"Out in space." She spoke with such incredulity that it reminded Xyon, ever so slightly, of the wonder of it all. To Xyon, space was simply something to survive in. An airless, freezing and unforgiving vacuum that was a sort of ever-present opponent. One mistake, one slip in his vigilance, and it would crush his ship and him without even noticing. He would just be another bit of space-going flotsam and just as important. It had not inspired in him any sense of awe for a very long time. But seeing it through her eyes made him recall, ever so faintly, the first time that he had set off into space. He hadn't been much older than she, as he recalled. Back then, it had all been a great adventure. In many ways, it still was. But these days he was more concerned with survival than anything else.

"I'm out in space," she said again. She shook her head. "You have . . . you have no idea . . . so many years . . . so many years, I wondered what it would be like . . . and my mother, she said that only fools would . . . would ever leave Montos . . . and I dreamed of other places, and the dreams frightened me, and I . . ."

He wasn't sure that he entirely knew what she was talking about. She was speaking so quickly, about so many things, and she didn't seem at all focused. He put a hand on her shoulder, and it felt remarkably cool to the touch. He was also a bit surprised to see that she was looking a little more tanned than she had earlier. Her skin was darkening a bit, and he wondered why that might be.

As caught up in the wonder of the moment as she was, she still shrugged his hand off her shoulder. Talk about presence of mind.

"Riella . . ." he began.

She turned and looked at him in surprise. "How do you know my name?"

"I have ways of learning things. Of learning your name . . . and learning of the Quiet Place."

The effect the mention of those words had upon her was electric. She shrank back from him as if he had pulled out a vicious weapon and was about to gut her with it. "How . . . how could you . . . it . . . how . . ."

"You tend to do that quite a bit. Stammer out a series of barely connected thoughts. You might want to work on that."

"Who are you?!"

"I'm Xyon."

"I know that!"

"Then why did you ask?"

She put her face in her hands, and her fingers brushed against where her antennae had been. As if touching the now vacant area reminded her, she backed away from him while never taking her gaze from him. She was acting very much like a trapped animal.

"Shouldn't you be demanding that I take you home

about now?" said Xyon, his arms folded across his chest. "I mean, that is where this is going, isn't it?"

"No. I . . ." She looked decidedly crestfallen. "I can't go home, I can't . . ." She turned and looked back at him as if truly seeing him for the first time. "What happened to those creatures? The ones who were chasing me?"

"I had a chat with them. They agreed to leave you alone."

She looked at him with a trace of the wonderment that she'd been gazing out at the stars with. "Who are you? I mean, yes, I know your name is Xyon. But who are you?"

"No one important. I do what I feel like doing. There's not much to say beyond that."

"It can't be that simple. You go around the galaxy helping people?"

"No. I just kill time, waiting to see what happens next in my life. Everything else is fairly incidental."

"You're lying. I don't know why, but you are. Did you . . ." She hesitated to frame the question. "Did you kill them?"

"Kill who?"

"Those creatures, who were chasing me."

"Oh. One of them, yes."

"I could never do that. Kill something."

"You would be amazed," Xyon told her, "what you're capable of killing when it's trying to kill you."

"I . . . suppose so. Have you killed a lot of people? Or things?"

"As many as I've had to." Making a quick effort to turn the subject away from himself to something he felt more comfortable with, he said, "What I want to know, though, is why they were interested in you. What is this 'Quiet Place?' "

"A place in my dreams." She was barely speaking above a whisper. "Words that mean something only to me. How could you know of it? Where did you find out?"

"From the Dogs. They got the information from someone else."

Slowly she sagged to the ground as if she had no strength in her legs. Her back slid against the wall until her rump thudded onto the floor. Then she sat and stared. "How could it be? It's . . . it's all in my head . . . I didn't . . . it . . . I couldn't . . ."

"You're doing it again. The fragmented sentence thing."

"Shut up!" she said, her temper flaring, and then she reined herself in, taking several deep breaths. Tears started to roll down her face and she quickly, firmly wiped them away.

"It's obviously not in your head. At least, not only there. Do you have any idea how the Dogs would have found out, or how—"

"No." Her fists thudded against her thighs. "I have no idea. None at all."

She looked back out the viewport at the stars, and then slowly she got to her feet. She moved to the port and stood against it, staring out at the gleaming array of stars before them.

Then she whispered something, so softly that he couldn't make it out. "What was that?"

"I need to sleep." It was as if she were addressing him from another quadrant.

"You just woke up."

"I know." Quickly she walked away from him and to the backroom. He heard the bed creaking and, moments later, looked in on her to see her with her eyes closed, her chest rising and falling in a steady pattern.

He walked away, shaking his head, not even pretending to understand what was happening . . . and then he jumped as he heard her cry out. Immediately, he ran back to the bedroom in time to see her sitting up, looking as if she'd been frozen into the upright position. "All right, what in hell is going on?" he demanded.

She didn't hear him, or if she did, she didn't acknowledge him. She seemed to be concentrating intently, although he couldn't quite determine what it was she was concentrating on. Immediately, she swung her legs down and off the bed and padded back up the hallway. He followed her, scratching his head. "Riella? Riella, would you mind telling me—"

Still no answer. Instead she had gone to the viewport and was staring out. This time, however, she didn't appear overwhelmed by the glory of all creation. She seemed to be concentrating, trying to pick something out. He didn't have a clue as to what she was doing.

"Turn us," she murmured.

"What?"

"Turn us. Around. I want to see everything. All of it."

He couldn't even begin to understand what she was talking about, but there was no harm in indulging her. "Lyla," he said. "Keep us stationary, give us a spiral survey of the area."

"All right, Xyon."

Riella jumped slightly at the unexpected female voice that seemed to emanate from right by her elbow. But then she promptly forgot about it as Lyla's systems guided the ship in a gentle spiral pattern, like a gyroscope. Riella scanned everything around her intently, and Xyon watched all of it with quiet bemusement.

Suddenly she cried out, "Go back! Go back!"

Obediently Lyla angled the ship back in the direction

that it had been pointing when Riella had shouted. The vessel froze in place as Riella stared, fixated, in one particular direction.

To Xyon, it seemed an eternity passed, and still she didn't speak. Just stared. Finally he offered, "Would you like to see some star charts?"

She looked at him blankly at first. "What? Star charts?"

"Maps. Visual indicators that give names of systems, planets, distances, travel times . . ."

"You have such things?" She sounded amazed.

"Of course. Anyone who travels in space does. Well, they do if they're interested in survival. I can punch up an overview of the general sector of space you were looking at, if that would be of interest to you."

"Yes. Very much, I'd like to see it."

"Lyla—"

"All right, Xyon," she said without his having to complete the question. "On the side screen."

He pointed to a screen just to the left of Riella's shoulder, and she turned and stared at it, wide-eyed, as a detailed schematic appeared on the screen. She regarded it fixedly, so much so that he thought her eyes were going to pop clean out of her head.

"What are you looking for?" he asked.

"I don't know."

"Yes, somehow I had a feeling you'd say that."

After that, she said nothing for quite some time, except to call for other star charts, or ask for closer studies of particular areas. Seeing that the conversation wasn't going any further, Xyon busied himself with his own duties. Working with Lyla, he scanned various broadcasts over the ether, seeing if there was any more activity on the part of the Dogs of War. He managed to pick up, through deft tapping of private transmissions, the results of the Dogs' recent visit to Montos. Apparently, a considerable portion of Montos City was in flames. Beyond that, things were unclear and contradictory. Some reports stated that the Dogs were running amok while others said that they had fled, although what they might be fleeing from Xyon could not even guess.

At that point, Xyon didn't have anywhere else in particular to go. There were a couple of worlds he had been thinking about visiting, but none of them were particularly high priority. Besides, what was he supposed to do? Drag Riella all over the place?

Indeed . . . what *was* he going to do with her?

Not for the first time, he cursed himself for his impulsiveness. He had hauled himself over to Montos to try and help someone he didn't know, to rescue her from a situation that he knew nothing about. He had actually managed to accomplish it, except now that he had done so, he didn't know how to proceed. Xyon had an annoying habit of following his instincts without giving any thought as to where those instincts might lead him. Consequently, he tended to find himself in situations where his instincts had run out and he had nothing left to substitute for them.

Hauling Riella from one end of the quadrant to the other didn't seem like much of an option. He could return her to Montos, but she didn't seem particularly inclined to go there. Besides, matters there seemed rather unstable, and he might very well not be doing her any favors by depositing her back in the middle of it.

For that matter, something seemed distinctly wrong. He wasn't entirely certain that Montos would be the right place for her in any event.

He was starting to realize that it wasn't his imagination at all. She was looking distinctly less Montosian. He was beginning to suspect that the antennae had fallen off because either they weren't real in the first place, or they had been grafted on somehow. And her skin color was deepening, darkening.

He had lost track of time when she suddenly said, out of the blue, "You really didn't cut off my antennae, did you."

"No, of course not."

She nodded absently, still staring at the star charts. "You don't seem the type to have done it."

"Really. What type do I seem like?"

"I don't know." She didn't even look in his direction. "I'm not sure what type you are ... except that you scare me."

"I scare you?" He laughed at that, and then she did look at him to fire an annoyed glare at him. But he was not particularly intimidated by the prospect of her anger. This was his ship, after all. If she got too much on his nerves, he could always punt her into space and be done with her. He couldn't envision himself doing so, but then again, who knew what lengths she might drive him to. "Sweetheart, you're the spookiest, weirdest thing on this ship, and it's not as if there's a great deal on it. You sleep, you scream, you study star charts for hours on end even though you've never been in space and have no idea where you would go even if—"

"Here."

He blinked. "What?"

"Here," she said again with greater emphasis, and she pointed at one particular sector. "Here is where I want to go. Take me there."

He stepped closer. "Magnify sector 18M, Marks 113–114, Lyla." The requested area immediately enlarged on the screen and he leaned forward to study it. "Why there?"

"There," was all she said.

"But there's nothing there. The star doesn't even have a name; just a locale." He glanced at the designation. "Star 7734. The system is . . . it doesn't even have a system. It's just there. There's nothing there, Riella. It's a waste of time to—"

She whirled on him, then, and there was something about her that was different. There wasn't simply anger in her tone; it was more like solid iron, and when she spoke, it wasn't begging or pleading or even petulance. It was with a voice of command that expected to be obeyed. *"Take me there!"* There was no mistake at all: it was, indeed, an order.

At which point Xyon toyed with the idea of tying her down or locking her away or in some other way endeavoring to teach her just who was running the ship and who had the right to bark orders at whom. Instead, Xyon was rather surprised to hear his own voice say, "All right. Lyla, set course for Star 7734."

"Setting course, Xyon."

"Let's go, then."

The fact that her rather strident command had been obeyed didn't relax Riella in the slightest. Instead she remained whipcord tense. She shifted her focus from Xyon back to the star charts and fixated on them for some time, even once the ship was well underway for the requested destination.

Not for the first time, Xyon wondered just what in the world he had gotten himself involved in.

Riella did not want to sleep. She knew what would happen, for by this point, it was happening every single time she went to sleep. No longer was she experiencing a calm, restful slumber, not ever. She would go to sleep and the dreams would haunt her, and then she would awaken and feel less and less herself.

Hour upon hour she had remained, staring at the star chart while the ship, the *Lyla,* headed on the course that she had so emphatically stated must be followed. Xyon, finally succumbing to exhaustion, had settled in his bed at the far end of the ship and gone to sleep. It wasn't as if he trusted her particularly; she had heard him muttering low commands to Lyla, caught the words, "Keep an eye on her," and knew that he had instructed Lyla to summon him if there was any untoward activity on her part.

In an effort to keep awake, she said, "Lyla."

"Yes," came the brisk voice.

"What are you?"

"Pardon?" the ship replied.

"Well, I . . . I mean, I don't pretend to be conversant with hardware throughout the galaxy. I probably know less than most people do about such things. But I was under the impression that there aren't any computers as sophisticated as—"

Lyla's voice interrupted. "What makes you think I'm a computer?"

Riella didn't know what to make of that. "I'm sorry—"

"A computer. Why do you assume that I am?"

"Well, aren't you?"

"I'm not exactly a computer."

Riella felt a chill go down her spine. "Then . . . then what . . . are you? Are you a ghost or—"

"Ghost?" And Lyla laughed. "No. No, quite the contrary. I am very alive."

"Alive?" Riella could scarcely believe it. "But . . . but how can you be alive? Is this entire ship alive, then?"

Again that eerie laugh. "Only in that I am part of it. The ship itself is not sentient. I, of course, am."

"Of course," said Riella, trying to sound casual even though the entire thing seemed insane to her. "Of course you're sentient. I mean . . . why wouldn't you be."

There was a hesitation on Lyla's part. Not a silence; Riella could sense it. The computer, the being, the . . . whatever it was . . . was hesitating.

"I used to be someone else," Lyla said. "Someone . . . very bad. I did not serve society. I did not help others. This . . . was my punishment . . . and my salvation."

Slowly the truth began to dawn on Riella. "You're . . . not physically here, are you . . ."

"Not really. But my personality engrams were built into the ship. Part of an experimental program run by scientists who were formerly part of the Daystrom Institute."

"And this ship was given to Xyon? Such a rare vessel? Why?"

"Given to Xyon? No. Xyon tends to acquire things in a manner other than having them given to him."

Riella's lips thinned. "So he is a thief, is what you are telling me."

"Oh yes."

Immediately Riella's opinion of Xyon (that was still in the process of forming) took a downward turn. A hero, an adventurer, an altruist . . . these she could appreciate, even admire, although there was still something about him that was unsettling. But someone of a moral character low enough to be a thief . . . that called into question everything else he said and did. Who knew what uses he intended to put Riella to? Perhaps he was hoping he could ransom her, or perhaps . . .

She didn't know. There were any number of possibilities, and none of them were especially pleasant.

But there was something that still eluded her. She wanted to ask more about Lyla's background, but couldn't quite bring herself to do so. Then she focused on something else. "I do not understand, though. If you are sentient, you can leave at any time. Or has he programed you in some way so that you—"

"Oh, no. No. My presence with him is purely voluntary."

"Then why do you remain with a . . . thief?" The word was so distasteful to her that she was having trouble forming it.

"Because," Lyla said matter of factly, "I like him."

"How can you like a thief?"

"I like Xyon. What he does is immaterial to me. I do not judge; I appreciate someone for who they are, not what they are."

"That is . . . very generous of you."

"Really?" Lyla paused to consider this. "Yes. Yes, I suppose it is. I never thought about it much before. Interesting, isn't it. As quickly as I think, with my computer mind . . . apparently I do not manage to think of everything."

"Yes. Very interesting." Actually, she wasn't sure that it was interesting, but at that moment, she wasn't all that sure of anything anymore.

The only thing that she was absolutely positive about was that she had to make it to that place on the star chart, the star that was designated as 7734.

The Quiet Place.

The words whispered in her head, and as she studied the star chart and saw the number 7734 glowing in front of her, the chart started to blur in front of her. She fought it off, rubbing her eyes. She had lost track of time. She had no idea of how many hours (days, it seemed) she had been awake. But she dared not sleep because she would dream of . . .

The Quiet Place, and the mists were congealing around her, moving through her and she felt a chill down to her very soul. And her soul was slipping away, being pulled from her body, she could feel it being dragged out. It sank its long fingers into her heart, trying to maintain its place, desperately striving to avoid its fate, but the mists were pulling on it, shredding it, and when she screamed it was in unison with herself. And there was the red-skinned man, there was Zoran (for he had a name now) and . . .

. . . another. Another red-skinned man, gods, no there were two of them? Twice the evil, twice the menace? But . . .

. . . but this one had different markings on him, and she had a different feeling from him. He was reaching out to her, this new red man, and he was crying her name, except he wasn't, and the mists seemed angry at him, as if he were trying to interfere with them. They came at him from all sides, and he was strong, but she had no idea how strong he was. She reached out towards him, and called his name, except how could it be that she knew who he was when she had never seen him before . . .

. . . and suddenly she was jolted

. . . to wakefulness, and she gasped as she tumbled off the chair. Her head snapped around as she looked up from her prone position on the floor and saw that Xyon was at the chair stationed squarely in front of the tactical array. He looked disheveled, his clothes hastily tossed on. Clearly whatever was happening had occurred while he was asleep. But despite his appearance, he was obviously fully awake and dealing with the situation, whatever the devil it was.

Then she heard an explosion that occurred in concert with the abrupt shuddering of the vessel. "What's happening?!" she called.

"Something's got a lock on us!" he shouted back. "Tractor beam . . . pretty powerful, too, from the feel of it!"

"I thought this thing had a cloaking device!"

"That's right, girl, but we don't have an infinite energy source, thank you very much," he snapped even as he obviously assessed their options. "We don't run cloaked all the time."

"Well, I guess you should have done it now!" she said sarcastically.

"I guess so," he shot back. "Next time you want to contribute something to a situation other than belated wisdom, I'd be happy to hear it! Lyla, full reverse thrusters!"

"Thrusters on full. No effect. We're being held."

"Full engines, then! Blast us out of here! Can you do that?"

"That depends, Xyon."

"On what?" he asked in exasperation.

"On whether you mind the ship being torn in half when I do it."

He exchanged glances with Riella. "Do I get a vote?" she asked.

"No. Lyla, what's the source on the beam! I'm not

getting any lock on . . ." Then the sensor readings suddenly snapped into focus. "Wait a minute. I see it. Damn!"

"What is it?" asked Riella. She was almost afraid to ask.

"From the configurations, it's a Redeemer ship," said Xyon, and he sounded rather worried.

She couldn't blame him. Even on the relatively isolated world of Montos, the might of the Redeemers was well known. An aggressive religious sect that maintained its home on Tulaan IV, the Redeemers were a missionary race intent on spreading the word of the return of their primary God, Xant. The only thing that had proven a deterrent to the Redeemers was the presence of the Thallonians.

But with the Thallonians out of the picture, the Redeemers very much believed that their time had come to seize their rightful place as the preeminent race in the galaxy. Using their homeworld as a base, they were prepared to launch a holy war, converting all nearby worlds to their beliefs through any means necessary. And if a selected world was populated by inveterate nonbelievers, then genocide was also an option.

Riella had never actually seen one of the Redeemers, although she had heard some fearsome stories. Meantime, Xyon seemed determined to find an upside, presuming there was one. "Not one of their megacruisers, thankfully, but still more than a match for this piece of tin."

"My hull is not composed of—"

"It's a figure of speech, Lyla." He thumped the viewport in frustration.

Riella thought she saw genuine fear in Xyon's face. On the one hand, the notion that Xyon was afraid of something was inexplicably daunting. He didn't seem like the type who was easily thrown. He looked over to Riella. "How lucky are you feeling right now."

"Why?"

"Well, if the Redeemers are grabbing hold of us, they obviously have some reason for it. They don't do anything without a reason. They may want me, or you, or the ship. Impossible to tell. There is a way of avoiding the problem, however."

Hope sprang within her. "What? What could we do?"

"Suicide. That way you don't have to face whatever they have in store for us."

"That's it?" Her voice went up an octave. "Either we submit to them, or we kill ourselves? There has to be some other option."

"None immediately comes to mind."

She took a step back from him, and there was pure fury in her eyes. She couldn't help it. In a number of ways, she had actually found herself admiring him, and the recent revelations—and his attitude now—were filling her with such contempt that she could barely see straight. "I should have expected it," she snapped. "From a thief like you . . . all thieves are cowards . . ."

"Who told you I was a thief?" he said.

"Lyla."

"And you believe her?"

For a moment, she hesitated. "Are you saying she's lying?"

"No, no, she's telling the truth. I was just curious as to whether you believe her."

She let out a howl of fury as the ship lurched, being drawn closer to the Redeemer vessel. They could see it now, dark and ominous, hanging there in space like a great, hulking creature, pyramidal in shape—frightening in that conquest by the Redeemer ship seemed inevitable. She lunged forward and thudded her small hands on his chest. Xyon could very likely have blocked her outburst, but he didn't even bother. Her hands made small, hollow noises that he didn't even appear to notice.

"You're so . . . so . . . ohhhhh!" she shouted. "Standing there, calm as you please, and saying we should be prepared to die!"

"I didn't say anything about 'we.' I'm not going to be dying now, this way. I have a different fate awaiting me, so I'm fairly safe, actually. What's going to happen to you, however," and he shrugged.

She drew in so close to him that her face was practically in his. "I thought," she said, her voice dripping with ice, "that you were a hero."

"I am," said Xyon. "I just may not be your hero, that's all."

IX.

THE OVERLORD WAS THE TALLEST of the Redeemers, and half again as wide. His skin was hardened and black, almost obsidian, and his eyes were deeply set and a soft, glowing red. Other races generally tried not to look directly into the face of a Redeemer; it was like experiencing a little foreshadowing of death. His clothing was as black as his skin, with a tunic that hung down to his knees and black leggings that were tucked into his high boots. He wore a large black cape draped around him, giving him—when he was in a contemplative, forward-leaning mood—a distinct resemblance to a crouching bird of prey.

"Prime One," he called. He knew he would not have to wait long; Prime One always remained an easy summons away. Sure enough, there was a quick scuttling of feet, and moments later Prime One entered. Prime

One bowed deeply and waited for the Overlord to speak.

The Overlord had been working on training the new Prime One. His predecessor had been a good and faithful servant, dedicated and with a healthy fear of the Overlord that kept him well motivated. Unfortunately, the previous Prime One had had a direct engagement with the starship *Excalibur,* and it had not gone especially well for the late Prime One. To be specific, the starship had outmaneuvered the Redeemer vessel, with the result that both the vessel and Prime One had been the victim of a solar flare created by a burst of energy generated by the *Excalibur.* The solar flare had effortlessly wiped out ship and crew, leaving the Overlord to find new help.

The Overlord, to put it mildly, had not been very happy about that. As a result, evening the score with Mackenzie Calhoun and his vessel had been uppermost in his mind. However, his summons to Prime One at this point concerned another matter.

"My understanding," he said in that remarkably soft tone of his, which commanded attention just by its lack of volume, "is that we have located the vessel with the girl aboard. Is that correct?"

"Yes, Overlord."

"And the ship has been captured and taken in tow?"

"Yes, Overlord."

"Why," asked the Overlord, leaning back and fixing a deadly stare on Prime One, "have we taken it in tow? Of what possible use is some space-fool's vessel to us?"

"With all respect, Great One, he is no mere fool. The ship's computer exhibits a sentience we did not think possible, and it also carries a Romulan cloaking device. I am not certain from whence it came, but it is functioning quite well. It is our opinion that there may be other such treasures aboard the ship, which would preclude the notion of simply leaving it derelict. Unless, of course, your greatness wishes for us to leave it behind."

The Overlord regarded him coolly for a moment. "What do you think?" he asked.

"I think," Prime One said with a slight bow, "whatever you wish me to think, Overlord."

The Overlord sighed heavily at this.

Once upon a time, he had enjoyed the fact that the Prime Ones—all of them—were totally subservient to him. They measured each word carefully, lest the slightest missplaced statement result in some hideous punishment. The Overlord had felt that that was the way it was supposed to be. Why shouldn't he feel that way, really? The Overlords who had preceeded him had left behind them a body of disciplinary tactics that suggested, even mandated such thinking.

But it was becoming a bit tiresome to the Overlord. How was he supposed to expand his thinking and leadership, how was he supposed to challenge his various preconceptions, if no one challenged him in return? How was one reasonably supposed to lead people who were afraid?

In a way, he admired Mackenzie Calhoun, the hated commander of the starship *Excalibur,* precisely because he was someone who went about his activities without giving a damn about the Redeemers, about the Overlord, even about the Great God Xant himself. If Calhoun were not his sworn enemy, the Overlord would almost be able to wish Calhoun were his ally.

"Let us say," the Overlord said slowly, "that I was not mandating your opinion. That I had no thoughts on the matter one way or the other. What would you say then?"

Prime One looked ever-so-slightly panicked for a moment, but then he smiled slowly, as if he had managed to see around a trap that was being laid for him. "Such a circumstance would be impossible, Overlord. For the Overlord is all-knowing. It would be impossible for the Overlord not to know something, and so the situation you describe . . . could not be." He even nodded to himself slightly as if personally approving of the way that he had just handled the challenge.

The Overlord sighed. "Very well said, Prime One. I would not presume to disagree with one as learned and perspicacious as yourself."

"Thank you, Overlord," said Prime One, bowing slightly.

"The reasons you have put forward are quite reasonable. Scan the vessel to make certain there is no risk of self-detonation, and then bring it into our docking bay for inspection. The girl, I shall attend to personally."

"And the young male?"

The Overlord considered that a moment. "What sort of creature is he?"

"Humanoid. We are not entirely sure of his planet of origin, although we have some speculation."

"It does not matter," the Overlord waved it off. "Bring him along to watch the interrogation. It may very well be that his presence will have some effect on the girl. Furthermore, if she does not respond well to questioning, we can always question him."

"In hopes of pressuring her to respond so that he will not suffer?"

The Overlord shrugged. "No. In hopes of killing him. I am in a bad mood today."

* * *

The Redeemers had an annoying habit of shoving Xyon, even when he was cooperatively moving along. "Will you please stop that?" he said in irritation as they prodded him forward. They seemed disinclined to attend to him. Instead, they just kept pushing him when he showed the slightest hint of slowing down.

The silence with which they moved was a bit disconcerting to Xyon. Each of them was sporting encompassing robes that hid their feet. The lack of noise made it seem as if their feet were gliding above the floor without actually coming into contact with it. Truthfully, even if they were all capable of defying gravity, that shouldn't have thrown Xyon off that much. God knew he had certainly seen stranger things than that in his life. Still, it certainly left him with a rather odd feeling that he couldn't quite articulate, not that anyone would have actually listened to him had he put words to it.

"So where are we going anyway?" he asked. "I don't suppose you guys are actually going to tell me just why you decided to grab me when I was minding my own business."

The Redeemers didn't respond. They didn't even look at him. That was about what he had expected, but he had really been hoping they'd say *something*. He might have been able to parlay that into some sort of useful information. Unfortunately, they didn't appear interested in cooperating.

He was shoved into a darkened room, but it only took his eyes a moment to adjust to the lack of light. What he saw there, however, froze him in place.

Riella was in some sort of heavy-duty chair, locked in at her hands and feet, angled back at a 45-degree angle. There was clear terror on her face, a face that was looking even more dark than it had been before. In fact, the tint of it was starting to change; she wasn't looking quite as tanned, but rather flushed. Then again, he could certainly understand it, considering the predicament in which they found themselves.

When she saw Xyon, he could tell that there was a momentary flash of hope in her eyes. Then she saw that he was bracketed by Redeemers, and her spirits visibly sank once more.

"My hero," she said bitterly.

"I'm pleased to see you're taking this so well," he replied, and instantly regretted it. Sarcasm was not what the girl needed. She needed kind or brave words, or some sort of assurance—no matter how insincere—that everything was going to work out fine. Unfortunately, he had not provided her with that, and now the moment was gone. She said nothing more. She didn't even glare at him; she just stared off into nothing.

A door at the far end of the room slid open and in walked the individual Xyon instantly took (by the way the others deferred to him) to be the leader. They stepped back as he glided to the middle of the room.

"I," he said in a surprisingly quiet voice, "am the Overlord."

"Really." Xyon studied him a moment and then shrugged indifferently. "I was expecting someone taller."

The Overlord came up to just under Xyon's chest.

When he had first been escorted by the Redeemers, Xyon had been struck by the fact that none of them seemed much taller than three-and-a-half feet. The Overlord was a comparative giant, standing at a relatively gargantuan four-and-a-half-feet tall. Nevertheless, that was hardly what Xyon would consider intimidating.

"Do you only have respect for an enemy, then, if it is someone who towers over you?" inquired the Overlord. Xyon shrugged. "I stand above you in many ways, young man. Physical height is very much the least of those things to be considered. I could kill you with a word."

"It would have to be a fairly formidable word."

The Overlord spoke a word.

Immediately Xyon felt as if a shovel had been slammed through his brain. The actual word spoken was immediately driven from his head, as if the mere memory of it would be too much for his meager faculties. He didn't quite realize that he was on the floor until he felt the cold hardness of it against his cheek. He shut his eyes tightly to try and clear his head, then slowly sat up. His arms were trembling as he pushed himself into an upright position. He had absolutely no idea what had just happened. He looked around, and then up at the Overlord.

"What . . . did you do?" Xyon said. He decided his voice sounded annoyingly weak when he said it, and so he forced his composure to take over as he slowly brought himself to standing, his legs shaking until he managed to command them to stop doing so.

"There are certain techniques privy to the Overlord," the Overlord said coolly. "You cannot stand against them. Even other Redeemers cannot. I do not suggest you tempt your fate again. I could have killed you just then. I still may. It depends whether you irritate me or whether it will serve our purpose. We do not like to take lives, you see."

"Oh, really," Xyon said. He was leaning against the

wall, trying to look nonchalant. In point of fact, he was doing so to make sure that he didn't topple over. He didn't completely trust his legs or his ability to remain upright. "As I recall, aren't you the people whose High Priests carry some sort of infection with them. A virus. And if their blood is spilled, the virus annihilates everyone on the planet? That doesn't indicate to me a tremendous reverence for life."

"We revere all life when it is life that will benefit Xant," the Overlord told him.

"Right. Xant. Your god."

"Your god, too." The Overlord smiled. It did not improve his expression in the least. "Your god, when and if you choose to accept him. All lives are in the service of Xant. Xant is everything, we are nothing. If your life will be spent in the service of Xant upon his return, then your life is sacred. Indeed, it would be a mortal sin to take a life under such circumstances. But if you refuse to accept Xant, or act against his interests, then your life is nothing. Less than nothing. One has no right to complain about the extinguishing of something that is less than nothing. Those who attack a High Priest have rejected the name of Xant, and so rejected life itself. Don't you understand? In such circumstances, we have not killed them. They have killed themselves."

"That's very considerate of you. I never thought of a race of beings who go around imposing their beliefs on others—or else—as being nothing but altruistic in their motivations."

"Then you have learned differently this day, haven't you." As if Xyon had lost interest for him, the Overlord turned to Riella. "Now you, child, present a different situation. You have knowledge that we desire."

"Do I." She was trying to make her tone sound defiant. She wasn't succeeding overmuch.

"Yes. Yes, you do." He was slowly circling her, never taking his eyes from her. "You know of the Quiet Place. We would know of it, too. We have sought it for a very, very long time. We know that you know of it. We know of the dreams that have haunted you—"

"How?" she whispered.

He waved off the question as if it were immaterial. "That does not matter. What matters is that we know. And we will do whatever we have to in order to pull the information from you. We are prepared to subject you to all manner of deep mental probes, many of which will be—regrettably—quite painful. We will, if necessary, reduce you to a sobbing sack of protoplasm, unless you agree to cooperate with—"

"Star 7734," she said immediately.

Xyon rolled his eyes. "That's standing up to torture, all right."

The Overlord frowned. "What do you mean, Star 7734?"

"Star 7734. That's where the Quiet Place is. You wanted to know. I've told you. Can I go now?"

The Overlord glanced at the other Redeemers as if checking to make sure that they had heard what he had. "The Quiet Place," he said slowly, "is one of the greatest secrets in the galaxy. She who knows of it possesses a sacred trust, passed on through generations since before anyone—even the first of the Overlords—can remember. You don't seriously expect me to believe that without the slightest act of torture, you would—"

"Seven. Seven. Three. Four. Aren't you listening? Are you stupid?" Riella said in obvious annoyance. "I don't know anything about generations or the first of the Overlords. I don't know anything about the greatest secret in the galaxy. All I know is that I have this place rattling about in my head, and no one's told me it was supposed to be a big secret. Even if they did tell me, I'm just a girl being plagued by terrifying dreams. I didn't sign on for torture and being turned into a sack of . . . what was it?"

"Protoplasm," offered the Overlord politely.

"Yes, thank you. A sack of protoplasm. That is not, frankly, my idea of fun."

"A sacred trust is not intended to be fun," said the Overlord.

"I don't care! I don't care!" She pulled in frustration against the bonds holding her to the chair. "I don't want this trust, sacred or otherwise! I never asked for this 'great secret,' this generational responsibility. The only thing I ever asked was for the dreams to stop. And they haven't! I don't owe anyone anything, and I certainly haven't promised anyone that I would keep silent about the Quiet Place. I was only trying to get there in hopes that, once I did, it would be satisfied—whatever 'it' is—and leave me alone for the rest of my life."

One of the lower orders of Redeemers was holding a padd in front of the Overlord and pointing. The Overlord was nodding slowly and then he looked at Riella. "Our star charts indicate that there is nothing at the designate 7734. A star, but that is all. No planets. Not even an asteroid. It's just dead space."

"Well, that's what you've got between your ears, so you should feel right at home there!"

Xyon winced when she said that. He had a sneaking suspicion that the Overlord was not going to take very kindly to that assessment of his mental capacity.

The Overlord actually chuckled slightly. It was not a pleasant sound.

"You sought to distract us," he said. "Make us waste time going to an empty system while the true location of the Quiet Place remains locked in your head."

"No, I didn't! I'm not that clever!"

"Obviously, since it apparently never occurred to you that we would check the location before going there." He drew close to her, then, and Xyon felt a chill going through him. He remembered what the Overlord had done to him just with a word or words. He didn't even want to consider what would happen to Riella if the Overlord turned his full attentions on her. "Where is the Quiet Place."

"She's telling the truth!" Xyon said, deciding there was no point in keeping silent. After all, if she—the keeper of this "sacred knowledge"—was more than willing to talk her head off about it, what purpose was there in Xyon's reticence? "That's where we were heading! That's where she told me to go!"

"Then she was lying to you."

"Or perhaps she was telling the truth, and you simply refuse to believe it, because you're sanctimonious fools!"

The Overlord spoke another word. This time it felt like a hammer blow, and it slammed Xyon against the wall with such force that it actually lifted him off the ground. He gasped from the impact, a sheet of white exploding behind his eyes. It was everything he could do not to fall. He had never been so grateful for the existence of a wall in his life. As before, the actual word, or words, slid out of his mind before he could even recall the slightest hint of it. He was starting to wonder whether that was actually an act of self-defense; that to remember the words being used against him would somehow cause the top of his head to blow off.

"You do not fall," the Overlord said. There was a hint of approval, even mild admiration, in his tone. "That is impressive. Most anyone else would. You would be a formidable servant of Xant if you were able to get past the fundamental anger that darkens your soul."

"Perhaps the reason I'm . . . getting angry . . . is because you keep throwing me around with your magic words."

"They are hardly magic. They tap into primal truths of the universe. Truths that we of the Redeemers instinctively grasp, and you, just as instinctively, reject. They are as consistent, as real, as reliable as the so-called 'laws of physics.' You would do well to remember that."

And you would do well not to let me get my hands around your throat, Xyon thought, but rather wisely he didn't say that.

"Now then, child," the Overlord turned his attention back to Riella. "We are going to try again. I will ask you—"

"I already told you!" she interrupted him. "I can't make up an answer. I wouldn't even know what answer to make up! The first time I saw a star chart in my life was when Xyon showed me one. If I just began manufacturing answers, you'd see through that in no time. So what is the point in lying?"

"What indeed? Then you will tell me."

"I can't!"

The Overlord sighed. He seemed rather sad about the situation. "Yes. Yes, I rather thought you would say that."

And that was when the first charges surged through the bindings that strapped Riella to the chair.

She arched her back, crying out, her eyes snapping

wide, and it seemed as if the energy itself was going to be sufficient to propel her right out of the chair. Her head snapped left, then right, and her mouth was so wide open that she seemed in danger of dislocating her jaw.

"Stop it! She's telling the truth!" Xyon shouted. He took a step towards the Overlord, knowing that the creature could stop him with but a word. As it turned out, though, the Overlord didn't even have to open his mouth, for Redeemers converged on him from all sides and thrust him to the ground, piling atop him. They might not have been terribly tall, but their strength was far more formidable than Xyon would have believed. He struggled in their grasp, cursed their names and ancestry. And while all this was happening, Riella was continuing to scream.

As if he were responding to an afterthought, the Overlord touched a small control pad on the chair. The energy immediately ceased its corruscation around her, and Riella sagged forward. Her eyes remained wide open; she appeared to be staring with great fascination at something that only she could see.

"Have you had a change of heart?" the Overlord inquired solicitiously.

She did not respond immediately, and Xyon took the opportunity to jump in. "How can she have a change of heart about something over which she has no control?! That place, that Star, 7734 . . . that's it! That's the place you want! All of this is unnecessary! You have no call to hurt her at all!"

"So you say. So she says. However," the Overlord continued, "what you say and what she says is not terribly relevant. What matters is what I say."

"And what do you say, Overlord?" asked one of the Redeemers.

The Overlord pondered that a moment, stroking his chin thoughtfully, and then he said exactly what Xyon expected him to say.

"Hit her again."

More energy, more screaming, more protests that she was telling everything she knew, and still the Overlord would not be deterred. And so it continued, and when Riella passed out from the increasing strain (which was often) the Overlord would politely wait until she had recovered, at which point the torture would recommence.

"Don't you have a word!" Xyon suddenly said at one point while Riella was out cold, being revived for the who-knew-which time.

The Overlord looked at him curiously. "A 'word?'"

"Yes! If you've got some sort of word that can inflict pain, don't you have something that can just . . . just force people to tell the truth? Without all of this barbaric torture?"

"We do, actually," the Overlord said thoughtfully. "Would you like me to use it?"

"Of course! If it'll end this, then definitely!"

"All right, if you're certain."

Something in the Overlord's tone caught his attention. "Why? What reason would there be not to use it?"

Riella's head was slowly being lifted up by one of the Redeemers, and she was staring bleary eyed at Xyon.

"Well," said the Overlord, "inflicting pain, you see—as I do with you—believe it or not does not require much effort. But controlling someone's mind, forcing truth from them, that can take something of a toll on the subject."

"How much of a toll?" Xyon asked cautiously.

"It's usually terminal, I'm afraid."

"You mean it would kill her?"

"That's correct."

Xyon looked helplessly at Riella, having no idea what to do. She was looking at him, through eyes that barely focused on him. Her mouth moved ever so slightly. He saw the words her mouth was making out:

Kill me.

Xyon felt awful. It was as if this girl's life were suddenly being thrust into his hands. Who was he to carry this sort of responsibility, to make this kind of decision. He hardly knew her, and what he did know of her, he wasn't really that crazy about.

He had lost track of time. He had no idea how long they had been subjecting the girl to this kind of treatment, but it was quite clear from her reactions and deportment that she was not some tough warrior who was laughing off pain and challenging enemies to do their worst. She wanted the torment to end, and even if it meant that she would feel nothing, ever again, obviously she didn't care anymore or didn't consider that too high a price to pay.

Now it had come to this: the helpless Riella begging him to allow her to be subjected to a treatment that would very likely mean her demise.

He felt a mental maelstrom beginning to build within him, emotions tumbling over each other. It was a sensation that he rarely felt, that only the most primal situations brought out within him. He never felt it when his own life was on the line, possibly because he had such utter confidence that his life was not at stake—not until the appointed time. But seeing others suffer to the degree that she was, it was threatening to overwhelm him, and he recognized the sensations that were rampaging through him.

Suddenly he said, "Me! Ask me!"

The Overlord had been reaching for the switch to apply more voltage to Riella, but his hand froze over it. He turned and looked contemplatively at Xyon. For his part, Xyon was doing everything he could to contain the raging emotions within. "You? . . ." he asked thoughtfully.

"Yes! Me! I was her pilot! What she knows, I know! Try it on me!"

"Knowing that it will very likely—"

"Yes, yes! I know! But it means you'll stop hurting her!" His long hair was falling in his face. He shoved it back and glared at the Overlord with such pure intensity of emotion that the Overlord actually took a step back. "Come on, then! Ask me what you want to know! If you think you can, that is! If you're not all talk! If you're really capable of—"

The Overlord spoke the word. It was not one word, actually it was several words.

Xyon felt as if his head, his brain, were being shredded. He could have sworn that the skin on his head actually peeled back, pink and throbbing, uncovering the skull beneath, and then the skull in turn cracked open and his mind just spilled out all over the floor.

He heard himself saying things, a torrent of words spilling out. It wasn't just the information about the Quiet Place that tumbled out of him, it was other things, things with no relevance whatsoever. Within seconds he had informed the Overlord of his favorite color, and his parents' names, and the last birthday present he'd gotten, and his favorite tune, and the things Lyla whispered to him at night that made the darkness seem less oppressive, and the sheer stinking fear that was wedded to his soul because what if he was wrong and he wasn't supposed to die at that particular time, and it was just a reflex action to prevent him from worrying that every hazardous situation he was in might actually be the beginning of his end.

All that and more was at the Overlord's feet in a matter of seconds, and then Xyon collapsed, as if there was simply nothing more in him remaining to keep him up. It was not the fall of someone who had just become unconscious. It was as if all the muscles and bones within him had simply disintegrated, and as a result, he had completely fallen apart.

The Overlord and the Redeemers stared at the insensate sack of meat that had once been Xyon. After a moment, the Overlord reached out with the toe of his boot and prodded him. It was hardly a final means of determining whether there was any life within him. It certainly wasn't scientific or medically sound. But somehow it seemed the thing to do.

Xyon didn't budge. His face was slack, his eyes open but looking at nothing.

"Is he dead, Overlord?" inquired one of the Redeemers.

"It would seem so," said the Overlord after a moment. "Interesting. His dying words reflected those spoken by the girl. He truly believes that the Quiet Place is at Star 7734."

"So she was telling the truth, then."

Riella was staring fixatedly at the unmoving body of Xyon. Clearly she couldn't quite grasp what she had just seen. The Overlord couldn't blame her, really. The young man had just sacrificed himself for her. It gave him a certain measure of nobility that the Overlord would never have assumed that he possessed.

"He believes that she was telling it," the Overlord said reasonably. "However, that does not mean she actually was. His belief does not make it so. The probe of the girl will continue."

She choked when she heard this, as he suspected she would. She started trying to utter a word, a single word.

"'Why'?" asked the Overlord. "Are you asking me 'why'? Why did I allow him to sacrifice himself in this way, when I knew that it would not necessarily provide a final answer?" She managed a nod. "Because," he told her in a matter-of-fact tone, "I was interested to see whether he would be willing to go through with it. And I was interested to see if he would survive it. Think of it as . . . scientific curiosity."

"You . . . bastard," she managed to get out.

"Your opinions do not matter particularly to me, but I appreciate the vehemence of your thoughts."

He reached for the switch on the back of the chair, and Riella stiffened in anticipation.

And that was when all hell broke loose.

X.

FOR SOMEONE WHO HAD LIVED in terror of her dreams for so long, Riella could not recall a time when she so very much wanted to be dreaming.

Every so often, back on her home (former home) of Montos, she speculated about what it would have been like to have lived previous lives. She now felt as if she were living through one of those earlier existences now. That she was observing the current events from very far away, from another life many years in the future, safe and distant. That she was not Riella at all, but someone else who had no emotional connection to these happenings whatsoever. That was certainly the way she would have preferred it.

Because what she was seeing now was just too brutal.

There was Xyon, having laid down his life, lying on

the ground. There was the Overlord and several of the Redeemers, staring down at him, at his body. It seemed so cruel, so . . . so disrespectful. They should have been looking anywhere else, rather than gawking at the corpse of someone so brave, so . . . so . . .

So stupid. How could he have been so stupid as to throw his life away? How could? . . .

All the questions tumbled in her brain, with no answers presenting themselves. And then it became clear that Xyon's sacrifice was in vain, that she was going to undergo still more torture. Her attention was immediately, and understandably, pulled away from Xyon and to herself. Why not? His pain and suffering was over. Hers was just beginning.

That was when the alarms went off.

The alarms seized the attention of the Overlord and his aides immediately. The Overlord did not appear particularly perturbed by the intrusion. Indeed, he seemed rather interested, even intrigued that someone would be so foolish as to launch an attack directly against the Redeemers. "It would appear we have visitors," he said. "One almost has to admire their audacity."

"Overlord," one of the Redeemers said, and he actually appeared a bit apprehensive. "This is not one of our primary battle vessels. It is designed primarily for short-range travel in friendly territory. We could be at a disadvantage."

"Are you questioning my choice of vehicles?" There was an amazing cool in the Overlord's voice, but also an unmistakeable warning.

"No, Overlord," the Redeemer said immediately.

"Good. That is good." The Overlord considered the matter a moment longer, and then said, "I shall attend to this present disruption. You remain here. Make certain that our guest is kept comfortable."

She wanted to laugh upon hearing that. She also wanted to cry. Comfortable? Bound hand and foot into a chair of torture, knowing that more suffering would be hers to experience very shortly. What sort of sick, sad world had grabbed hold of her? She should never have left her mother. She should never have fled her home, never allowed herself to fall in with these various bizarre beings who wanted her to provide answers, and then disbelieved her when she provided them. She had totally lost track of herself, no longer had any idea whom she could trust. The depressing truth was that she couldn't trust anyone.

Well . . . maybe Xyon. He'd been willing to lay down his life for her.

But he was dead, dead and gone.

The Overlord swept out of the room, leaving the three Redeemers alone with Riella and Xyon's corpse. The Redeemers looked a bit disconcerted now that their leader had walked out, their purpose placed in abeyance for the time being.

"We should get him out of here," one of them said, indicating Xyon's unmoving form.

"The Overlord did not tell us to."

"True. But he did not tell us to leave him here, either."

This was an indisputable rejoinder. It gave them something to ponder for a few moments, and finally the first Redeemer said, "There is another room in the back. We can throw him in there. That way if his body begins to smell, we do not have to concern ourselves with the stench."

The plan met with immediate approval, and the three

Redeemers reached down to haul Xyon up and out. They dragged him up so that he was almost in a standing position, dangling there like a rag doll.

That was when he abruptly planted his feet.

Riella gasped, positive beyond all certainty that she had fallen asleep and was dreaming once more. Except this time, instead of dreaming about the Quiet Place, she was dreaming of a very unlikely rescue by an equally unlikely rescuer.

Xyon's eyes were open and filled with fire. There was a Redeemer on either side of him, and arms that had been draped loosely around their shoulders suddenly tightened. The third Redeemer was standing directly in front of him. Xyon swung his feet up and slammed them against the Redeemer's chest, knocking him clear across the room. The Redeemer crashed into the far wall, his head making a peculiar and most satisfying crunching sound before he sagged to the floor. Before he had even hit, though, Xyon was already gripping the heads of the Redeemers next to him. He angled backwards and brought their heads slamming together. The noise their skulls made when smacking into one another was really rather hideous. One of the Redeemers went down immediately; the other was staggering, but still managing to stay on his feet. Xyon did not hesitate. He drew back a fist and slammed forward as hard as he could, catching the Redeemer squarely on the point of his chin. The Redeemer's head snapped around, and the rest of his body followed suit. Consequently, he looked a bit like a top as he spun in place and then toppled over.

Xyon took a deep breath and a moment to steady himself before turning his attention to an incredulous Riella. He studied the bonds as she gaped at him. "Hold on . . . I think I see how to open them," he told her.

"You're dead," she told him.

"You'd better hope not because if I am, then you're hallucinating all this, which means you've got bigger problems than you already think you do."

"You're dead," she said again, lacking the tools at that moment to latch onto his sense of the ironic.

"No. I'm not."

"I saw him . . . saw what he did to you. Something mental. Something—"

"I'm not without mental resources myself," Xyon told her. "Unfortunately, I've never had any real training with them. They're a bit catch-as-catch-can. But he got me angry enough that I was reasonably sure I could erect barriers when he went after me. I was right. Lucky me," he added with no trace of sarcasm. "Okay. Got it."

Seconds later, the bonds lifted clear of the chair. Riella still didn't move. She was too busy staring at Xyon. "I . . . I thought you were dead," she whispered.

"Yes, that was more or less the idea," he told her. "Get up. Come on, get up," he said again, showing no signs of patience.

"I . . . can't move my legs." Her arms were clear, but she was shaking her legs and not getting much response from them.

"Circulation problems. Come on." He hauled her to her feet and she immediately sagged against him. He held her up effortlessly. He felt so strong to her. She bumped up against his chest, and it seemed rock solid. She traced the feel of his muscles beneath the sleeves of his tunic. They were not overlarge, but what was there was taut, cablelike. Why hadn't she noticed it before?

"Who are you?" she asked.

It was clear from his expression that he considered it a rather odd question. "You have this endless need to find a slot to tuck me into," he said. "Hero or thief or noble martyr or whatever handy label you want to slap on me. I'm Xyon. That's all. Accept that or don't, as you see fit. Now let's get out of here."

Without further conversation, he went to the door, which slid open obediently. No reason it shouldn't have; the Overlord didn't lock it when he exited. Xyon glanced right and left, up and down the hallway, and then held out a hand to her. "Come on," he said urgently.

"Coming," she said, gripping his hand firmly. Everything seemed to be happening too quickly for her to get a true handle on it all, but she knew two things beyond a doubt: first, sticking with Xyon would probably be the wisest course of action; second, anyplace had to be better than where she was right then.

They started racing down the hallways, Xyon pulling Riella so firmly that he almost hauled her off her feet. She had enough presence of mind to call, "Do you know where you're going?"

"Not a clue," he shot back. "I know I want to get to the ship and get out of here. I haven't worked out much beyond that. I . . ." Then he paused and suddenly flattened against the wall of the corridor. Riella needed no encouragement to follow suit.

An instant later, a Redeemer charged around the corridor. Xyon halted him through the simple expedient of sticking out his foot. The Redeemer took a header over it and hit the floor hard. Immediately, Xyon was on his back, pinning the back of the Redeemer's skull so that he didn't wiggle beneath his grasp. Then he frowned, his face a mask of concentration, and the Redeemer stiffened beneath him. The Redeemer's mouth moved, but no words emerged from it. Then he sagged, Xyon breaking contact with him. It took Xyon a moment to compose himself, and during that time the Redeemer was suddenly on his feet, turning towards Xyon and yanking out a rather fearsome-looking cudgel. Riella sensed that it was more for decoration than actual combat, but nevertheless it could be quite nasty if it came into contact with, say, the side of Xyon's skull. Xyon made sure, however, that such an opportunity never arose, for he blocked the downward thrust of the cudgel with a deft defensive move and then swung a quick right that dropped the Redeemer cold.

"Down," he said, sounding vaguely distracted.

"Down?"

"This hallway. This corridor. Down this way, and there's a lift at the end that we take. That'll bring us to the landing where the ship is."

"How do you? . . ." But a glance from him silenced her. She was rapidly learning not to ask.

They bolted down the corridor and, sure enough, there was a lift at the far end. In the distance, they could hear the sound of running feet. There were weapons being discharged, the sounds of scuffling . . .

. . . and snarling.

Riella immediately recognized the sound. "Gods . . . that's those creatures, isn't it. From back on Montos."

Xyon listened carefully, and then nodded. "Yes. I think so. The Dogs of War."

"What are they doing here?!"

" I couldn't care less what they're doing here as long as we manage to get ourselves somewhere else. And with any luck, we'll be long gone before they even knew we were here."

The doors to the lift slid open.

Two dogs were in there. One was monstrously huge. The other Riella knew all too well . . . the one with the swords strapped to his back. Their eyes widened. Their nostrils flared.

"So much for luck," muttered Xyon.

Atik couldn't believe it when the doors slid open. The creature was there, right there, next to the very quarry they had come for.

"Get the female, Vacu! Leave the male to me!" shouted Atik, and even as he spoke, he had both his long fangs out. He wasn't taking any chances this time. He would bisect the creature before it had the slightest chance to get away.

He swung one of the swords . . . and the blade struck some sort of cudgel that the creature was wielding. The creature deflected the strike, quickly, cleanly, almost effortlessly. Atik came in with the other sword, and then the club was blocking that one, too.

It wasn't possible, nor was Atik willing to believe it. He pressed the attack, both swords flashing, taking turns one for the other. All the creature had for his defense was some sort of club that couldn't have been more than three-feet long. He kept backing up, backing up.

But blocking. Blocking the entire time. The creature's face was a mask of concentration, a fine bead of perspiration appearing on it, but otherwise giving no indication that his brilliant series of parries was anything of a strain. High, low, left, right, up, down, the swords flashed this way and that, and every single time, the damned creature blocked it. Atik was moving the blades so quickly that even he couldn't keep track of them. Just on the basis of the odds alone, he should have at least drawn blood, but still the creature frustrated him by keeping the swords at bay with nothing more than a fancy stick.

Atik howled in frustration, crisscrossed the swords, tried to come in even faster. The creature, astoundingly, stepped between the swords, which missed him clean on either side, and then he struck Atik on the side of the head with the cudgel. Atik's head spun and the Dog went down. The creature hit him again and Atik tumbled back, unable to believe the shocking turnaround that events had taken.

Then the creature shouted, "Riella!" and Atik heard the door to the lift slide shut. Vacu, bless his thick hide, had done exactly what he was supposed to do. With a frustrated cry, the creature ran to the doors and pulled at them. They wouldn't budge. He shouted "Riella" again as if the repetition would somehow cause her to materialize back there in the corridor.

Atik took a chance. He drew back an arm and hurled one of the swords. It spun through the air perfectly, whirring 360 degrees like a vicious wheel of death. The creature saw it coming at the last second, but there was no room for him to dodge it completely. He tried to knock it aside with the cudgel, but he was only partly successful as the whirring sword sliced across his upper arm before clattering to the floor a short distance away from him. Atik was pleased to see that it was a fairly nasty gash, blood flowing freely, and he had every intention of taking advantage of it.

The creature, seeing Atik coming, snagged the fallen sword by sliding his toe under the blade, and then he kicked it upward into the air. With a deft move he snagged it in midair, but he was trying to do too much at once, and he barely got the sword up in time before Atik clashed against him, hilt to hilt.

"We just keep getting in each other's way," Atik snarled.

"I was thinking the exact same thing," shot back the creature. But it was more bravado speaking than anything else. Atik knew that the wound was nasty, and that the creature's strength was leaking away along with its blood. Another minute, maybe even seconds, and Atik would finally be able to dispose of this smooth-skinned irritant.

Suddenly, from the far end of the corridor, there was the sound of weapons' fire discharging. Atik was a weapons master. He knew the sound that each and every one of the Dog's weapons were likely to make, and that noise wasn't one of them.

The door to the lift slid open. There was no sign of Vacu. He had obviously managed to get away with the girl, and that left the Dogs to get clear of the ship and complete their mission. From the far end of the corridor, a squad of Redeemers emerged, their weapons blasting. Neither Atik nor the creature had the slightest choice. They hurled themselves into the open lift door, and it slid shut, closing the Redeemers out . . .

. . . closing them in.

The car started down.

Each of them was holding a sword. There was barely more than a foot between them.

Neither of them moved. It was almost as if they were each daring the other to attempt the first strike. They could have been carved from ice.

"This is not an ideal combat situation," Atik said.

"Not much room for style," agreed the creature.

"We are great enemies, we two."

"We certainly have a knack for running afoul of each other."

Neither of the swords wavered. Neither of the potential combatants moved.

"Tell me your name."

"Again?" said the creature. "Why does that interest you?"

"One should know the name of one's nemesis."

"I'm honored," the creature said tightly. He paused a moment more, and then said, "I will tell you . . . if you tell me why you want the girl."

"She knows the secret of the Quiet Place. Of how to get there, where immortality and untold riches await," Atik said immediately.

"And you intend to have her lead you there."

"Yes."

The creature considered that a moment. Then, almost as an afterthought, he said, "Xyon. My name is Xyon."

"Zzzyyy—ohnnn." Atik rolled the unusual syllables across his lips. "Xyon . . . Atik of the Dogs of War salutes you. We have wounded each other in respective encounters. We will face each other again in a situation that will allow us more style. We deserve that."

"You have interesting priorities," Xyon said. "I want the girl back."

"Get her if you can."

The door slid open and Atik immediately backed into the hallway to have more room. Xyon emerged quickly, keeping the sword up and in front of him . . .

. . . and found himself facing a half a dozen Dogs of War. They were growling in unison. Unlike previous encounters, they were heavily armed and armored. They did not look like they were in a mood to bargain, discuss, or—most important of all—attack with style.

Xyon backpedaled rapidly, practically throwing himself into the car as the doors slammed shut.

"Leave him!" shouted Atik. "We have what we came for! Let's get out of here!"

"But your long fang!" Omon called out, standing there as part of the pack. "He has one of your long fangs!"

"Let him keep it. I'll have the opportunity to get it back. If I'm sure of one thing, it's that," said Atik confidently.

As part of its automatic cycle, the lift started back up again. This was not something that particularly enthused Xyon, for he knew that there were very likely Redeemers clustered at the top, waiting for his unwilling return. And he strongly suspected that he was not going to stumble too soon upon the unique set of circumstances that had resulted in his current (and possibly short-lived) freedom.

He glanced upward and saw a standard-issue emergency trapdoor in the ceiling of the car. Quickly, he tested the tensile strength of the newly acquired sword, flexing it in his hands. It seemed fairly strong, ideally strong enough to accomplish what he needed it to do without breaking. He jammed the sword into the narrow space between the lift doors and pried with all his strength. He was fully prepared for the sword to snap; instead, a bit to his surprise, it remained intact and he actually managed to force open the door.

"Detecting passenger emergency," the lift's onboard computer spoke, and the lift car immediately came to a halt.

Once he had managed to get the door open, it was not a particularly difficult matter to keep it that way. He simply shoved his hand against it, and that kept the lift securely in place while he reached up with the sword and pushed open the trapdoor overhead. "Detecting emergency escape hatch open," the computer told him, just in case he had been unaware of his own actions. Xyon paid it no mind. He took two quick steps and vaulted through the open door. Moments later he was scrambling around in the shaft; he had come upon an emergency ladder that seemed to run the length of the shaft. It was exactly what he was looking for, and seizing the opportunity, he started clambering down.

He was, of course, taking a chance. There was a possibility that the Dogs had clustered at the bottom and were waiting for him to return. He did not, however, think that was going to be the case. They had managed to get their hands on what they wanted, namely Riella. Now it was just a matter of their getting clear of the ship . . .

. . . the ship.

How in the world had the Dogs managed to get on board the Redeemer ship? What sort of resources did they have at their disposal, anyway? There were a goodly number of Dogs, true, but it wasn't their method of operation to attack a foe so much more powerful than themselves—and the Redeemers certainly fell into that category. They must have wanted Riella quite desperately to deviate in that way from their standard tactics.

And how had they known that Riella was there, anyway? The more he thought about it, the less sense it made to him.

He continued to dwell on it, though, for doing so was much easier on him than thinking about just how much his shoulder was hurting him. The slice had been vicious, and he had already lost a good deal of blood. It had stopped flowing, apparently, but his upper shirt-sleeve was red and sodden, and every move he was making with his arm was a fire of agony up and down his biceps and triceps. "I'm going to kill him," he muttered, "presuming I don't get myself killed first."

He got to the bottom of the shaft. The ladder ended about ten feet above the bottom, for no reason that he could think of other than that it had been constructed that way for the sole purpose of annoying him. Realizing that he had no choice, he dropped the sword down first, waited until it had clattered flat on the bottom, and then dropped down after it. Under ordinary circumstances such a drop wouldn't have been particularly daunting. But he had almost been killed by a few words from the Overlord, almost lost an arm in a sword fight, and was now trying to make his way to his ship without getting himself killed. This was not developing into one of his easier days.

He landed in a crouch and remained that way for a moment, making sure that he hadn't twisted his ankle or in some other way injured himself. When he was satisfied that he was intact, he picked up the fallen sword and then stood in front of the door that was blocking his exit from the shaft. He started prying at it with the sword, as he had done with the lift door.

The lift above him chose that moment to start to move. Descending, of course, straight towards him. Well, naturally that would happen. Heaven forbid it might actually go in the opposite direction and spare him a few moments of aggravation.

He worked faster at the door. The sword wasn't sliding in as smoothly this time as it had with the other one. He worked as quickly as he could, trying not to think about the heavy lift car descending upon him. It seemed as if he could almost feel its weight crushing him. The wall at the bottom of the shaft curved inward; there was no space for him to angle himself away from the descending car.

He pushed with the sword, growled in fury as he saw the car coming right at him. He wasn't going to make it.

Desperately, not expecting anything except the terminal sensation of the car crushing down on him followed by the blackness of oblivion (which, frankly, he was ready to welcome at this point) Xyon flattened himself on the floor of the shaft, grimaced, gritted his teeth and waited. The one thing he refused to do was cry out in frustration or anger or pain.

Well, maybe pain.

The lift came closer . . . closer still, and now he could sense the car directly above him. He closed his eyes, prepared himself.

The lift car came to a halt half an inch above his head.

He opened his eyes, not quite able to believe it. The car remained there a moment longer; he could hear the sound of running feet, very likely belonging to Redeemers as they pounded out of the lift and down the corridor.

He had caught a break. The lift's natural motion brought it to a halt just above the floor of the shaft. In retrospect, it made perfect sense. Why have the thing banging up against the floor of the shaft every time, after all? But he hadn't been considering such niceties of design when he'd been busy flattening himself on the floor to avoid being crushed, even though it turned out that there was no danger of that happening.

After a few moments more, the car reversed itself and started back up again. Instantly Xyon was on his feet, and this time—without the pressure of the oncoming lift car—he was able to use the sword to pry open the door out of the shaft. He braced himself, waiting to see if a barrage of ammunition from the Redeemers would be waiting to greet him. If that happened, he had no defense handy. He would wind up more pitted than an asteroid.

But such was not the case. Instead the corridor was mercifully empty. He stepped out of the shaft, allowing the door to slide shut behind him, and offered up a prayer that that would be the last time he'd have to deal with rooting around in a turbolift shaft. Then, gripping the sword firmly, he dashed down the corridor.

As he ran, he felt the ship shuddering around him. It was a series of quick, sudden sensations, and he was sure he could hear in the distance quick rushes of air. Then he realized what was happening, and he couldn't help but be amazed at their ingenuity. The Dogs had arrived in some sort of vessels that had actually attached themselves to the hull of the Redeemers' ship, like so many parasites. They had then burned their way through the hull, creating small enough holes for them to clamber through and into the ship.

Except . . .

Where had the Redeemers' shields been? Had the Dog ships actually been able to penetrate the Redeemers' shields? It was remotely possible, particularly if the Dogs had found some way to jam the harmonics, alter them in some fashion that allowed the ships to slip through. But even so, it seemed terribly unlikely. The pieces of the entire business were just not fitting together for Xyon.

Ultimately, though, it didn't matter. His major concern had to be getting off the ship and going after Riella. The latter should not prove to be too major a problem. After all, he knew where they were going. Unlike the Overlord, who refused to believe the answers that were being handed to him, Xyon knew perfectly well that the Quiet Place (whatever it was) was where Riella said it was. Or, at the very least, that it was where Riella was going to take them, even though the general environs didn't seem particularly promising, considering the fact that there didn't appear to be any sort of planet there. That, and the fact that—even though he had been running around like a lunatic ever since stumbling over the phrase—Xyon still had no really clear idea of just what in the world the Quiet Place was. Or what it represented. He knew of the offhand comments by the Dogs and the vague allusions made by Riella, but that was pretty much it.

He heard Redeemers shouting in the distance, heard the calls going out for repair crews. Clearly they had bigger things to worry about than Xyon making a break for it, considering the fact that their ship suddenly had an array of holes in it. Xyon made it to the docking bay without incident. Once he entered, however, there was a serious incident awaiting him: two heavily armed Redeemers standing on either side of the door just inside.

He could tell from their attitude that they had not been waiting for him. They had just been mindlessly following their orders, doing their duty, guarding the door. They hadn't really expected any intruders; so when Xyon entered the first thing they reacted with was surprise. It is always dangerous to take a follow-up action while surprise is setting in, but that was the unfortunate decision that the two of them made. They swung their weapons up and aimed them squarely at Xyon. Xyon, for his part, hesitated only a moment, to make sure they had a lock on him, and then he simply ducked, throwing himself flat on his back and shutting his eyes tight. The blaster bolts crisscrossed directly over him, his eyes slammed shut against the impact. When he opened his eyes, he looked to either side and discovered that (to his astonishment) the manuever had worked. The guards had been far more concerned with aiming and firing on Xyon. When he had managed to absent himself from the paths of the weapons, the two Redeemers had rather deftly managed to blow each other out of existence. There was still enough left of them, what with their shreds of uniform and such, that Xyon was confident they could still be identified.

In the meantime, however, he dashed across the bay to his ship. "Lyla!" he shouted, and for a moment he felt a cold, clutching sensation in his stomach as he wondered if somehow they had managed to wipe out the ship's personality or, worse, physically remove the bodily remains that was Lyla from the ship herself. Either move, particularly the latter, would be nothing short of catastrophic for Xyon. Fortunately, however, neither seemed to be the case. Apparently, they just hadn't been there long enough, for the door obediently opened. "Hello, Xyon," Lyla's voice said pleasantly. "Did you miss me"

"Terribly," said Xyon, all business. "Get us out of here."

"The bay doors are not open."

Xyon did not even hesitate. He tapped the weapons array, bringing a plasma discharger on line as it snapped into view on the underside of the vessel. Pushing a button, he blasted apart the offending door with no effort. "They are now," he said sanguinely.

With no further hesitation, the ship lifted off and angled towards the shattered door and out into space.

"Did it!" called out Xyon. "Lyla, take us to cloak and bring us around to—"

He did not, however, have the opportunity to complete the thought. Just before the ship went invisible, an array of heavy-duty fire power erupted from the Redeemer vessel. The impact was so severe that it knocked Xyon clean off his feet. He skidded across the floor of the vessel and had the misfortune of smashing his already throbbing shoulder against the far bulkhead. He let out a yelp of pain.

"You have injured your—" began Lyla.

"*I know, I know!*" shouted Xyon, cutting her off. "Are we cloaked?"

"Yes. But they are bracketing the area. It would appear they know generally where we are."

"Then get us out of here! Right n—!"

Before he could get out the rest of the sentence, the ship was hammered once more. He heard something then that was truly frightening: He heard Lyla scream. It wasn't in panic; more a shriek of general alarm. But it was a disconcerting sound nevertheless, and one that he had never thought he would hear emanating from the ship's onboard personality.

Looking out the viewing port, he saw the Redeemer ship spiraling away into the distance. There were a few stray Dog ships as well; the Redeemers were fighting a multifront war, and that was the only thing that Xyon had going for him. The Redeemers were firing at everything in sight rather than any one thing. Xyon saw one of the Dog ships blow up, then a second. The rest of them angled away, and Xyon then found himself in a curious position. On the one hand, he wanted to pray that, of the ships that had been hit and destroyed, Riella hadn't been on one of them. On the other hand, the prospect of the poor girl in the hands of the Dogs of War wasn't particularly appealing either. For all he knew, the moment she told them what they wanted to know, they might tear her apart just for sport.

No. No, they wouldn't do that. He was suddenly certain of that. It would just be bad tactics, that was all. They couldn't go on the assumption that she was telling the truth until they saw it with their own eyes. At the very least, Riella was safe until they managed to get to the legendary Quiet Place.

The Redeemer ship had moved off completely, absenting itself so quickly (perhaps going in pursuit of a Dog vessel) that in no time at all, Xyon found himself alone in space. "Lyla," he called. "Are you okay? I heard you scream."

"Do not be absurd, Xyon," Lyla said with just a hint of primness. "I am incapable of any concern over my personal well-being anymore. A scream would indicate alarm, even fear, and these are not aspects of—"

"Fine. It was my imagination. Set course and head for Star 7734. Move us out."

"Unable to comply at this time, Xyon," Lyla said.

"Unable? Why?"

"Damage to operational systems, including warp drive, navigation, and life support."

It was the last one that immediately caught Xyon's attention. "Life support?"

"That is right."

"How much damage?"

"Estimated repair time, twenty-seven hours, once replacement parts are found."

"Once replacement parts are—" He couldn't quite believe it. "Where would we find those?"

"Closest reliable merchant is in the Apel system, nineteen hours from here—"

"And the opposite direction from Star 7734."

"It doesn't matter all that much, Xyon, since our engines are also down. I am working on rerouting through subroutines in hopes of bringing them back on line. At the very least, we will have impulse power back in two hours, twenty-seven minutes, allowing for full repair time."

"So we're dead in space at the moment."

"That is correct. That situation, however, is only temporary."

"Uh-huh. And just out of curiosity, with damaged life support the way it presently is, how long before I'm dead?"

"Nine hours, eleven minutes."

He rubbed the bridge of his nose. "Terrific. Lyla, has it occurred to you that death is a situation that is most definitely not temporary?"

"I have considered that," Lyla said reluctantly. "I was, to be honest, hoping you would not notice that part of the problem."

"Well, it was pretty hard to miss. A distress signal, Lyla," he added after a moment. "Can you send one?"

"Yes."

"Then do it. And drop the cloak; it's not going to do us a great deal of good if someone shows up to try and rescue us, and they can't find us."

"Xyon, have you considered the possibility that either the Redeemers or the Dogs of War might detect the distress signal, return and destroy you."

"Yes, I've considered that, Lyla."

"If that happens, do you have any plan?"

"Yes. If that happens, then I plan to die."

Lyla appeared to consider that for a moment. "I can't say that's one of your better plans, Xyon."

"You're absolutely right, Lyla. Hopefully, should the circumstance arise, I'll be more inspired."

Xyon lapsed into silence then. He puttered around the ship at first, but he knew better than to try and aid in the ship's repair. The nano-based technology that Lyla had at her disposal was hopefully going to be more than enough to get the job done. Instead he found his thoughts turning towards the missing Riella.

"Do you miss her?" It was as if Lyla was capable of reading his mind.

"Who?" he asked.

"Riella. Do you miss her?"

"No, Lyla, I don't. But she's a loose end, and I wound up taking her in. I owe it to her to try and see this through."

"Do you?"

"Yes. I do."

"Why?"

He sighed. "Lyla, it's been a long time since you had a normal body. But if you'll cast your memory back, you'll recall that sometimes there are things you do, not because they necessarily make logical sense, but just because you feel you have to do them. Helping Riella is one of those things."

She pondered that one. "I suppose you are right, Xyon."

"I'm glad you underst—"

"It makes no logical sense."

He sighed once more. "No. It doesn't, does it?"

"Riella reacted negatively when she learned that you were a thief. Why would she feel that way?"

"Because," Xyon told her, "she's lived in a nice, isolated little existence where everything she ever wanted has been handed to her. She's never had to fight for anything in her life. She doesn't know how difficult or harsh or cruel the universe can actually be. Because of that, it's easy for her to stake out the moral high ground and look down disdainfully at those of us who have been living in it for years just trying to survive."

"I see."

"It must be nice to live on the moral high ground."

"Perhaps, in my old age, I'll move there myself."

XI.

RIER STRODE INTO THE HOLDING FACILITY in which Riella was being kept, Atik and Krul flanking him. He stopped at the entrance, however, and stared uncomprehendingly.

The girl was lying on the floor, which was odd considering that there was actually a couch and chair available. Her eyes were closed, her body trembling. Her hands were clenched into fists so tight that her fingernails were digging into her palms and small trickles of blood were flowing from the wounds. She was whispering things, but the words were incomprehensible. Every so often she would mutter something that Rier was barely able to make out, but then the rest of it was lost.

"I'll wake her," Krul said, and took a step forward.

But Rier put a hand on his shoulder and stopped him. "No. Let it run its course, whatever it is."

And so the Dogs stood there, watching the girl writhe about for some minutes, in the throes of something they could not even begin to guess at. Suddenly she sat up, her eyes not focusing on anything at first. It seemed as if she was looking inward somehow. And what she was seeing within was possibly the most frightening thing of all. Then she looked up at Rier and became fully aware of her whereabouts.

"Do you know where you are?" Rier actually sounded remarkably solicitous.

She nodded.

"And do you know why you're here?"

"You brought me here." Her voice cracked slightly, as if her throat were constricted.

"Yes. And do you know why?"

"Does it matter?"

"We want to know of the Quiet Place."

She laughed softly at that. "Do you. Do you now. And what is the point of my telling you?"

"The point? The point is that we will not kill you if you are cooperative."

"I was cooperative with the Redeemers. They did not believe me."

"The Redeemers are fools," Atik spoke up.

"They can actually be a guide to us in their actions," sniffed Krul. "All we have to do is observe the way they go about their business, and then do the exact opposite." He then chuckled at his own joke.

"But I warn you," Rier said intently, and he approached Riella slowly, ominously, looming over her. "If you lie to us . . . I will know."

"Oh really." She seemed curious rather than intimidated. "And how will you? Know, I mean."

"Because when one lies, there is a certain scent of fear that is inevitable. And I can smell fear."

"And you like the smell, don't you."

"What?" He inclined his head slightly. "What do you mean?"

Rier was accustomed to an assortment of behaviors among prisoners, but he'd never encountered anything quite like this before. From the girl's voice, from her attitude, it really seemed as if she did not give a damn what he thought or what happened to her. It was as if she was addressing him from some great, lofty place that he could not even begin to aspire to. He wasn't sure how to react to it.

"I mean," she said, "that the smell entices you. Excites you. That is why you so enjoy attacking people face to face. It's not simply the destruction, or the acquisition of other people's property. You like the smell of fear when they see you approaching. The fear when they panic, the smell they produce when they beg for their lives or soil themselves in terror. That is something you simply cannot resist. You love it. You live for it. Do you not?"

Rier, Atik, and Krul looked askance at each other, and then back to her.

"Yes," Rier said slowly.

She nodded. He might not even have been in the room for all the difference it seemed to make to her.

"I will lead you to the Quiet Place," she said after a short time. "You will go there without question. If it is not there, as I assure you now that it is, kill me. Don't kill me. I don't really care anymore. What you do to me is of absolutely no consequence anymore. I'm beginning to understand just how irrelevant this," and she plucked at the reddening skin on her arm, "is."

"The Quiet Place," Krul said eagerly, "will we find

immortality there? Riches? There are so many things whispered about it."

"You will find all that and more," she said. "You will find a place of joy. You will find riches beyond the dreams of avarice. It will be as close to heaven as you will know on this side of the great and final curtain. All this and more will be yours."

The Dogs looked at one another, Rier's nostrils flaring. He detected no sign of deceit from her. Either she was telling the absolute truth or she certainly believed she was telling the truth, which worked out to the same thing.

"You," he said, "are rather intriguing for a non-Dog. I like you," he decided, his lips drawing back to reveal his fangs.

"My," she intoned. "What big teeth you have."

"The better to rend the flesh from my quivering prey."

"I am terrified," she said flatly.

She wasn't, of course. That much he could tell. He had never encountered anyone so serenely confident. In truth, he found it a bit annoying, perhaps even ever-so-slightly intimidating. Except he had no reason to be. She was entirely within his power, and he was Rier, leader of the Dogs of War. She posed no threat to him. He, Rier, was the master.

"As well you should be," he told her. He tried to maintain the stridency in his voice, but he wasn't quite able to do so. He cleared his throat and said, "Where, then, is the Quiet Place?"

"Set your heading for the star designated 7734."

"What? There's nothing there!" Krul snarled. "Rier, this is a trick. She's wasting our time!" He turned back to her. "I don't know what you're playing at, but—"

"Rier, get this thing out of my face," Riella said flatly. "At this point in your life, you need me far more than you need this mangy creature."

"You'll have to excuse his belligerence," Rier said. "His brother was killed recently, by your companion, actually. He cries out for blood. He cries out for revenge."

"He's not the only one," Riella told him.

Rier felt a distinct chill, and he had no idea why.

"The fact is," Riella continued, "I have no choice at this point. I have to get there. It's gone beyond my dreams. It's a compulsion that is threatening to consume me if I don't attend to it. If I resist it, or forestall it . . ." She sighed. "I will die. That is all there is to say, really. I will die. You think of yourself as my captors, but you're not. Not really. You are simply . . . a means to an end."

Her words hung there for a moment, and then Rier turned to his associates and said, "Have our course set for Star 7734."

"There's. Nothing. There," said Krul, very deliberately.

"If there isn't, then you may have the honor of punishing her for her lack of forthrightness," Rier said.

Krul turned his malevolent gaze upon her. "I look forward to that," he snarled.

"As do I," Riella suddenly said. She met his gaze, unintimidated, even slightly amused. "I hope we all get what is coming to us."

Rier and the others departed the room then, and Rier knew that he should have felt some measure of triumph since that had gone more smoothly than he could possibly have anticipated. Unfortunately, that gave him no explanation at all as to why he felt the fur on the back of his neck standing on end.

XII.

THE WORLD WAS STARTING TO FLOAT around Xyon. He was losing his sense of where he was. For a time, he was convinced that Riella was sitting right next to him. She was looking at him in an annoyingly accusatory fashion, and he said angrily, "What do you want from me? Hmm? I did my best. And I guess my best wasn't good enough for you, was it? Busting my ass to save you from all manner of insanity, and for what? Why should I? It's not as if you're that attractive. Your skin doesn't seem to know what color it is; hell, your whole body doesn't seem to know what race it is. And it's not as if you have a particularly pleasant personality, you know. You complain about things that aren't my fault. On the one hand, you whine that I should save you; on the other hand, you don't seem to appreciate it when I do. You're no prize, Riella! What do you think of that!"

She didn't say anything. Just sat there.

He made an impatient grunt and waved her off. She didn't go away. That was always her problem. She never went away.

"Xyon."

"Shut up, Riella!"

"Xyon," came Lyla's voice, a bit more urgency in it this time. "Someone is responding to your distress signal."

It took a few moments for what she was saying to filter through his clouded mind. He forced himself back to full wakefulness and awareness. He wasn't sure how much of his semi-delusional state was due to the air becoming stale and how much was because of fatigue. "Someone is?"

"Yes."

Immediately he was on his feet. He wasn't sure why he felt the need to stand; he wasn't speaking to anyone yet, and even if he was, this was hardly what anyone would term a formal occasion. "Do you know who it is? Dogs or Redeemers or maybe someone who might not actually want to kill me."

"The third category, I think. They're identifying themselves as being from Starfleet."

Xyon moaned when he heard that.

"Is there a problem with Starfleet, Xyon?"

"No," he said in annoyance, leaning against the starboard bulkhead.

"Why do you say things that way, Xyon?"

"What things, what way?"

"For instance, although your voice says that nothing is wrong, your tonality indicates that, in fact, the situation is bothersome to you. You do not say what you mean."

"People oftentimes don't say what they mean. That's how we manage not to kill each other," Xyon told her.

"Oh. So honesty leads to homicide?"

He gave that one some thought. "More often than you'd think, actually," he admitted. "This Starfleet vessel . . . where are they? Is it a starship?"

"No, Xyon. They're identifying themselves as a runabout on their way to rendezvous with a starship. They're offering their assistance."

"I don't see that we've got a great deal of choice," Xyon said. He rubbed the fatigue from his eyes. "Lyla . . . there's a likelihood we may have to leave you here."

"Why, Xyon?"

"Because . . ." He looked at the empty chair which, in his imaginings, had been occupied by Riella a short time earlier, ". . . we may have to go after Riella, and I doubt the runabout has the towing capabilities necessary to bring you along. And time might very well be the most important factor. Will you be all right out here?"

"I am a ship, Xyon. Space is my natural environment."

"You're more than a ship, Lyla." He affectionately patted the control console. "We both know that. Sometimes I think you're the only thing that keeps me sane."

"Xyon . . . you are preparing to leave me behind in order to go aboard a runabout with strangers from an organization for which you apparently harbor some antipathy, all for the purpose of saving a young female whom you would seem not to particularly like."

"What's your point?"

"The point is, how do you know I managed to keep you sane?"

Xyon considered that a moment . . . and then started to laugh.

"Is that funny, Xyon?"

"You know what, Lyla?" he said, endeavoring to calm himself. "Believe it or not, I think it is funny, yes."

"Xyon?"

"Yes, Lyla."

"Don't leave me."

He had been sitting at the console, and something in Lyla's voice prompted him to sit up straight, tilting his head curiously as if he couldn't quite believe what he'd heard. "What?"

"Don't leave me." As an afterthought, she added, "Please."

"You mean in space?"

"Yes. If it is indeed a starfleet runabout, very likely they may have the parts on hand I need to effect repairs. Then I can follow you. It will take additional time. Perhaps you can take me in tow just during that time. It will slow you, I know, but—"

"Lyla—"

"Please." This time the word was more than an afterthought. She sounded . . .

Frightened? Was it possible for Lyla to feel that range of concern? She was organic at heart, he knew, but she had never . . .

"All right," he said slowly. "All right, Lyla. I won't leave you."

"Promise me."

"I promise you."

He actually heard a sigh of relief. "Thank you, Xyon."

"You're welcome."

* * *

Zak Kebron had not known what to expect when he beamed over to the stranded ship. Part of him had wondered whether this might be some sort of elaborate ruse or trap. But he took one look at the disheveled young man and knew immediately that this was no more and no less than what was advertised: A space traveler in trouble. Kebron could also tell that the young man had never seen a Brikar before. He could always discern that because of the astounded looks people gave him upon first encountering him. Sometimes he wished he could take himself out of his body just to see himself the way others saw him . . . and be properly impressed.

"Lieutenant Zak Kebron, of the Starship *Excalibur.* You are?"

"Xyon. Captain . . . and crew, pretty much . . . of the good ship *Lyla.*"

Kebron glanced around with a critical eye. "Our instruments indicate that your engines are not fully functional. Your impulse engines are on line, but you have no warp drive capacity."

"That's about right."

"Well, we can take you aboard our ship and bring you back to the *Excalibur.* At that point—"

"I'd rather not leave my ship, if that's okay."

"I appreciate your not wanting to jeopardize your property by leaving it as derelict, but towing your vessel will slow us down considerably."

"If you have some additional hands that could pitch in, some key elements, we could probably get her up and running," Xyon said with some urgency.

"You may be correct. But if we do not rendezvous with our starship on schedule—"

"That's the other thing—"

Kebron looked at him warily. "Other thing?"

"There's a girl who's been kidnapped by the Dogs of War. Have you heard of them?"

"I have some passing familiarity with them," Kebron said dryly.

"Well, she needs our help . . . my help . . . although you can help if you want. Considering the circumstances, I could really use—"

"Hold on. I appreciate the concern you're showing for your girlfriend—"

"She's not my girlfriend. She's someone who needs help, that's all."

"Altruism in deep space. A rare attribute. Would that I had it."

"But they may kill her!"

"Xyon," Kebron said with rapidly waning patience, "we have a runabout. That is all. That is hardly sufficient firepower to travel to the home planet of the Dogs of War and—"

"They're not going there! They're heading for somewhere called the Quiet Place."

"That may be, but . . ."

That was when Kebron stopped dead, and stared incredulously at Xyon. His gaze was so intense that Xyon actually took a step back. "What is it?"

"The Quiet Place."

"Yes. That's right. What? Has everyone heard of it?"

"The girl. What is her name?"

"Riella. Why, does that name mean anything?"

Kebron slowly shook his head, which, of course, required that his entire upper torso sway from side to side. "Tell me, Xyon, do you believe that there is a great purpose in the universe that brings people together in unexpected but predestined ways?"

"No."

"Good. Neither do I. We'll chalk this one off to weird coincidence. Beam back with me to the runabout and tell my associates precisely what you've just told me. And when you do, watch the face of the red-skinned one in particular. It should be interesting."

Si Cwan became aware that his mouth was hanging open, and he closed it. "Are you sure about this?" he asked Xyon.

Xyon looked at the three individuals grouped around him and said flatly, "Yes, of course I'm sure. I knew the girl's name, I know where she said she wanted to go. God knows that enough people have been bandying about the name of the place. Considering it was some-place I never even heard of before, a sizable number of folks seem rather interested in it. Can any of you tell me the truth behind this place?"

Si Cwan was quite aware of the eyes of Kebron and Soleta upon him. He did not, however, allow it to out-wardly disconcert him. Instead, he circled the interior of the runabout slowly, thoughtfully.

"Is this pause for dramatic effect?" inquired Kebron. "Or are you trying to manufacture a story that will sound plausible?"

"I resent the implication, Kebron," Cwan shot back. "I may be many things, but a liar is not one of them. The fact is that the Quiet Place is a somewhat personal aspect of Thallonian tradition."

"The Redeemers, the Dogs of War, and some woman on Montos all know about it," Xyon pointed out. "How intensely personal can it be?"

"The fact that so many are aware of it is simply an-other example of the losses suffered by the Thallonians.

Our loss of homeworld . . . of our privacy . . . of our dignity . . ."

"Get to the point," said Kebron.

Si Cwan shot him a disdainful look.

"The truth is—"

"Finally."

He ignored Kebron's comment. "The truth is that even the truth about the Quiet Place may sound a bit . . . preposterous. The Quiet Place is heaven. Or Hell. Or a bit of both. At least, that's what a number of races in the former Thallonian empire believe. It is a mysterious place, the whereabout of which is not generally known. Some actually claim to have been there, although there's never has been a way to confirm it. But those who say that they have been there, whether by intent or accident, claim to have been transformed in some way, although for good or ill is not always easy to discern at first. Some return claiming to have seen the dead, or are able to read the future, or possess arcane knowledge that they'd never had before. Some claim . . ." He hesitated, as if knowing that he was pushing the limits of credulity. But by that point he was more or less in deep, so he continued, "Some claim to have looked upon the face of their God or Gods. Others come back as pale and wretched things, shadows of their former selves who can barely string two sentences together. There are also rumors of a race of beings who actually reside beneath the surface of the Quiet Place, although it would seem somewhat unlikely."

"Considering how far over the edge the things you've been telling us so far are, that would actually be believable," said Kebron.

"Where is this place?" asked Soleta. "I've not read of it in any scientific text."

"Nor will you. There is no scientific proof of its existence. The Quiet Place cannot be found. You have to receive the Summons."

"As with all beliefs that depend solely on faith," Kebron said skeptically. "When even the slightest suggestion of proof is put forward, the tale descends into vagueness."

"Have you no faith in anything, Kebron?" Cwan inquired. He sounded almost a little sad.

"In myself. That's all I've ever needed."

Soleta was unable to keep the doubt from her voice. "And who receives this . . . Summons."

"I cannot speak for others," Si Cwan said, "but in the ruling family of Thallon, every third or fourth generation a princess of the line, upon reaching a certain age, receives the Summons. There is never advance warning. She simply disappears one night, sometimes to return, sometimes never to be seen again. If the princess returns, she never speaks of what she has witnessed, except in the vaguest of terms. But at this point, the tradition and knowledge of its occurrences is enough for us to determine what's going on."

"How utterly convenient," Kebron said. "So, if the princess in question just desires to go off for a weekend with her beau, she can come back wide-eyed and confused, and you will assume it's this Quiet Place."

"Kebron," Cwan said slowly, "If you had any beliefs, I would show respect for them. Kindly pay me the same courtesy. In point of fact, the Summons and its advent is one of the reasons, the many reasons, that I was so desperate to find my sister, Kalinda. She was just reaching the appropriate age when the Thallonian Empire fell. She may well have received the Summons—"

Xyon suddenly stiffened, as if jolted. "She would have red skin? Like yours?"

"Of course. Why?"

"Patch me through to your comm system. I need to communicate with my ship."

They didn't understand the urgency in his tone, but there was no reason to deny his request. Within moments, he was saying, "Lyla. Access the shipboard visual log. I keep a visual log of everything that goes on in my ship," he said to them in an offhand way.

"That is fairly standard operating procedure for Starfleet," said Soleta. "Perhaps you should consider a career in the fleet."

"Don't even joke about it," he said with unexpected vehemence. "Lyla, do you have it?"

"Of course, Xyon," her voice came back.

"Put an image of Riella on the screen over here, would you, please?"

"Coming through now, Xyon."

The viewscreen on the runabout rippled for a moment, and then the picture of a young girl appeared on it. Her skin was rather pale, and she had an odd bump on her forehead as if something had been there before but no longer was.

Slowly Si Cwan approached the screen. His face was utterly impassive, but it was clear to the others that he was forcing himself to maintain that cool exterior, particularly when he extended his hand toward the screen. His hand was trembling, betraying the emotions roiling through him. He touched the screen gently, as if afraid that somehow the image upon it would ripple and disappear if he touched it too forcefully.

"Kally," he whispered.

"Who?"

He turned to Xyon. "What did you call her? What name?"

"Uhm . . . Riella," said the plainly confused Xyon.

Si Cwan shook his head. "No. No, her name is Kalinda. Kally, we . . . I call her. She is my sister."

"Your sister? But she doesn't look like—no. No, of course." Clearly it was all making sense to Xyon even as he spoke. She underwent some sort of treatment, some sort of conditioning. It changed her appearance. That's possible, isn't it?" He turned to Soleta since she appeared to be the most likely to have an answer to that question.

She nodded slowly. "Yes. It is possible. But the maintaining of the . . . 'illusion,' as it were would vary, depending on how it was done. She might very well have had to undergo some sort of continuing treatment."

"What would the treatment have been like?"

"Hard to say. Some sort of radiation process, perhaps. If cellular regenesis was utilized, the daily ingestion of certain extracts would perpetuate it. Absent those, however, the subjects own DNA would reinforce itself and the facade would begin to dissipate."

"So, if her mother was keeping it going—"

"Her mother?" Si Cwan shook her head. "Her mother—our mother—is dead. I held her in my arms when she passed away."

"It is becoming rapidly obvious that we will not have all the answers until we have caught up with the girl. Where is she?" asked Soleta.

"I'll tell you as soon as you fix my ship."

Si Cwan moved so quickly that Xyon never even saw him coming. One moment Xyon was just standing there, and the next Si Cwan had both hands on the young man's chest and had hoisted him off his feet, thumping him up against the bulkhead. "Don't issue conditions if you prefer to breathe," he snarled as his calm exterior cracked. "Where is she? Where *is she?*" and he thudded him against the wall once more for emphasis.

But Xyon wouldn't back down. "You want her? Then help repair my ship. The sooner you do that, the sooner we can find her."

"We can take it in tow and fix it en route," Soleta said quickly, obviously seeking the fastest compromise to forestall further violence. "Will that suffice?"

"How do I know, once I tell you the heading, that you won't just cut and run? Leave my ship. Leave me."

"You have my word," Soleta said, "as a duly authorized repre—"

"I want *his* word," Xyon said, inclining his head towards Si Cwan.

Si Cwan growled low in his throat, and then released Xyon. The young man landed lightly on his feet. He straightened his clothes and looked imperiously at Cwan, waiting.

"You have my word," said Cwan. "As if I have a choice."

"I don't recall your asking my preferences when you were throwing me around a few moments ago," Xyon pointed out. He clapped his hands briskly. "All right. Set our course for Star designated 7734, and let's get to work on my ship."

"Star 7734?" Soleta said, sounding mildly confused. "But there's—"

"Nothing there, yes, I know. But that's where she's heading, or at least where she believes this Quiet Place is. If she's the one you want, that's where we're going."

"If you are lying . . ." Si Cwan warned him.

Xyon turned towards Si Cwan and said impatiently, "Has it occurred to you that I might actually be anxious to find her, too? My own neck has been on the line in all this, believe it or not. Just to clue you in, I was willing to sacrifice my life to save her. And I saved her from the Dogs of War, too."

"I see." Si Cwan studied him a moment. "But you're still here, so obviously you didn't sacrifice your life. And who has her now?"

"The Dogs of War," admitted Xyon.

"It sounds to me, then, as if you haven't been doing a particularly good job."

"Hopefully, I'll be able to live up to your exacting standards," Xyon said sarcastically.

Si Cwan ignored the sarcasm and said, "I wouldn't bet on it."

In the meantime . . .

. . . elsewhere . . .

In his ship—a small vessel of his that he had salvaged from his days as a Thallonian noble—Zoran stared fixedly at the transmission signal coming over his scanner.

It had been a testament to Zoran's skill as a pilot, and the quality of his tracking equipment, that he had been able to keep so far back from the Dogs of War that they had not detected his presence. The subcutaneous tracking device that remained lodged beneath Kalinda's skin was sending out a steady signal fortunately, considering that the rest of the antennae graft had fallen off. Only the implant bump remained. Fortunately, that was where the tracking device was.

The Montos experiment had been a complete disaster. He had sought to handle the princess carefully, craftily, and had gone to great effort to do so.

He had been certain that, sooner or later, she would receive the Summons. And like many others, he sought the powers and secrets that were legendarily part of the Quiet Place. But Kalinda had always been a stubborn little cretin, and he had been certain that she would be less than cooperative with his plans. It was possible that, even upon receiving the Summons, if she had known that would lead Zoran there, she would have resisted the call. Of course, if one resisted it for too long, it could rend one's mind to ribbons and leave the subject a blithering idiot who would remain little more than an empty shell for the rest of her wretched life.

But Zoran had been willing to take that chance.

He had employed the services of a psi-surgeon to implant an imagined history for Kalinda. Everything that she remembered of her life on Montos—her childhood, her loving mother, all of it—was mere fiction. The expert geneticist had done the rest, transforming her into a passable Montosian, with Malia's daily tonic providing the stability that the process needed to maintain itself. The plan had served a twofold function. It neatly kept Kalinda hidden away from the efforts of her annoying brother to find her. And it enabled her to live an easily observable life while Zoran, through Malia, waited for some sign of the Summons to manifest itself.

Which it had. With a vengeance.

But it had all come unraveled. Even with her false identity of Riella firmly in place, Kalinda had proven too intractable, too difficult to control. She had never fully trusted the woman she had believed to be her mother, not really. And with the intervention of the Dogs of War, the entire plan had come undone.

Sumavar. Who would have thought that Sumavar, that tough old warrior, the one who had put Zoran together with the geneticist . . . who would have thought Sumavar would prove to be the weak link?

Zoran had not killed Sumavar after he had served his need (as he had done with the geneticist and the psi-surgeon) out of a sense of loyalty and apparently misplaced confidence. And this debacle was a hard-learned lesson about the pointlessness of softer emotions. It was not one that Zoran would soon forget.

Fortunately, the tracking device provided him a fail-safe. Wherever Kalinda was brought, that was where Zoran would be.

And soon the secrets of the Quiet Place, whatever they were, would be his, and only his.

XIII.

"THERE'S NOTHING HERE. Can I kill her now?"

Krul's obvious irritation seemed well founded, indeed, there appeared to be nothing of remote interest nearby Star 7734. It was a fairly bright star, but no planets had come into formation, nor did there seem to be anything particularly suggestive for the renowned Quiet Place.

They were standing upon the bridge of Rier's personal cruiser. Carrying a crew complement of seventy, it was the sister ship to the one that had been destroyed back on Barspens, and he had kept it primarily in reserve. But the botched mission on Barspens had forced him to make use of it. He kept telling himself that that was what spares were for, nevertheless it didn't sit well with him. On the view screen, Star 7734 sat there in space, continuing to appear no more interesting than it had when they first arrived.

"Bring the young lady to us," Rier said coolly.

Moments later Riella was standing before Rier. She didn't even seem to be paying much attention to him, her focus was on the rather boring star in front of them.

"Thus far," he said, "I am not impressed. For your sake, it would be best if you could impress me, sooner rather than later."

He wondered if she had even heard him. He was about to repeat himself, which was not something he was accustomed to doing, when she pointed to her right. "That way," she said.

The Dogs glanced at each other. "In space, we generally prefer something a bit more specific than pointing and saying, 'That way,' " Rier informed her.

"If you want to put me in a small ship, so that I can go there and you can follow me, feel free."

"So that you can attempt to bolt? I don't think so."

"If you're that stupid that you would think I would try to outrace you—"

Rier stepped in close to her then, and the gaze from his black eyes lanced into her without so much as a hint of pity. "Perhaps," he said slowly, "you've mistaken my patience for weakness. My civility for actually being civilized. Make no mistake. I'd as soon tear you apart myself as look at you. You can only act fearlessly because I've given you that luxury. If I choose to, I can make certain that you feel very, very afraid. Have I made myself clear?"

He waited for her to argue, for he knew at that moment that the slightest wrong word from her, and he'd tear a chunk out of her face just to amuse himself. But instead, she offered no protest, no sarcastic or defiant word. She simply said, "Yes," so neutrally that it was impossible for him to take it at anything other than face value (although he very much suspected that it was meant as anything but).

He considered the situation a moment and then said, "If I put you at a navigation station, do you think you could navigate us wherever you wish to go?"

"I've no experience with it at all."

"Then you're going to learn on the fly. Omon," he called to the Dog who was seated at navigation. "Work with our passenger here as best you can. See if you can reach some mutual agreement as to where we're headed . . . before I become bored with her."

If she was intimidated by the thinly veiled threat of that last comment, she didn't let it show at all. Instead she walked over to the navigation station. For some minutes, Omon showed her the basics, and she nodded steadily in comprehension. It was something of a crash course, but she kept nodding steadily. "Do you truly understand all of this?" Omon asked her at one point. "You said you've never done anything like this before."

"I know. I haven't. But nevertheless it seems . . . vaguely familiar. I'm not sure why it does, but it does." She paused a moment, and then pointed and said, "Here. At 418 Mark 3. Take us over there, but slowly. Very slowly. I don't want to rush us into anything."

"Very considerate," Rier said. "Omon. Is there anything where she's indicating?"

"A nebula. That's all."

"Sensor probes?"

"Less than effective with a nebula."

Rier nodded. He knew that, of course. Still, he felt he had to ask.

As the ship inched towards the nebula, Rier's brow furrowed as he studied it. It did not look unique. It was a standard issue, gaseous nebula, as near as he could tell. A gigantic cloud of gas and raw cloud material, but that was all.

"Sensor sweep, as much as you can discern," said Rier. He took a step closer to the screen, as if somehow the additional proximity would make a difference.

Atik checked the sensor array. "Still nothing. I'm not . . ."

The fact that his voice trailed off was enough to command Rier's attention. "What is it?"

"Getting something, on the outer rim of the nebula . . . dead ahead. Except . . ." He shook his head. "This isn't possible."

"What isn't?"

"The sensors are telling me now that it's not there."

"Impossible. Either it's there or it's not. It can't be there and not there."

"It's possible that it could," Atik said reasonably. "If there's some sort of field distortion, the planet itself could be in a state of quantum flux somehow. Or it could be something as simple as the make-up of the nebula itself. The cloud could be bouncing our tactical signals back at us, causing a sort of . . . of ghost planet."

"And no one has ever detected this 'ghost planet' out here before?"

Atik shook his head. "A simple charting sweep of the region wouldn't necessarily detect it. The nebula is thousands of miles wide. You'd have to know exactly where you're looking, and even then—"

"All right, all right," Rier waved off further discussion impatiently. Instead he turned to Riella. "Is that it? Is that the Quiet Place?"

He excepted some sort of cryptic response, but instead she simply nodded.

"It is?"

"Yes."

"Focus full sensor probes on that world!" ordered Rier. "If there's some sort of cover, if there's something resisting our probes, punch through it!"

The nebula was becoming more and more distinct on the screen the closer they got, and Rier could even make out the general outlines of the planet. The screen began to fuzz over slightly, but Atik made some adjustments and the picture snapped back into view.

Unfortunately, that was all Atik was able to accomplish. He shook his head in frustration and said, "I'm not getting anything on it now. It's like a sensor black hole. It's absorbing all my probes and not giving anything back."

"Assemble a team," Rier said. "Transport them down and they can see what is and isn't there."

Omon turned to Rier and said, "Are you sure that's wise?"

Immediately, there was dead silence among the half-dozen dogs on the bridge. All eyes went to Rier as he said very calmly, very dangerously, "Are you questioning me, Omon?"

"No," Omon said immediately.

Slowly Rier nodded. "Good. That would be unfortunate."

"I know."

The pack, consisting of three dogs, was quickly assembled and brought to the transporter room. They stood there on the transporter pad, dressed in environmental suits since none of them had the slightest idea whether the planet could support life or not—although, considering the conditions around it, it seemed rather unlikely.

"Remain in constant touch," Rier said, pacing back and forth slowly. Riella was standing off to the side, saying nothing, as he continued, "If there is the slightest problem, we will bring you back up. If we don't hear from you, we will bring you back up."

"Will you be able to maintain transporter lock even though we're having troubles with our sensors?" asked one of the Dogs. He didn't seem challenging; just a bit apprehensive. Truly, it was hard to blame him.

Rier glanced to the transporter chief, who nodded. "I am told that we will," Rier said confidently. "Good hunting."

The pack snapped off a salute and moments later the transporter beams flared to life. The dogs dissolved in a burst of molecules . . .

. . . and immediately ricocheted back.

It happened with no warning at all, and the transporter chief yelped out, "Something's wrong! They're coming right back! And their patterns are all over the place, I can't lock down, I can't—!"

What appeared on the transporter pad then did not look remotely like the pack who had been standing there a moment earlier. It was all three of them, slammed together as if redesigned by an insane child with a Dogs-of-War-parts kit. One of them was making something vaguely akin to a howling noise, while the others were just flailing about, an arm here, a leg there, a finger protruding from the eye of one of them. A huge, throbbing, gelatinous mass of fur and bone with a pulse.

"Get it out!" shouted Rier. "Beam it into space! Beam it anywhere! Get it off the ship!"

The abomination that had once been three individual dogs vanished before it became fully formed. Rier gasped in revulsion over what he had seen, and then he turned on Riella and snarled, "Did you know that was going to happen!"

"No."

"Did you think it might?"

"I thought it possible, yes."

He waved his paws around in fury. "Then why didn't you say so!"

"You didn't ask."

He tried to contain his fury over her calm answer, and failed. Instead his arm lashed out, struck her across the chest, and knocked her down. She fell against the wall, but didn't utter a sound. Instead she just stared blandly up at him, as if daring him to do it again . . . or, more likely as if she didn't care whether he did it again or not.

Rier took a long moment to compose himself, and when he finally managed to do so, he said to her levelly, "What would you recommend we do?"

"Shuttle to the surface. Send me down in the shuttle. I, after all, am supposed to be there. So no harm will come to me."

"Your confidence in your imperviousness is truly charming. Do you share similar sentiments for us?"

"No. But I was unaware that the Dogs of War only did that which was safe."

There was no challenge in her voice, no sense of derision. She had spoken calmly, even with a mild air of curiosity, as if trying to determine what was and was not acceptable to the Dogs of War. Still, there was something about her attitude that Rier didn't entirely like. But he couldn't help but feel that attacking her just because of a passing remark might come across as a bit of an overreaction.

"Very well, then," Rier said. "We shall make a survey of the world from a shuttle. See if it is habitable or capable of being surveyed. The Dogs of War do not court merely safety, but we have not survived as long as we have by garnering a reputation for foolhardiness, either."

She inclined her head slightly to accept what he was saying, although he still wasn't certain whether she was simply being deferential or subtly sarcastic. He decided that if she was so subtle that no one realized it, then it really didn't matter all that much.

Moments later, Rier was back on the bridge, informing his crew of the new plans. There was a singular lack of enthusiasm among them.

"It's a trick! It's some sort of trick, it has to be!" said Krul.

Omon indicated the image on the screen that continued to flicker in definition. It was no wonder that the sensors were so pathetic as far as the nebula was concerned; it was tough enough just maintaining a visual lock. If they had actually had to enter the nebula in order to get within range of the planet, they'd probably have almost no visual to speak of. All they would see would be a large, fuzzy spot that might or might not be a planet. "Somehow, this is not what I was expecting when I first heard the legends of the Quiet Place. This world barely seems as if it's there at all."

"What did you expect, then?" inquired Rier. "A plethora of riches and immortality, there for the taking, easily located upon a world in well-traveled spaceways with great lights arcing from it and giant letters in orbit spelling out 'Welcome to the Quiet Place'?"

Openly annoyed, Rier stalked the bridge and sneered, "Look at you, quivering! Are you Dogs? Or are you men?"

And then Atik was on his feet. "I am with you, Rier."

There was only a moment's hesitation, and then Omon said, "Speaking my mind is not the same as being craven. My fangs and claws are yours, Rier, as always."

There were similar shouts of affirmation from throughout the bridge, and Rier nodded in approval.

"Omon and Krul, you're with me. And Krul go down and roust Vacu, in case we're in need of muscle. Atik you will remain in charge here until my return."

Atik nodded and saluted. "What about the girl?"

"The girl will come with us. She will lead us to the Quiet Place, as she has claimed she will."

"And if she does not?" asked Omon.

"Then she will die."

"And if she does?"

"Then she will die."

"A simple, elegant plan," said Omon.

Rier smiled as much as his maw would allow him. "I am so pleased you approve."

As the shuttle angled downward, the sensor arrays of the vessel swept the surface of the planet. Rier studied it thoughtfully, his dark eyes narrowing, and he glanced over at Riella. She no longer seemed quite as detached as she had earlier. She actually seemed involved in the moment, even a bit excited. "Feel as if you're coming home, do you?" he asked.

She nodded but didn't speak.

Rier turned in his chair and faced Omon. "What have you got so far?"

Omon shook his head. "It's a fortunate thing we brought the environment suits. So far, from the look of it, the surface is completely uninhabitable. Frankly, even the suits might not do us much good. A great deal of magma on the surface, and much of the—"

Riella suddenly gasped, putting her hand to her breast. "What's the matter with you?" demanded Rier, but still she said nothing. She just shook her head slowly, like someone in a daze.

"Rier—"

He looked back to a clearly puzzled Omon. "What now?"

"Hold on . . . let me double check," said Omon, as if not quite trusting his readings. He nodded once more to confirm it for himself. "I have no idea how it got there . . . I didn't see it on the first sweeps—"

"See what? What are you talking about?"

"A small section of the planet. Very small, not more than a mile or so in diameter. It's some sort of anomaly . . . like an atmospheric oasis."

"A what?"

"I'm not quite sure how else to describe it," said Omon.

Krul growled softly. Obviously, he was less than enthused about the entire business, but he wisely said nothing, less it be misinterpreted as cowardice. Vacu, over in a corner, snored softly, doubtlessly waiting for someone to awaken him at some point and tell him what needed to be crushed, hit, or destroyed.

"I don't understand it," admitted Omon. "It's possible that I missed it on the first sweep. It's small enough. Or perhaps, it simply . . . appeared."

"How very mysterious," said Rier. He looked to Riella. "Is that where we're supposed to go, eh? It seems to be inviting us."

Still she did not speak. Rier was beginning to lose patience with her. He went to her and, gripping her by the shoulders, half pulled her from her chair. "Well? Is that it? Is that where we're supposed to go?"

She looked at him then—really looked—and Rier suddenly felt as if her gaze was boring straight through into the back of her head. He released her without even knowing that he had done so, and she slid noiselessly back into her seat.

Suddenly the communications board crackled to life. Atik's voice came over it, and it was difficult to make out anything he was saying as the nebula interfered mightily with the transmission. It was all Rier could do to piece together what was being said. "Encountered . . . resistance. Two ships—"

"Two ships, yes, I hear you," said Rier quickly, wanting to get as much of the message as possible should he lose the band entirely.

"Small Thallonian vessel . . . and a Federation shuttlecraft . . ."

The Federation again! His teeth hurt with a longing to tear apart some of the Federation bastards who had made their lives so irritating. "And what happened?"

"We're fine. No significant damage. Thallonian vessel crippled—"

"And the Federation ship? The shuttle?"

There was a pause, more crackling.

"Say again?"

"Shuttle destroyed."

Rier nodded approvingly. "Well done. If the Thallonian ship somehow managed to survive, we'll easily be able to dispense with him. As for the shuttle, the less of those sniveling cretins running about, the better." He laughed softly at his own small jest.

"Nice piloting there, Kebron."

Zak Kebron said, "It's the name."

"What name?"

"The *Marquand*. It's the second shuttle we've lost by that name. It's cursed."

"I don't believe in curses."

"I do," said Xyon at the helm of the *Lyla*.

"Don't be a fool."

"A fool, Cwan? Excuse me, but need I point out that this is my ship? That you people beamed over here when your shuttle was about to be blown out of space?"

"While your ship was hiding safely under its cloak," Cwan said disdainfully.

"Right. And I can't understand why you haven't outfitted all your Federation vessels with similar devices."

"We of the Federation have a policy of approaching situations in an open and above-board manner. Such a policy is antithetical to the technology of the cloaking device," Soleta informed him. "We have to offer an alternative to such nefarious races as the Romulans."

"Right, an alternative. You're targets, they're not."

"Can we stay focused?" said Si Cwan. "Bickering isn't going to find Kalinda." He stepped forward, leaning over Xyon who was at the helm. "That shuttle that left the Dog war vessel, can you keep up with it?"

"It's not easy," Xyon said reluctantly. "Sensor tracking is sketchy at best. I'm relying mostly on sight and gut instinct."

"Gut instinct. Wonderful," said Kebron.

"I would not be quite so dismissive, Zak," Soleta

said. "McHenry pilots the *Excalibur* with much the same method."

"Don't remind me."

"There was another vessel in the short-lived encounter with the Dogs," Soleta said. "Kebron, Cwan. Do you have any speculations as to who it might have been?"

"Zoran," Cwan said immediately before Kebron could even take a breath. "It has to be. I will find him and kill him."

"If we encounter him and he can be made a prisoner, that will be the direction taken. You cannot simply kill him in cold blood," Soleta said.

"He is my oldest friend. I have earned the privilege."

Kebron glanced significantly at Soleta. "Now you see why I have no interest in being his friend."

"The shuttle is heading towards the planet," said Xyon abruptly. "Lyla, track ahead on their course. Are they heading towards anything?"

"There is a small area on the planet surface that appears to contain breathable atmosphere," Lyla promptly responded. "If they maintain their current heading, that will be their landing point."

"What could cause something like that? A small area of breathable atmosphere on a world so inhospitable otherwise?" Xyon wondered.

"A freak atmospheric occurrence," suggested Soleta. "Or perhaps some sort of terraforming experiment, left behind by a race long gone."

"Or a race that's still there," Kebron warned.

"That place has to be it: the Quiet Place." Si Cwan could not entirely keep the sense of wonder from his voice. "The Quiet Place. I can hardly believe it . . . I never thought I would see it myself—"

"What do you think you'll see there, Cwan? The face of God?" Kebron snorted. "Absurd. Right, Soleta?"

"Oh, I don't know," said Soleta. "I am a woman of science. I try to keep myself open to all possibilities."

"You, Soleta?" Kebron rarely sounded surprised or at least allowed himself to sound that way. "You're a scientist. Your discipline is the antithesis of religion."

"Not necessarily. After all, for example, in the Judeo-Christian Bible, God charges Adam—the metaphor for the beginning of humanity—with the responsibility of naming everything in Creation."

"So?"

"So . . . that is, fundamentally, what I do. I research, I study, and I try to put names to things. They are scientific names, but they are names nonetheless. My life is defining that which is already there. In a way, you could say that I am doing God's work."

Kebron rolled his eyes. "Religious . . . nonsense. I hate when you do that, Soleta."

"Do what?"

"Play devil's advocate."

"Whose advocate?" she asked, with a slight, puckish raising of one eyebrow.

"Devil's . . ." He stopped and then snorted once more.

Soleta walked up to the viewing port and studied the planet ahead of them. "I am just getting a feeling about this world. That is all."

"What sort of feeling?" asked Cwan.

"The feeling . . . that we are going to encounter something extremely unscientific."

XIV.

THE SCREAMING DID NOT BEGIN immediately; when it did begin, it did so quietly . . .

Riella felt as if the fog in which she had been living for many, many years was slowly lifting from the moment she set foot on the planet. The ground was surprisingly soft beneath her feet, almost spongy.

"I'm home," she whispered.

Rier was significantly less enthused by what he saw, for what he saw was a considerable amount of nothing.

He could not recall having seen a more desolate and uninteresting piece of real estate in his life. It was impossible for him to believe that there were any riches, any treasure, any secret of immortality there. There was nothing there.

Nothing. Not a damned thing.

The entire area was completely uninteresting. A few rises, a few crevices, that was all. No brush, no shrubs. Not a single animal of any sort was crawling across the slightly soggy ground.

The only intriguing thing was the sky. In the distance, high above, the clouds seemed to be whirling in a slow but steady vortex. They were dark, flashing every so often with lightning from within like a storm perpetually on the brink of opening up, but never quite getting there.

But they made no sound.

Rier's ears, sharp as they were, were strained to the utmost, and still he could detect no sound. Something was blowing the clouds, but there was no wind. Lightning crackled from on high, but there was no thunder. All was silent. All was quiet.

"What kind of place is this?" Omon said. He was clearly trying to keep the apprehension out of his voice.

"I have no idea. But I'm going to find out." He turned and strode towards Riella. "All right, girl," he said. "We're here in this world of oddity. You have led us here. Is this the Quiet Place?"

"You knew the answer to that question before you asked it," she told him.

It was odd. She seemed . . . taller somehow when she said that.

"Where are the riches, then? Where is the immortality?"

"All around you. Can't you feel it? Can't you sense it? For one such as yourself, who prides his senses, I can't understand how you can been so unsighted."

"You're the one who's going to be unsighted, girl,"

Rier told her sharply. "Once I rip your eyes out for playing games with us."

She drew herself up, straight and proud and disdainful, and said, "I don't need eyes to see far more clearly than you."

She was not acting like a victim. She was not behaving in a manner appropriate to someone whose life was hanging by a thread. Rier felt it time to make certain she understood just how precarious her personal situation was. He stepped forward and grabbed her by one arm with such force that it would have taken the smallest effort to rip it from her shoulder. "You will tell me," he said, "what I want to know! Or you will die, here! Now! Right on the site of this precious Quiet Place that you have led us to! You—"

"Let her go."

Rier, Vacu, Omon, and Krul reacted to the unexpected voice. Rier let out a low growl of anger.

There was a ship sitting on the ground not far away, and it was just rippling into visibility. A door had irised open, and standing just outside, weapons leveled at the Dogs, were two people in Federation outfits, a Thallonian, and a fourth whom Rier didn't recognize.

But Krul did immediately. "Him!" he said in alarm. "Rier . . . that one assaulted me! The one with the long hair! And he's the one who killed my brother! He's just as Rier described him!"

"And he was on the Redeemer ship!" Vacu spoke up. "He was fighting Atik, when I took the girl!"

"Well well," Rier said. "So you're the near-legendary Xyon. You have caused us a great deal of inconvenience."

"We want the girl," the Thallonian said. "Believe it

or not, that's all we want. Then you can have this place to yourself. You can stay here and rot for all we care. Let her go. Otherwise—" and he held his phaser straight at Rier.

"Otherwise . . . what?"

It was a new voice, from another direction. Judging by the reaction of the Federation representatives, the owner of the voice was not someone they wanted or expected to see. It was another Thallonian, and he had a disruptor aimed squarely at the other Thallonian who was still aiming at Rier. The newly arrived Thallonian, though, was one Rier recognized. He had been back on Montos. They had endeavored to get information from him and he had resisted until the unexpected attack from the locals had driven the Dogs off. He had not provided them with so much as his name.

"Zoran," said the Thallonian who was aiming at Rier. There was cold disdain in his voice.

"Si Cwan . . . milord," Zoran added in a voice dripping with sarcasm. He glanced in the direction of the Dogs. "Your war vessel crippled my ship. I barely managed to bring it down in one piece. You did me quite a bit of inconvenience, for which I would like to take the opportunity to repay you. And you, Si Cwan . . . you did not answer my question. Otherwise . . . what?" His disruptor did not budge in its targeting of Si Cwan.

"Otherwise I will kill him. And you, if need be," said Si Cwan.

"Not with that." It had been Riella who had spoken. She didn't seem aware that Rier was gripping her arm. She didn't seem aware of anything, really. It was as if she had withdrawn completely into herself. "That weapon will not work here."

"Oh, really," said Zoran.

"Kally," Si Cwan spoke directly to the girl. "Kally . . . it's me. It's Si Cwan. Do you recognize me, Kally?"

"That weapon will not work here either," she continued as if he hadn't spoken. "This is the Quiet Place. No weapons will function here."

"Let's test that little notion, shall we?" said Zoran, and he squeezed the trigger of the disruptor that was aimed at Si Cwan.

Nothing happened.

Riella closed her eyes, closed them very, very tightly. The screaming had begun. She was the only one who could hear it, though. But that would change, very soon.

Soleta saw Zoran try to fire and saw that nothing happened. She looked at her own phaser and saw that the energy gauge was high. It had full power. She tried to fire it into the ground, just as a test. Nothing. She cast a confused glance at Kebron. Kebron, normally the most inscrutable of beings, was for once visibly confused, for his phaser likewise wasn't functioning.

"Kalinda!" Si Cwan called out, and took a step towards her.

The largest of the Dogs stepped in between Si Cwan and Rier and let out a warning snarl. He was a head taller and considerably wider than Si Cwan and looked to be a formidable opponent.

"Hold it, Vacu," Rier said approvingly as he pulled Kalinda more tightly against him. His claws were at her throat. "I assure you all, that your phasers and disruptors may be nonfunctional, but my claws are working just fine. So all of you just stay right where you are, before it's—"

"Too late," Kalinda said. Her eyes were still shut tightly. Her voice sounded hollow. In the distance, Soleta could have sworn that the vortex of the sky was whirling even faster.

"That's right, before it's too late for your precious little girl here."

"Not for me," said Kalinda to the Dog, her eyes still squeezed shut.. "For you. It is too late . . . for you. They have come. They are here. They know you . . . all of you. And they are very . . . very . . . Quiet."

"What is the girl blathering about?" demanded Zoran.

Kalinda's eyes snapped open.

Her pupils were gone. Instead, against the whites of her eyes, there was a tempestuous swirling image akin to the clouds from on high.

Rier saw the bizarreness of her eyes and reflexively released his hold on her, took a step back and gaped in confusion.

"You killed me," whispered Kalinda. Her voice echoed, reverberated in itself, as if many of her were speaking at once.

"I didn't!" said Rier. "You're alive! You're . . . you're right here! What sort of?—"

"You killed us . . . and us . . ." Kalinda's voice tripled, quadrupled in its resonance. It sounded as if a mob were speaking through her in unison. "You all did . . ."

"Kally," Si Cwan called to her.

Kalinda's body began to tremble, her arms spread wide. Her eyes were beyond frightening. When she spoke, it was almost deafening. "We died screaming.

We died sobbing. We died *begging*. *All of us, from all over . . . we died as loudly as we could. And then we came here, to his place of quiet, in order to seek the silence in death that we could not have at the end of our lives. And you . . . all of you . . . were responsible for sending us here. You had your reasons. You thought them good. You have killed, or helped others to kill, or served with those who sent us here, and we welcome you and you will stay here forever, with us, and in that way have the immortality you so richly deserve. For you took our lives, and in doing so, you took all our hopes, and our love, and our hatred. We will never love again, never feel again, and we have you to thank for that. Welcome to the Quiet Place. Stay . . . forever . . ."*

XV.

You see them sometimes.

They're just out of the corner of your eye, when you're not expecting them, and sometimes if you close your eyes very, very tightly, and then open them quickly, there will be a quick flash of them behind your eyelids before they dissipate.

They are the echoes of déjà vu, they are the regrets that are fleeting, they are that which you didn't know you missed . . .

They are everywhere and nowhere, and they have come to the Quiet Place, and they are quiet no longer . . .

"Atik! We're losing all sensor trace of the planet!"

Atik sat forward, confused. "How is that possible?"

"The nebula is thickening around the world. Obscuring it further."

"Try to raise Rier on communications link. Let him know . . . and distance ourselves from the planet. If something goes too wrong, we don't want to be sitting on top of it when it happens."

Rier didn't know where to look first.

They were coming from everywhere, from all around, and they were screaming his name and screeching their fury. The Dogs drew together, confused, terrified.

From all over, they were attacking, and their eyes were missing, their arms were torn out, their intestines were trailing behind them, blood fountaining from hundreds of wounds. Everyone the Dogs had ever attacked and tortured and tormented, all of their victims, everyone who had suffered at their claws—all screaming, all screaming in fury, protesting their fate. They were pouring from the girl, they were arcing toward the skies and descending towards the Dogs, tearing at their fur, howling at them, and the smell of blood and fear was thick in the air . . .

And the Dogs screamed.

Xyon didn't know where to look first.

There was the Dog of War he had killed, coming right at him, except it didn't quite look like him, it was a shade of him, twisted and distorted, but him, and there was Foutz, whom he had killed with his bare hands, and there were others, so many others, and he tried to explain, tried to tell them that he had been trying to help others, or just defending himself, and he had never been happy over anything that he had done, but it had been necessary, and please, don't rip his soul from him, don't punish him, leave him, leave him, take the others, take the Federation people, take the girl, just leave him . . .

And Xyon screamed . . .

Zoran and Si Cwan didn't know where to look first . . .

All the victims of the Thallonian Empire, swirling towards them, permeating them, and they felt cold in their bones, crushing them, turning their muscles to jelly, turning their souls to small, blackened husks that would stay in the Quiet Place forever, to join the other tortured, shrieking beings who screamed quietly unto eternity . . .

The Thallonian Empire, which had destroyed so many in order to maintain its hold, that had ruled oppressively, and there was to be suffering and punishment for eternity . . .

And Zoran and Si Cwan screamed . . .

Zak Kebron knew exactly where to look first. . . .

He saw shades coming at him, the howling images of people he had killed. People whose heads he had crushed, people whose guts he had personally removed . . .

He looked through them. He ignored them.

They screeched at him. They howled at him. Their screams permeated to his innermost being.

He pushed them away with an annoyed grunt and, unsure of how long he could maintain his sanity, started toward Kalinda with the intention of breaking her in half.

Soleta didn't know where to look first.
At the screaming Dogs.

At the screaming Xyon.

At the screaming Si Cwan and Zoran.

At the unscreaming, but implacable Zak Kebron who was striding towards the screaming Kalinda.

She felt something pushing in at the outermost edges of her consciousness, but her mental shields easily blocked it. Other than that, however, there was nothing particularly inconvenient for her.

She looked at her tricorder, stared at the readings. She was detecting some sort of huge outpouring of psionic energy, but she couldn't lock onto the source. One moment it seemed to be Kalinda herself, and the next, it appeared to be coming from all around her. The one thing she was certain of, however, was that everyone else was seeing something that she wasn't. She supposed she should have felt a bit left out.

Then it fully dawned on her that Kebron was not about to pull punches with Kalinda. Holstering her tricorder, she darted towards him and interposed herself between the quivering body of Kalinda and Kebron's considerable bulk. "Don't touch her, Zak," she warned.

"She's causing this," Kebron said over the shrieking of the confused creatures he heard around her. He spoke thickly, as if concentrating on forming the words.

"Perhaps. Or the planet is. We don't know."

"Won't wait . . . to find out."

And Kebron lunged at Kalinda.

And Krul and Xyon slammed into each other and went down, Krul's outrage and terror pouring from him as he tried to silence his brother's howling by slaying the slayer . . .

And Si Cwan and Zoran slammed into each other and went down, the two friends-turned-enemies trying to settle old scores, moved and tormented by the souls around them demanding blood vengeance . . .

And Rier and Omon slammed into each other and went down, the latter blaming the former for every death he'd ordered, every grisly raid, and the souls wanted them to join them . . .

And Vacu, for no particular reason, slammed repeatedly into the ground, like a blazing person trying to extinguish the fire . . .

Soleta knew she had absolutely no hope of blocking Kebron. So instead she grabbed Kalinda by the arm, yanked her out of Kebron's path. Kebron, not exactly built to turn on a dime, charged past her, and then Soleta lost her footing on the spongy ground and fell, and Kalinda fell on top of her . . .

. . . and their minds merged, and suddenly *Soleta saw it all, knew it all, felt the psychic assault from all sides, all of the creatures of the damned whipping past her . . .*

. . . and, struggling to her feet, Soleta half pulled, half dragged Kalinda toward Xyon's ship. As she did so, she shoved her mind into Kalinda's, envisioning a fortress, erecting barriers, and she felt something, somethings, battering against them, trying to tear them down, but she wouldn't let them. The howling was everywhere, and over and over, Soleta kept saying firmly, *I do not believe, this is unscientific, fear comes from lack of knowledge, that is all, and once something is understood, there is no need to fear it, and someday I shall understand what is happening here, and when I do, there will be nothing to fear, nothing to fear, nothing to fear* . . .

She hammered that concept over and over into

Kalinda's mind . . . Kalinda, the conduit, Kalinda, the receiver of the Summons . . .

And Xyon suddenly saw Krul clearly above him. Moving entirely on instinct, he coiled his legs under Krul's chest and thrust upwards with all his strength. Krul tumbled back and off him, and Xyon scrambled to his feet . . .

And Si Cwan suddenly saw Zoran below him. His hatred for his greatest enemy abruptly seemed inconsequential, a trivial thing, for his sister was there, right there, being hauled away by Soleta. Her safety was all that mattered. Si Cwan drew back a fist and delivered a crushing blow to the side of Zoran's head, stunning him momentarily, and that was all he needed to leap clear of the Thallonian and dash after Soleta . . .

And Rier suddenly saw Omon with his teeth at his throat, and he saw Vacu rolling about like an idiot. He shoved Omon off him, pointed and shouted, "There! Over there!"

The Federation people were heading towards the ship that had been cloaked. Rier charged at full speed. He was doing everything he could to focus, his mind still scrambled over the images that had been barraging him moments before.

He was within a few feet of Xyon and, confident that the human couldn't produce a weapon and shoot at him, he leaped through the air, a howl of fury torn from his throat.

Xyon spun and Rier only had a second to see the gleaming blade, one of Atik's long fangs, in Xyon's hand, and then the blade was through Rier's chest. Rier clawed at it, confused and stunned, and Xyon yanked the blade back, blood spraying.

"Play dead," he said, and darted into his ship.

The other dogs clustered around as the door irised shut. The ship lifted off quickly and smoothly . . . and silently, as if its engine noise was being absorbed into the eerie silence that was all around. Within seconds, the ship had faded out, consumed by the cloaking device.

"Get . . . after them," gasped Rier. "We still . . . the riches . . . immortality . . . it's . . . it's all around us . . . we can . . . we can touch it . . ."

"We'll get them . . . we'll get it, Rier . . . I promise," said Vacu. The big Dog who had been virtually impossible to hurt felt nothing but pain as he looked upon his fallen leader. He scooped up Rier's body and, jaw set, repeated, "I promise. We'll get them. All of them." He drew himself up and in a voice of surprising command, said, "Let's go!"

They started towards their ship, which was sitting a short distance away.

Something crushed it.

They gasped collectively as the top of the shuttle craft caved in, as if a gigantic weight had slammed down upon it. Within seconds, the shuttle had been reduced to little more than scrap.

"The ship! The invisible ship! They did this!" shouted Omon, but by that point it was too late to do anything about it. The Dogs were stranded.

They turned towards Zoran. The Thallonian was sitting there, staring off into nothing. Omon went to him quickly, grabbed him by the throat and snarled, "Your ship. Where is it? Get us off this damned place."

Zoran laughed.

"What's so damned funny!"

"My ship?" chuckled Zoran. "You mean the one that your vessel crippled? I crashed here, you idiots. I'm as stranded as you!" And then he laughed very, very loudly.

"No. You're not stranded here. Not anymore," said Omon, and his teeth flashed.

The *Lyla* tore up and out of the planet's atmosphere, calling on all its power to slam through the nebula. Xyon was piloting entirely on instinct, determined that nothing was going to stop them from breaking free after all they had been through. He heard Si Cwan murmuring Kalinda's name as he held Riella (Kalinda, damn it!) tight against him.

Kebron was now at Xyon's side. "Can this get us out of here?"

"Absolutely," Xyon said, sounding confident, feeling less so. Then he frowned. "Do you—?"

"Yes. I see it."

The nebula seemed to be getting thicker and thicker around them. It was as if they were piloting through increasingly thick fog . . . fog that pounded at them, fighting their every effort to get through. They were flying completely blind. "Lyla! Can you be of any help here?" shouted Xyon.

"Yes. Of course."

Music promptly filtered through the ship. A woman's lilting voice crooned a song.

"Lyla! What the hell is that?"

"It's a jazz rendition of a song called 'Namely You.' "

"I mean, why are you playing it?!"

"You seem upset. Music tends to calm down one's nerves."

"Well, it's not helping!"

"Perhaps an instrumental then . . . how about 'Nearer My God to Thee'?" Violin strains poured out of the speaker.

Before Xyon could tell her to shut it off, the nebula suddenly cleared in front of them . . .

. . . and the Dog warship hovered bare kilometers away, dead ahead.

With a yelp Xyon angled the ship as fast as he could. Fortunately, Lyla was aiding him, and consequently the ship managed to avoid collision . . . albeit barely. Safely under cloak, the smaller ship hurtled away without detection.

Xyon let out an unsteady breath. "I wasn't expecting that," he said.

"Frankly," muttered Soleta, as "Nearer My God to Thee" played, "I was expecting an iceberg."

"What was it? What was down there? You're a scientist. You tell me. I mean . . . it couldn't have been ghosts. That couldn't be . . . could it?"

"The Pilgrims who settled America would have taken one look at me and burned me as a demon creature," Soleta said coolly. "A supernatural mystery one day is scientific explanation the next. One never truly knows, or understands, everything."

"I don't accept that. That's no answer. Do you truly believe that could have been what . . . what we thought it was?"

Soleta pursed her lips, and then said, "There is a university on earth, called Yale. I was there once, in its theater building, which had been renovated many times during its existence. I was visiting a friend who was an actor there. One day, while I was waiting for her to come offstage, I noticed someone just out of the corner of my eye. A woman, a fleeting image, running up a flight of stairs. She was dressed in a costume replete with a high collar and odd frills. Obviously period garb. It was not remotely in keeping with the play that was being performed at that moment. My friend came offstage and I asked her who that person had been. My friend looked at me very oddly, and then smiled and said, 'Congratulations. You've just seen the Yale ghost.' According to local legend, several centuries earlier, the wife of a drama professor had been struck and killed by a vehicle while crossing the street. She had been on her way to the theater where she was rushing to make her curtain; she was acting in a production of a play by a 20th Century Russian writer named Anton Chekhov. I saw her wearing the costume she had been wearing in the play."

"So you imagined it," said Xyon skeptically. "So what?"

"But I didn't know of the legend before she told me."

"Oh."

"Have you no legends or tales of that which you do not understand in your homeworld?"

"A few," he admitted. "Places where visions of the future can supposedly be seen. That sort of thing. But I never . . ." He sighed. "I guess I'm going to have to give this some thought."

"That's all that anyone can ever do," replied Soleta. "That's all."

Xyon then blinked in confusion and checked the long-range scanners. "I don't believe this."

"What is it?"

"The planet. The one with the Quiet Place. It's . . ."

"It's gone? That's impossible."

Atik got out of the command chair and crossed

quickly to the sensor array. It was difficult to believe . . . but it was true. As untrustworthy as the sensors had been, they had at least enabled them to detect something earlier. But now there was no sign of it. The nebulae, having become thicker in the area of the planet, had now thinned once more . . . and there was no sign of the world at all.

And then, before anyone on the bridge could say anything, Atik suddenly gasped. His hands went to his throat and he collapsed. The other Dogs gathered around him, whimpering in confusion, and then Atik whispered words that chilled them.

"Xant . . ." he said. "Xant . . . the Great God Xant . . . the Redeemers . . . were right . . . I see him, so clearly . . . Xant is light . . . we are darkness . . ."

Then he passed out.

XVI.

THE OVERLORD WAS QUITE PLEASED.

The Dogs of War had been a consistent irritant for the Redeemers. Constant.

But they could be saved. Anyone could be saved. They simply needed a lesson.

So when Atik, who aspired to become leader of the Dogs of War, had quietly approached the Overlord with his own ambitions, possibilities had presented themselves. Ambitious as he was, Atik had been perfectly candid that he did not wish to go head-to-head with Rier, or Rier's inner circle of supporters. He claimed that it would not have been honorable. The odds were that he was just concerned, not without cause, that he would lose.

The Quiet Place had been a logical, elegant solution to the problem. The Quiet Place, feared even by the Redeemers. Sought after by Rier and the Dogs. The Quiet Place where, if everything went perfectly, Rier and his ilk would find and never return from again.

And everything had gone perfectly. The Overlord sat in his chamber and smiled a rare smile. It had all gone perfectly because Xant had wanted it that way. And by this point, Atik had had his little "vision" and was likely in the midst of converting the Dogs to the cause of the Redeemers. Who could ask for better than that?

And now . . . now, with the Dogs of War well along the way from having been a nemesis to becoming, instead, a resource, all the Redeemers had to do was deal with the *Excalibur* and their hold on Sector 221–G, formerly known as Thallonian space, would be complete.

The Overlord was so caught up in his thoughts that it was some minutes before he noticed the trembling Redeemer standing in front of him. "Yes? What is it?" he asked with obvious irritation.

"There is . . . no other way to say it, Overlord. There is dire news from Tulaan IV."

The Overlord sat straighter in his great chair. "What ails homeworld?"

"The Black Mass, Overlord. The Black Mass is on the move . . . and it appears that Tulaan IV is squarely in its path."

He couldn't believe it. After all this . . . with everything coming together so beautifully . . . something like this had to happen? He sagged in shock. "Are they sure?"

"Yes, Overlord. If we are not able to do something, our ages-old homeworld will be completely obliterated."

"Then," said the Overlord with conviction, "we will have to stop the Black Mass."

The Redeemer looked stunned. "But . . . but Overlord . . . no one has ever managed such a feat. Ever."

"There is . . . a possibility," said the Overlord. "The problem is . . . it will require help."

"Whose help, Overlord?"

The Overlord grimaced at the irony of his reply. "Captain Mackenzie Calhoun of the *Excalibur.*"

"Captain Mackenzie Calhoun, of the *Excalibur.* Welcome aboard. I've heard a great deal about you."

In the transporter room, Calhoun bowed slightly to Kalinda, who was leaning on Si Cwan's arm. Her skin was not quite as dark red as Si Cwan's, although it was Calhoun's understanding that that was due to some sort of genetic treatment she had undergone.

Kalinda nodded in acknowledgment of his gesture of respect. "I am . . . afraid I'm not quite myself at the moment, Captain. There's . . . a lot I still have to sort out."

"And you will certainly have the time to do so."

The door to the transporter room hissed open and Shelby hurried in, to see Si Cwan and his sister, as well as Soleta, Kebron, and an odd-looking young man just stepping off the transporter platform. "Sorry I'm late. Elizabeth Shelby, Second in Command."

"A pleasure, Commander," Kalinda said.

"Yes, Commander, I was just in time to commend Lieutenants Kebron and Soleta on their fine work," Calhoun said drily. "You lost yet another shuttlecraft while embarking on a side mission that ran contrary to my orders that you should report back here. You violated regulations and risked your safety out of a misplaced sense of heroism."

"We've tried to learn from your example, sir," said Kebron.

"I've taught you well," Calhoun said approvingly. He turned to the young man. "And you would be?"

The young man slugged him.

Calhoun managed to dodge most of it, his reflexes as sharp as they ever were, but he was still partly tagged on the jaw. He staggered slightly but then regained his footing, rubbing his chin.

"I'm Xyon of Calhoun. I'm your son," he said.

Without batting an eye, Calhoun said, "A pleasure to meet you, too."

To Be Continued . . .

OUR FIRST SERIAL NOVEL!

Presenting, one chapter per month . . .

The very beginning of the Starfleet Adventure . . .

**STAR TREK
STARFLEET: YEAR ONE**

A Novel in Twelve Parts

**by
Michael Jan Friedman**

Chapter Four

Chapter Four

As Connor Dane slipped into an orbit around Command Base, he saw on his primary monitor that there were still a handful of *Christophers* hanging around the place. He glanced at the warships, observing their powerful if awkward-looking lines.

"Can't hold a candle to you, baby," Dane whispered to his ship, patting his console with genuine affection.

Then he punched in a comm link to the base's security console. After a second or two, a round-faced woman with pretty eyes and long dark hair appeared on the monitor screen.

"Something I can do for you?" she asked.

"I believe I'm expected," he said. "Connor Dane."

The woman tapped a pad and checked one of her monitors. "So you are," she noted. "I'll tell the transporter officer. Morales out."

With that, her image vanished and Dane's view of the base was restored. Swiveling in his seat, he got up and walked to the rear of his bridge, where he could stand apart from his instruments. After all, the last thing he wanted was to materialize with a toggle switch in his belly button.

Before long, the Cochrane jockey saw the air around him begin to shimmer, warning him that he was about to be whisked away. The next thing he knew, he was standing on a raised platform in the base's transporter chamber.

Of course, this chamber was a lot bigger and better lit than the ones he was used to. But then, this was Command Base, the key to Earth's resounding victory over the Romulans. It didn't surprise him that it might rate a few extra perks.

The transporter operator was a stocky man with a dark crewcut. He eyed Dane with a certain amount of curiosity.

"Something wrong?" the captain asked.

The man shrugged. "Honestly?"

"Honestly," Dane insisted.

The operator shot him a look of disdain. "I was wondering," he said, "what kind of man could see a bunch of birdies invade his system and not want to put on a uniform."

The captain stroked his chin. "Let's see now . . . I'd say it was the kind that was too busy popping Romulans out of space to worry about it." He stepped down from the platform. "Satisfied?"

The man's eyes had widened. "You drove an escort ship? Geez, I didn't—"

"You didn't think," Dane said, finishing the man's remark his own way. "But then, guys like you never do."

Leaving the operator redfaced, he exited from the chamber through its single set of sliding doors. Then he looked around for the nearest turbolift.

As it turned out, it was just a few meters away, on the opposite side of a rotunda. Crossing to it, Dane went inside and punched in his destination. As the doors closed and the compartment began to move, he took a deep breath.

He would get this over as soon as he could, he assured himself. He would satisfy his curiosity. Then he would get back in his Cochrane and put as much distance between himself and Command Base as he possibly could.

The lift's titanium panels slid apart sooner than he had expected, revealing a short corridor shared by five black doors. Dane knew enough about Command protocol to figure out which one he wanted.

Advancing to the farthest of the doors, he touched the pad set into the bulkhead beside it. Inside, where he couldn't hear it, a chime was sounding, alerting the officer within that he had company.

With a rush of air, the door moved aside. Beyond it stood a broad-shouldered man in a black and gold admiral's uniform, his hair whiter than Dane remembered it.

Big Ed Walker's eyes narrowed beneath bushy brows. "Connor," he said. He indicated a chair in his anteroom. "Come on in."

Dane took the seat. Then he eyed the admiral. "I'm glad you recognize me, Uncle Ed. For a moment there, I thought you were confusing me with someone who had some ambition to be a star fleet captain."

Walker chuckled drily as he pulled up a chair across from his nephew. "Funny, son. But then, you always did have a lively sense of humor."

"I'm glad I amuse you," said Dane. "But I didn't come here to crack jokes, Uncle Ed. I came to find out how my hat got thrown in the ring. I mean, you and I haven't exactly been close for a good many years now, so I know it wasn't a case of nepotism."

The admiral nodded reasonably. "That's true, Connor. But then, you can't call that my fault, can you? You were the one who chose to leave the service and strike out on your own."

"I had no desire to be a military man," Dane tossed back. "No one seemed to believe that."

Walker smiled grimly. "I still don't. What you accomplished during the war, the reputation you earned yourself . . . that just proves you had it in you all along. You're a born officer, son, a natural leader—"

"So are dozens of other space jockeys," Dane pointed out, "guys who'd give their right arms to join your star fleet. But you picked me instead." He leaned forward in his chair, deadly serious. "So tell me . . . what's the deal, Uncle Ed?"

Alonis Cobaryn grunted softly to himself as he studied the scale hologram of the *Daedalus*-class prototype. Somehow, the two-meter-long hologram had looked more impressive in the darkened briefing room where he had seen it the day before.

Here at the center of Earth Command's primary conference room, a grand, solemn amphitheater with gray seats cascading toward a central stage from every side, the hologram seemed small and insignificant. And with two dozen grim, lab-coated engineers occupying a scattering of those seats, already making notes in their handheld computer pads, the Rigelian had to admit he was feeling a little insignificant himself.

He saw no hint of that insecurity in the other captains standing alongside him. But then, Hagedorn, Stiles and

Matsura were used to the soberness of Earth Command environments and engineers. And while neither Shumar nor Dane could make that claim, they were at least Earthmen.

Of all those present, Cobaryn was the only alien. And while no one in the facility had done anything to underline that fact, he still couldn't help but be aware of it.

For some time, the Rigelian had been fascinated by other species. He had done his best to act and even think like some of them. However, after having spent an entire day on Earth, he was beginning to wonder if he could ever live as one of them.

Abruptly, Cobaryn's thoughts were interrupted by a loud hiss. Turning, he saw the doors to the amphitheater slide open and produce the slender form of Starfleet Director Abute.

As the dark-skinned man crossed the room, the engineers looked up from their pads and gave him their attention. No surprise there, the Rigelian reflected, considering Abute was their superior.

"Thank you for coming, ladies and gentlemen," the director told the lab-coated assemblage, his voice echoing almost raucously from wall to wall. "As you know, I have asked the six men who are to serve as captains in our new fleet to critique your work on the *Daedalus*. I trust you'll listen closely to what they have to say."

There was a murmur of assent. However, Cobaryn thought he heard an undertone of resentment in it. Very possibly, he mused, these engineers believed they had already designed the ultimate starship—and that this session was a waste of time.

However, Abute disagreed, or he wouldn't have called this meeting. The Rigelian found himself grateful for that point of view, considering he was one of the individuals who would have to test the engineers' design.

The director turned to Matsura. "Captain?" he said. "Would you care to get the ball rolling?"

"I'd be happy to," said Matsura. He took a step closer to the hologram and pressed the flats of his hands together. "Let's talk about scanners."

It seemed like a reasonable subject to Cobaryn. After all, he had some opinions of his own on the matter.

Matsura pointed to a spot on the front of the ship. "Without a doubt, the long-range scanners that have been incorporated into the *Daedalus* are a big improvement over what we've got. But we can go a step further."

Abute seemed interested. "How?"

"We can devote more of our scanner resources to long-range use," Matsura answered. "That would allow us to identify threats to Earth and her allies with greater accuracy."

The engineers nodded and made notes in their pads. However, before they got very far, someone else spoke up.

"The problem," said Shumar, "is that additional long-range scanners means fewer short-range scanners—and we need that short-range equipment to obtain better analyses of planetary surfaces."

Cobaryn couldn't help but agree. Like his colleague, he was reluctant to give up any of the advantages Abute had described the day before.

Matsura, on the other hand, seemed to feel otherwise. "With due respect," he told Shumar, "you're equating expedience with necessity. It would be nice to be able to get more information on a planet from orbit. But if we could detect a hostile force a fraction of a light-year further away . . . who knows how many Federation lives might be saved some day?"

Shumar smiled. "That's fine in theory, Captain. But as we all know, science saves lives as well—and I think you would have to admit, there's also a tactical advantage to knowing the worlds in our part of space."

Matsura smiled too, if a bit more tightly. "Some," he conceded. "But I assure you, it pales beside the prospect of advance warning."

Cobaryn saw the engineers trade glances. Clearly, they hadn't expected this kind of exchange between two captains.

Abute frowned. "Perhaps we can table this topic for the moment." He turned to the engineers. "Or better yet, let's see if there is a way to increase both long- and short-range scanning capabilities."

Grumbling a little, the men and women in the lab coats made their notes. Then they looked up again.

The director turned to the Rigelian. "Captain Cobaryn? Can you provide us with something a bit less controversial?"

That got a few chuckles out of the engineers, but not many. They seemed to the Rigelian to be a rather humorless lot.

As Matsura stepped away from the hologram, looking less than pleased, Cobaryn approached it. Glancing at the crowd of engineers to make sure they were listening, he indicated the hologram's warp nacelles.

"While I am impressed," he said, "with the enhancements made in the *Daedalus*'s propulsion system, I believe we may have placed undue emphasis on flight speed."

Abute looked at the Rigelian, his brow creased. "You mean you have no interest in proceeding at warp three?"

His comment was met with a ripple of laughter from the gallery. Cobaryn did his best to ignore it.

"In fact," he replied diplomatically, "I have *every* interest in it. However, it might be more useful to design our engines with range in mind, rather than velocity. By prolonging our vessel's ability to remain in subspace, we will actually arrive at many destinations more quickly—even though we have progressed at a somewhat slower rate of speed.

"What's more," he continued, "by shifting our emphasis as I suggest, we will be able to extend the scope of our operations . . . survey solar systems it would not otherwise have been practical to visit."

Stiles chuckled. "Spoken like a true explorer," he said loudly enough for everyone to hear him.

Cobaryn looked back at the man. "But I *am* an explorer," he replied.

"Not anymore," Stiles insisted. "You're a starship captain. You've got more to worry about than charts and mineral analyses."

Abute turned to him. "I take it you have an objection to Captain Cobaryn's position?" he asked a little tiredly.

"Damned right I do," said Stiles. He eyed the Rigelian. "Captain Cobaryn is ignoring the fact that most missions don't involve long trips. They depend on short, quick jumps—at ranges already within our grasp."

"Perhaps that is true now," Cobaryn conceded. "However, the scope of our operations is bound to grow. We need to range further afield for tactical purposes as well as scientific ones."

Stiles looked unimpressed with the argument. So did Hagedorn and Matsura. However, Stiles was the one who answered him.

"We can worry about the future when it comes," he advised. "Right now, more speed is just what the doctor ordered."

There was silence for a moment. Without meaning to do so, the Rigelian had done exactly what Abute had asked him not to do. Like Matsura, he had become embroiled in a controversy.

"Thank you, gentlemen," the director said pointedly. "I appreciate the opportunity to hear both your points of view."

Cobaryn saw Stiles glance at his Earth Command colleagues. They seemed to approve of the concepts he had put forth. But then, that came as no surprise. It was clear that they were united on this point.

"Since Captain Stiles seems eager to speak," Abute added, "I would like to hear his suggestion next."

"All right," Stiles told him. He came forward and indicated the hologram with a generous sweep of his hand. "Two hundred and thirty people. Entire decks full of personnel quarters. An elaborate sickbay to take care of them when they get ill." He shook his head. "Is all this really necessary? Our Christophers run on crews of thirty-five—and most of the time, we don't need half that many."

"Your Christophers don't have science sections," Shumar pointed out abruptly, his arms folded across his chest. "They don't have laboratories or dedicated computers or botanical gardens or sterile containment chambers."

It was a challenge and everyone in the room knew it. Stiles, Shumar, the other captains, Abute . . . and the gathering of engineers, of course. Their expressions told Cobaryn that this was much more entertaining than any of them might have expected.

Stiles lifted his chin, accepting the gauntlet Shumar had

thrown down. "I read the data just as you did," he responded crisply. "I heard the argument for all those research facilities. My question is . . . how much of it do we need? Couldn't we cut out some of that space and come up with a better, more maneuverable ship?"

Shumar shook his head. "Maybe more maneuverable, Captain, but not better—not if you consider all the capabilities that would be lost if the *Daedalus* was sized down."

"And if it's *not* sized down," Stiles insisted, "the whole ship could be lost . . . the first time it engages the enemy."

Again, Director Abute intervened before the exchange could grow too heated. He held up his hand for peace and said, "I would say it's your turn, Captain Shumar. To make a suggestion, I mean."

Shumar cast a last baleful glance at Stiles. "Fine with me," he replied. Taking a deep breath, he pointed to the hologram. "As we learned yesterday, we've improved our tactical systems considerably. Thanks to all the extra graviton emitters on the *Daedalus,* we've now got six layers of deflector protection—and as someone who's been shot at with atomic missiles, I say that's terrific."

Cobaryn hoped there was a "but" coming in his colleague's declaration. He wasn't disappointed.

"But what if we were to covert one or two of the extra emitters to another use?" Shumar suggested. "Say . . . as tractor beam projectors?"

Matsura made a face. *"Tractor* beams?"

"Tightbeam graviton projections," Hagedorn explained, his voice echoing easily throughout the amphitheater. "When their interference patterns are focused on a remote target, they create a certain amount of spatial stress—

which either pulls the target closer to the source of the beam or pushes it farther away."

Shumar nodded approvingly. "That's exactly right."

"However," said Hagedorn in the same even tone, "tractor beams are very much in the development stage right now. Some people say it'll be a long time before they can be made practical . . . if ever."

The Rigelian saw some nods among the engineers. It wasn't a good sign, he told himself.

Shumar frowned. "Others say tractor beams will be made practical in the next few months. Those are the people I prefer to put my faith in."

Hagedorn shrugged with obvious confidence. "I was simply putting the matter in perspective, Captain."

"As we all should," Abute said hopefully.

"Is it my turn now?" Hagedorn asked.

The director shrugged. "If you like."

Hagedorn began by circling the hologram in an almost theatrical fashion. For a few seconds, he refrained from speaking . . . so when he began, his words had a certain weight to them.

"You've made some interesting improvements in the ship's transporter function," he told the assembled engineers. "Some *very* interesting improvements. For instance, it'll be a lot easier to shoot survey teams and diplomatic envoys to their destinations than to send them in shuttles.

"But frankly," he continued, running his hand over the *Daedalus*'s immaterial hull, "I don't think these enhancements will be of any use to us in combat. As we proved during the war, it's impossible to force-beam our personnel through an enemy's deflector shields."

"Not everything is intended to have a military application," Director Abute reminded him, anticipating an objection from Shumar or Cobaryn.

"I recognize that," Hagedorn told him, as expressionless as ever. "However, transporters *can* have military applications. Are you familiar with the work of Winston and Kampouris?"

Abute's eyes narrowed. "It seems to me I've heard their names . . ."

So had Cobaryn. "They are military strategists," he stated. "They have postulated we can use transporter systems to penetrate deflector shields by sending streams of antimatter along their annular confinement beams."

Shumar made a sound of derision. "Talk about being in the development stage," he said. "Transmitting antimatter through a pattern buffer is and always will be suicide."

Hagedorn shrugged. "Not if the buffer has been built the way we might build a warp core?"

"In which case it would have to *be* a warp core," Shumar insisted. "The same elements that would protect the pattern buffer would make it impermeable to matter transmission."

"Not according to Winston and Kampouris," Hagedorn remarked.

But this time, Cobaryn observed, the engineers seemed to rule in Shumar's favor. They shook their heads at Hagedorn's comment.

Taking notice of the same thing, Abute scowled. "Which leaves us at another impasse, I take it."

Shumar eyed Hagedorn, then Stiles and Matsura. "I guess it does."

The director turned to Dane. "We have one more captain to hear from. Perhaps he can put forth a design recommendation on which we can all agree before we call it a day."

He didn't sound very optimistic, the Rigelian noted. But in his place, Cobaryn wouldn't have been very optimistic either.

Like everyone else in the amphitheater, he looked to Dane. The man considered Abute for a moment, then glanced at the engineers. "Communications," he said simply. "You say you can't do anything to improve what we've got. I say you're not trying hard enough."

The director seemed taken aback—but not nearly as much as the crowd of engineers. "I've been assured by our design team," he replied, "that nothing can be done at this time."

Dane regarded the men and women sitting all around him in their white labcoats. "I've got an assurance for your engineers," he said. "If they don't come up with a quicker way for me to contact headquarters, they can find themselves another starship captain."

Cobaryn had to smile. The Cochrane jockey had not shown himself to be a particularly charming individual. However, he did seem to have more than his share of vertebrae.

Abute looked at Dane for a second or two. Then he turned to his engineers. "You heard the man," he told them. "Let's see what we can do."

There was a rush of objections, but they died out quickly. After all, any engineer worth his degree relished a challenge. Even Cobaryn knew that.

"Thank you again," the director told the people in the gallery. "You may return to your work."

Clearly, that was the engineers' signal to depart. The Rigelian watched them toss comments back and forth as they descended to the level of the stage and filed out of the room. Then he turned to Abute, expecting to be dismissed as well.

But Abute wasn't ready to do that yet, it seemed. He regarded all six of his captains for a moment, his nostrils flaring. Finally, he shook his head.

"Gentlemen," he said, "we obviously have some differences. Honest ones, I assume. However, we must make an effort to seek common ground."

Cobaryn nodded. So did Shumar, Hagedorn, Stiles and Matsura—everyone except Dane, in fact. But the Rigelian knew that Dane was the only one who was being honest with the director.

After all, there was a war raging. The first battle had been fought to a standoff there in the amphitheater, but Cobaryn didn't expect that it would be the last.

Look for STAR TREK Fiction from Pocket Books

Star Trek®: The Original Series

Star Trek: The Next Generation®

Star Trek: Deep Space Nine®

The Search • Diane Carey
Warped • K. W. Jeter
The Way of the Warrior • Diane Carey
Star Trek: Klingon • Dean W. Smith & Kristine K. Rusch
Trials and Tribble-ations • Diane Carey
Far Beyond the Stars • Steve Barnes
The 34th Rule • Armin Shimerman & David George
What You Leave Behind • Diane Carey

Star Trek®: Voyager™

Flashback • Diane Carey
The Black Shore • Greg Cox
Mosaic • Jeri Taylor
Pathways • Jeri Taylor
Equinox • Diane Carey

#1 *Caretaker* • L. A. Graf
#2 *The Escape* • Dean W. Smith & Kristine K. Rusch
#3 *Ragnarok* • Nathan Archer
#4 *Violations* • Susan Wright
#5 *Incident at Arbuk* • John Gregory Betancourt
#6 *The Murdered Sun* • Christie Golden
#7 *Ghost of a Chance* • Mark A. Garland & Charles G. McGraw
#8 *Cybersong* • S. N. Lewitt
#9 *Invasion #4: The Final Fury* • Daffyd ab Hugh
#10 *Bless the Beasts* • Karen Haber
#11 *The Garden* • Melissa Scott
#12 *Chrysalis* • David Niall Wilson
#13 *The Black Shore* • Greg Cox
#14 *Marooned* • Christie Golden
#15 *Echoes* • Dean W. Smith & Kristine K. Rusch
#16 *Seven of Nine* • Christie Golden
#17 *Death of a Neutron Star* • Eric Kotani
#18 *Battle Lines* • Dave Galanter & Greg Brodeur

Star Trek®: New Frontier

#1 *House of Cards* • Peter David
#2 *Into the Void* • Peter David
#3 *The Two-Front War* • Peter David
#4 *End Game* • Peter David
#5 *Martyr* • Peter David
#6 *Fire on High* • Peter David
#7 *The Quiet Place* • Peter David
#8 *Dark Allies* • Peter David

Star Trek®: Day of Honor

Book One: *Ancient Blood* • Diane Carey
Book Two: *Armageddon Sky* • L. A. Graf
Book Three: *Her Klingon Soul* • Michael Jan Friedman
Book Four: *Treaty's Law* • Dean W. Smith & Kristine K. Rusch
The Television Episode • Michael Jan Friedman

Star Trek®: The Captain's Table

Book One: *War Dragons* • L. A. Graf
Book Two: *Dujonian's Hoard* • Michael Jan Friedman
Book Three: *The Mist* • Dean W. Smith & Kristine K. Rusch
Book Four: *Fire Ship* • Diane Carey
Book Five: *Once Burned* • Peter David
Book Six: *Where Sea Meets Sky* • Jerry Oltion

Star Trek®: The Dominion War

Book 1: *Behind Enemy Lines* • John Vornholt
Book 2: *Call to Arms . . .* • Diane Carey
Book 3: *Tunnel Through the Stars* • John Vornholt
Book 4: *. . . Sacrifice of Angels* • Diane Carey

Star Trek®: The Badlands

Book One: Susan Wright
Book Two: Susan Wright

Star Trek: *Strange New Worlds* • Edited by Dean Wesley Smith
Star Trek: *Strange New Worlds II* • Edited by Dean Wesley Smith